I0579274

A Valentine for One

Wisteria Tearoom Mysteries

A Fatal Twist of Lemon
A Sprig of Blossomed Thorn
An Aria of Omens
A Bodkin for the Bride
A Masquerade of Muertos
As Red as Any Blood
A Black Place and a White Place

Intermezzi (Interludes)

"Intermezzo: Spirit Matters"
(to be read between *A Masquerade of Muertos*
and *As Red as Any Blood*)

"Intermezzo: Family Matters"
(to be read between *As Red as Any Blood*
and *A Black Place and a White Place*)

A VALENTINE FOR ONE

PATRICE GREENWOOD

Evennight Books
Cedar Crest, New Mexico

This is a work of fiction. All of the characters, organizations, and events portrayed in this novel are either products of the author's imagination or are used fictitiously.

A VALENTINE FOR ONE
Copyright © 2021 by Patrice Greenwood

This book is set in the Alegreya typeface, a font originally intended for literature, designed by Juan Pablo del Peral for Huerta Tipográfica.

An Evennight Book

Evennight Books
P.O. Box 1644
Cedar Crest, NM 87008-1644

Cover photo: Pati Nagle
Map illustrations: Chris Krohn and Patrice Greenwood

ISBN: 978-1-952653-06-3

First Edition August 2021

for Emmai

Acknowledgments

My thanks to:

Chris Krohn and Deborah Ross
for their kind assistance with this long-awaited book,

The Treehouse Writers
for their helpful input on marketing matters,

The St. James Tearoom
for making their afternoon tea available for takeout,

and to my readers for their infinite patience and their kind support.

"To-morrow is Saint Valentine's day,
All in the morning betime,
And I a maid at your window,
To be your Valentine."

—Ophelia, in *Hamlet*, Act IV, Scene 5
by William Shakespeare

AT A QUARTER TO ELEVEN on the first Tuesday in February, I stood at the hostess station in the Wisteria Tearoom's gift shop, attired in my best lace dress. A whisper of macaron aroma—sugar and almonds, with a hint of elderflower—reached me from the pastry case nearby, and I swallowed. I'd had a light breakfast in anticipation of my tea date that morning.

The macarons were featured on the February menu, debuting that day. Normally I would not have made a date to entertain a guest to tea until the menu had settled in for a few days, but this was a busy month and Tuesday was the quietest day of the week for us, usually. I trusted Julio to make sure the food was perfect, especially since my guest was his roommate (and partner), Owen Hughes.

The bells on the front door tinkled and I glanced toward the hall. Women's voices murmured in pleased tones. I looked at the reservations screen, checking for the name Olavssen out of habit. The Bird Woman was a top customer, and also a wild card. I was guiltily relieved to see that she did not have a reservation this morning.

Three ladies stepped into the gift shop: an older woman escorting two teens, their eyes gleaming with delight. Probably they'd gotten out of school to celebrate a birthday, I surmised from the gift bags carried by one of the teens. I barely had a chance to wish them good morning before Rosa, one of my servers, whisked them away to the main parlor.

My stomach rumbled. Resisting the urge to dash down the hall to the butler's pantry and grab a cup of tea, I prowled the gift shop, looking for things to straighten. They were in short supply this early in the day, but I managed to distract myself by rearranging the valentine cards.

"Choosing one for your fiancé?" asked Dale behind me. I glanced at him, taking in his dark gray vest and slacks, silvery satin dress shirt, and burgundy bow tie, all setting off his slightly rakish curling hair. Dapper as usual, and I loved the masculine touch he brought to the tearoom staff.

"Which one do you like best?" I countered. I'd already picked a card to give to Tony, but I was always interested in the male point of view.

"That one," he said without hesitation, reaching past not only the flowery-hearty cards, but also the plaid and the scene of ducks that were there as more masculine offerings. His fingers tapped the top edge of a Mucha reproduction, a voluptuous woman in flowing pink silks, standing on tiptoe and looking coyly over her shoulder at the viewer, framed by an Art Nouveau crescent. Meeting my inquiring gaze, he added, "But then, I've always been partial to nymphs."

"A sign of excellent taste," remarked another voice. Owen's.

Dale and I both turned. Owen stood in the doorway, dramatically formal in a black morning coat with his long, dark hair loose over his shoulders, an elegant turquoise bolo tie the only touch of color about him.

"Good morning," I said, smiling as I stepped forward.

Owen bowed slightly, returning the smile. Dale clicked into server mode and bowed as well.

"May I show you to your alcove?"

Owen and I followed him through the ghost of the Poppy alcove and along the short, drapery-defined passage that gave privacy to Dahlia and led to the Violet alcove. Both areas shared views of the fireplace, but the drapes kept them separate, at least symbolically. Dale stood by the fire while Owen stepped to the chair by the window, leaving me the nearer chair. As soon as we were settled, Dale lifted the cozy from the waiting teapot on the low table before us and filled our cups, then covered the pot again.

"I'll be right back with your tray," he said, and slipped out.

I picked up my cup and saucer and took a sip of tea: Darjeeling. Owen's gaze met mine as I glanced at him. Once again, I was struck by his...I had to call it beauty. He was not effeminate, but "handsome" wasn't the right word. His face reminded me of illustrations of fae that I'd seen in the books I devoured in my youth: slender, high-cheekboned, and slightly ethereal. His every movement was elegant, a studied grace. And while his attire was old-fashioned, it was not the least bit dowdy—quite the opposite. He looked sleek.

"Well," he said, cradling his own cup and saucer in long-fingered hands.

"Well," I replied. "Thank you for joining me."

"The pleasure is mine. I've looked forward to an hour or so of your company." A quiet smile lingered on his lips.

"So have I," I said. "Actually having tea is a rare treat for me, these days." I sipped again, knowing he knew I meant the meal and not the beverage.

"I'm afraid I haven't come to tea here since October."

I nodded. None of Kris's Goth friends had come to tea since then. Not surprising—the death of Gabriel Rhodes on Halloween night had sent a shock through their circle, and although Gabriel hadn't died at the tearoom, his death had arisen from of events that had taken place at the masquerade here that night.

Dale returned, carrying our three-tiered tea tray laden with savories, breads, and sweets. He set it on the low table with the teapot. "This is our Valentine menu, which I hope you'll enjoy. May I get you anything else?"

I looked at Owen. "Would you like some sherry or port? Or champagne?"

His smile took on a mischievous dimple. "I was about to decline, but champagne is always a temptation."

"Two glasses, please," I said to Dale, who bowed himself out.

I had emptied my teacup, so I picked up the pot. "May I warm up your tea?"

"Thank you."

He set his cup and saucer on the table and I filled it, then filled mine. Now that he was closer, I saw that his bolo was spiderweb turquoise, a rare variation with webbed threads of silver inclusion. It was a magnificent stone, not so large as to be vulgarly ostentatious, but certainly valuable.

"That is a gorgeous bolo," I said.

"Thank you."

"My mother had a necklace of spiderweb turquoise."

"Is it yours now?"

"Yes, but I haven't worn it in ages."

I hadn't worn it at all, actually. I treasured it, but I had not been able to bring myself to wear it after Mom's death, and had put it away. Now I wanted to get it out, at least to look at it. Maybe I'd even put it on.

Dale returned with two flutes of champagne on a small silver tray, which he presented with a flourish. He set a glass before each of us, bowed once more, and withdrew.

I picked up my glass, then hesitated, wondering if I should propose a toast. Owen lifted his own flute, relieving me of the indecision.

"Here's to good neighbors," he said.

"Yes." I smiled, sipped, and set down the glass, knowing I should eat something before drinking more. I carefully took the savories plate out of the serving tray.

"Ah," Owen said, gazing at his flute, watching the bubbles climb up it. "Gruet. *Blanc de Noirs*, yes?"

"Yes. It's my favorite."

"Will you serve it at your wedding?"

"We should. Good idea."

Fortunately I could order it wholesale through the tearoom. It was nowhere near as expensive as Dom, or even Veuve Cliquot, but it wasn't dirt cheap either.

I offered the savories to Owen, who carefully transferred his share of the treats to his plate.

"I have so much to thank you for," I said. "The townhome, the photos..."

He waved a dismissive hand, laughing softly. "No need. You'll find, as you get to know me better, that I am largely motivated by self-interest."

"You spent a lot of time photographing and processing Maria's letters," I said as I moved my the savories to my plate. "I don't think you billed me enough."

"I was curious. I wanted to read them. I wouldn't charge you for that."

"You read Spanish?"

He nodded. "Señorita Hidalgo was most expressive."

"I need to find a translator. I can't quite manage her Spanish."

"Well, it's archaic. I would offer, but my Spanish isn't *that* good. I might be able to recommend someone."

"That would be lovely."

I picked up a miniature *bastilla*, a Moroccan spiced chicken pastry, and carefully bit half of it, managing to minimize the filo explosion. Cinnamon and a hint of sugar made it exotic. I gave a small sigh of pleasure as I savored it.

Owen chose to begin with our nod to salad for the month; an endive leaf filled with a Waldorf-style fruit salad, enhanced by fresh currants. My uncle Manny, from whom we ordered most of our produce, must have found those for Julio, in February no less.

We continued to chat as we worked our way through the savories and moved on to the breads. Dale arrived just as I emptied the teapot, and whisked it away to refill it. I took a bite of my scone and looked at Owen, who was gazing at the portrait of Vi over the mantel.

"That's Julio's work, isn't it?" he asked.

"Yes."

"I remember her—the singer. She was brilliant at the party you gave."

"You were there? I don't remember seeing you that day."

"I came stag."

Ah. Yes, perhaps the Goth crew were not into opera, though I would have expected to remember Owen, anyway. They had all been at the tearoom's grand opening celebration earlier last year. That was the first time I'd met Owen, and he had looked—well, much as he did today. Perhaps it was the same coat, in fact.

"You're an opera fan?" I asked, not surprised at all.

"Season tickets every year. My mother taught me expensive tastes, alas."

Well, he could afford them. He was stunningly rich, apparently, though to his credit he didn't flaunt it.

"I usually go once a season," I said. "I haven't decided about this year. Maybe *Romeo and Juliet.*"

"Not *Don Giovanni?*"

"I don't love it. I went to *Tosca* last year—I'd rather see something lighter."

"Have you seen *Cappriccio?*"

"That's the Strauss? No, I haven't."

"I recommend it. You'd like it, I think." Owen smiled. "Will Tony escort you?"

I took a sip of tea. "I hope so."

"Definitely *Cappriccio*, then. It'll be good for him. *Romeo and Juliet*'s a little on-the-nose."

I chuckled, setting down my cup. "True. And the ending is a downer."

"And on that note, a toast." Owen picked up his glass. "To a brilliant, delightful wedding."

"I'll drink to that." I finished my last sip of champagne and sighed, thinking of all the must-do wedding tasks on my list.

"That may be his best painting," Owen said. He was looking at Vi's portrait again.

"Well, they were friends. He put a lot of love into it." I refreshed our tea, then took the sweets plate out of the tiered tray. "Did you give him a studio space at your place?"

The townhomes in his neighborhood were not large, but they did have two bedrooms. The night Tony and I had gone to dinner at Owen and Julio's, Owen had shown us a vacant one he owned, and then offered it to us for far less rent than he could have made on it. I'd been thinking about the second bedroom. We hadn't toured Owen and Julio's home, and I wondered—had Owen been generous enough to give Julio a room of his own?

"Well, actually," he said, looking sheepish, "we have a shared studio. It's a couple of doors down from your townhome."

I managed not to goggle, distracting myself with the sweets. "How many of those townhomes do you own?" I asked as I offered the plate to Owen.

"Um. Six."

"*Six?*"

"Inherited." He moved his strawberry puff, mini Sachertorte, and macarons to his plate. "The other three are rented at the moment. No one you know, but long-termers. I don't like to rent them to vacationers—too disruptive."

I nodded, put my sweets on my plate, and took refuge in my tea, momentarily bereft of speech.

Six townhomes. On Artist Road, one of the more expensive areas in an expensive town. And season tickets to the opera, and who knew what else. Oh, the Mercedes. Ai, yi, yi.

"My photography stuff takes up a lot of space," Owen continued. "Too much, probably. And I have all my musical instruments there, except the little harp that you saw. That was my first harp."

"Oh," I said. "You have others?"

"A couple. The concert harp I played in high school, and a larger Celtic harp, levered. And a baby grand piano."

"Oh!"

"You play the piano, yes? There's one in the big room." He nodded toward the main parlor.

"It was my mother's," I said. "Yes, I play, but I haven't practiced in ages."

"You should come over some time and jam with us."

"Julio plays music?"

"Drums and bass."

"Tony plays guitar," I said shyly.

Owen grinned. "All right! We've got a band!"

I chuckled. "Only one problem. No time for rehearsals."

"Well, we can be a half-assed band. Oh, sorry. That wasn't polite."

I laughed, oddly relieved. "I'm not *always* polite myself."

Still smiling, Owen picked up a cream-colored macaron and took a bite. "Oh! Mmmm!"

I watched his face as he enjoyed the flavors, which were subtle and took a moment. He closed his eyes, chewing slowly, and finally sighed.

"What was that?"

"Elderflower. I told Julio it might be too subtle. The almond can overpower it."

"No, no, no! It's perfect!"

"That's what he said."

I picked up my pink macaron, examining its lovely, smooth shape before destroying it with my teeth. Owen took a bite of his as well, frowning thoughtfully. "Raspberry. And something else…"

I waited. Julio had said Owen was a connoisseur. He'd been speaking of wine, but I suspected Owen might also be an epicurean.

"Rose!" he said, looking to me for confirmation.

"Correct."

"Hah!" He popped the other half into his mouth and chewed in ecstatic triumph, then washed it down with tea. "I will have to ask Julio to bring some of those home."

"We have them in the gift shop. I'll pack some up for you."

"Excellent!" He reached for the strawberry puff. "I remember these."

"Yes. An encore. I considered saving them for the tearoom's first anniversary, but they really are perfect for Valentine's."

"Indeed. And the chocolate I reserve for last, of course."

A soft sound of chimes wafted in from the direction of Dahlia. Dale was ringing the first warning bell.

"Out of time already?" Owen said. "Alas!"

"Well, we're nearly out of food, too," I said, picking up the teapot. "But we have a few minutes still. A final warm-up?"

He nodded. I filled his cup, and poured the last of the pot into mine. Owen took a sip and sighed.

"This has been delightful. Thank you, Ellen."

"I'm glad you enjoyed it."

"I could make a habit of it. Especially with such congenial company. Oh, before I forget…." he set down his cup and pulled an envelope out of his breast pocket, handing it to me. "Keys to the townhome. It's been cleaned, so it's ready for you."

"Thank you. I'll give Tony his—he'll probably want to start moving in this weekend."

"Let me know if you need help with that."

"Thanks. My uncle has a big truck, so I think we'll be good."

Owen nodded, then picked up his Sachertorte. I had fallen behind—I ate my strawberry puff while I watched him savor the chocolate. Again, he closed his eyes, and gave a soft moan as he slowly chewed. I felt a little voyeuristic, watching him. He seemed not to care that I observed his quite evident sensual pleasure.

Maybe I'd give Tony a Sachertorte.

Owen swallowed, and remained still. Oddly, he reminded me a little of Kris's print of the Drowned Ophelia—resting back in his chair, face upturned, hair spilling over his shoulders.

I quietly devoured my own torte, too shy to close my eyes, though I made an effort to pay more attention to the sensations of eating it. Smooth texture, the slight tang that accompanied the rich dark chocolate, the hint of apricot—definitely a tour de force of flavor and mouthfeel. Owen stirred, looked at me, and smiled.

"That was bliss. Thank you."

"You're very welcome. You can thank Julio, too."

"I most certainly will."

The chimes sounded again. Owen sighed, drained his teacup, and stood, offering a hand to me. I took it, though I was perfectly capable of rising from my chair on my own. His fingers squeezed mine slightly before he let go.

Abandoning the emptied plates, cups, and glasses that were all that remained of our feast, I led him out to the gift shop. There I slid eight macarons—two of each flavor, including the chocolate varieties that we hadn't had with our tea—into a small pastry box.

"Ah-ah!" I said, when Owen reached for his wallet. "My gift."

He smiled, accepting the box with his signature slight bow. "Many thanks. I'm looking forward to seeing more of you—once you've settled in."

"That may take a little while, but yes. Eventually I'll reciprocate on your dinner invitation."

"That was all Julio."

"Was it?"

An impish quirk raised one corner of his mouth. "Well, mostly. He wanted to make you dinner, and I wanted a chance to show you the townhome."

"And I'm deeply grateful. You're giving us a tremendous gift. I intend to ply you with all the tea you can manage."

He laughed, then leaned forward and planted a swift kiss on my cheek. "Au revoir, neighbor," he said, and slipped out of the gift shop before I recovered from my surprise and the flush of adrenaline.

A whisper of scent had accompanied the kiss. Something herbal, slightly pungent. Evergreen.

I became aware of Dale watching me from the checkout counter. He wore a bemused smile.

"I'd better get back to work," I said briskly. "You're all right here?"

Dale nodded. I nodded as well, then marched myself upstairs to my desk.

At 3:30, my cell phone rang, pulling my attention out of the web, where I'd been surfing potential wedding venues. I glanced at the caller ID. It was Tony, so I answered.

"Hi!"

"Hey, babe. You free for dinner?"

"Yes."

"How about that Italian place near the Federal building?"

"La Osteria? Nice!"

"Well, I'm sort of celebrating. Got a big report turned in."

"Shall I call and see if they have a table?"

"I already reserved one. Six-thirty okay?"

"That'll work." I glanced toward the window, checking the weather. The sun was starting to dip toward the western horizon. "Shall I drive? We can meet here."

"Sure," Tony said.

"Great!"

And, silence.

"Bye," I said anyway, and put down the phone.

"Mew," called Minuit from her playpen. She'd been napping, but my voice must have awakened her. I got up and went over to her, picking up her feather wand before unzipping the lid of the pen and wiggling the feathers over her head. I didn't want to get black fur on my lace, so I left her in the pen and teased her until she got bored with the toy, then gave her a few scritches and a treat, and closed the pen again.

We were coming to the end of the day. I checked the teapot that lived atop the samovar. It held dregs; time to wash it out. I turned off the samovar and looked into Kris's office, teapot in hand. My office manager was at her desk, glowering at her computer screen. Behind her a row of boxes were stacked against the wall that divided her office from the storeroom.

"Did those arrive today?" I asked.

She glanced at them. "This morning, while you were having tea."

"I'm going out to dinner, but I can put them in the storeroom tonight, after I change."

"There's no room. It's full."

"Oh!" I set the teapot on her credenza and went to examine the labels on the boxes.

"It's all the Valentine cra—uh, stuff," Kris said.

"Maybe we can move some of it down to the gift shop?"

"Everything down there is full, too. Rosa and Dale worked on that today."

"OK. I'm sorry, Kris. It'll move out fast."

"Yeah."

I watched her for a minute, her fingers flying over the keyboard, a small frown line between her brows. She had on a black sweater and black jeans, with her hair caught back in a barrette, a bit more casual than usual for her, but it was Tuesday. The jet beads of the necklace she had worn almost every day since Gabriel died glinted against her sweater. Her sleeves were pushed up, revealing the tattoo on the inside of her left forearm: a wiggle-bladed dagger that Dee had told me was called a "kris." She had a letter opener shaped like the same kind of knife.

"You OK?" I asked softly.

She paused and looked up at me in mild surprise.

"Yeah."

I tried to remember the last time I'd seen her smile. She hadn't been with Gabriel that long, but they had been living together when he died, and I'd expected—hoped—that it would become a lasting relationship. She'd been all right over Christmas, with the exception of a few rough days, but since New Year's her mood had gotten darker. I knew from experience that grief came in waves, and won if the approach of Valentine's Day was bothering her.

"OK," I said. "Let me know if I can help with anything."

"Thanks." She went back to crunching whatever numbers she was working on.

I picked up the teapot and stepped out into the upper hall. Its spaciousness struck me, coming from Kris's cramped office. My little TV area, with the wing chairs that had been in Hyacinth, was separated by a screen from the sitting area that faced the windows. The hall was my ersatz living room, but visitors rarely saw it. The extra boxes could easily have gone out here, against the wall, instead of in Kris's space. I'd move them out after dinner, I decided.

In my suite, I rinsed out the teapot and rubbed away the tea stains with a clean cloth. I never put soap in my teapots—it could stick and alter the flavor of the tea. Returning the pot to its place on the samovar, I headed downstairs to check on things. The four o'clock reservations would be arriving, and the morning staff would be going home. Dee and Iz had taken over for Rosa and Dale in the parlors and the butler's pantry, and Mick was alone in the kitchen, working his way through the day's dishes. He'd already done the kitchen equipment—big bowls and baking sheets were drying in the rack.

The aromas of Julio's food mingled with the scent of piñon logs gently turning to coals in the fireplaces. The day had been fairly mild, but it would get cold after sunset. I'd be wearing my long wool coat to dinner.

I stepped into the dining parlor, which was empty. The table had been cleared of all but the lace tablecloth and the centerpiece of pink and white roses glowing softly beneath the chandelier. Not many walk-ins on Tuesdays, especially late in the day. At four, the last seating of the day, we would have people who liked to take tea at the traditional time and had planned ahead, making reservations for their favorite alcoves.

Looking up at the chandelier, I watched for any movement of the crystals, but they were still. Captain Dusenberry, my ghostly housemate, had nothing to comment on today, apparently.

I walked up to the gift shop to confirm that all the storage space was full. A young woman was browsing the valentine cards, and the servers were both busy, so I lingered at the counter, tidying supplies and glancing at the reservations list. None of the names were familiar.

The customer brought two cards over, and I rang them up for her, then closed out the register for the day and carried the bank bag —slightly more slender than usual—up to Kris's office.

"Thanks," she said as I laid it on the corner of her desk.

I had caught up on my messages, so I went back to surfing wedding venues. I was looking for a garden, but the search results were mostly hotels, B&Bs, casinos, a couple of museums. Most of those places would want to cater, and I wanted Julio to do the food. The Santa Fe Botanical Garden was a maybe, but the amphitheater just didn't sing to me. And the plantings were pretty deserty. I wanted something a little more lush.

Santa Fe Baldy might be my best bet after all.

Sighing, I closed the browser and went downstairs again to the kitchen. Mick, plugged into his music as usual, glanced up at me, gave a wave, and went back to the dishes. I nodded back, then blithely took a small plate from a cupboard, crossed to the refrigerator and helped myself to two Sachertortes. One for me, one for Tony.

Maybe I'd tell him to close his eyes.

*L*A OSTERIA WAS WARM and cozy. The candle in the center of our table pushed back the darkness just enough so we could see what we were eating—chicken picatta for me, pasta bolognaise for Tony—and the Sangiovese lit a gentle glow in my stomach. Tony had changed into a dress shirt and tie, and looked quite handsome, I thought. His leather motorcycle jacket was draped over the back of his chair. Probably his warmest coat, and I didn't begrudge it on this chilly evening.

"So that report I turned in wraps up a case I've been working on for eight months," he said.

I lifted my wine glass. "Congratulations!"

"I may actually have a couple of free days this week."

"You could spend them packing." I reached for my purse, took out a key, and offered it to him. "Owen brought these by today. Here's yours."

Tony met my gaze, then picked up the key from my palm. He turned it over in his hand.

"Here's to the new place," I said, raising my glass in a toast.

Tony nodded and emptied his glass, and a waiter stepped out of the shadows to refill it, then slipped away again.

"Let me know if you need boxes," I said. "We have lots."

"I could probably use some."

I could not picture Tony carrying a load of cardboard across town on his bike. "I'll bring a stack over for you. We break them down for recycling. Do you have wide tape?"

"I don't."

"We have a tape gun. I'll lend it to you."

"Thanks." He shot me a shy glance. "God, it's getting real."

"Yes."

I'd have to pack, too, but I had no time constraints, unlike Tony. I'd probably start with furniture.

"When is your rent due?" I asked.

"The fifteenth."

"Do you want to try to be out before then?"

"Could try." He shrugged, then looked up at me. "You ever... done this, before? Moved in with someone?"

I sipped my wine. "I've had roommates, but that's not the same."

"No."

"How about you?"

Tony shook his head.

"An adventure for both of us, then."

The adventure of a lifetime, I hoped. Tony took out his keychain and added the townhome key to it.

"Did Owen say when the rent is due?"

"I imagine he'll let us decide when to pay."

Tony frowned briefly, then straightened his shoulders and met my gaze. "The max we agreed on, I told him we'd pay that."

"Okay," I said.

We had calculated that number as the most we could comfortably afford, when we were looking for a place to rent together. Owen's townhome would easily have brought him more, but he cared more about having friends as neighbors than about making money. He'd told us he'd be donating our rent money to charity, which was certainly an incentive to pay promptly, to me at least.

"If I'm in by the fifteenth, we'll pay then," Tony said.

"I won't be in that fast. I'm sure Owen would give us a little extra time."

Tony's frown returned. "We'll pay as soon as we can," he said.

"Okay."

Tony was still uncomfortable about accepting Owen's generosity, I knew. He dug into his meal again. Watching him, I took a bite of chicken.

He was nervous about this transition. Heck, I was nervous about it, too. I could start by moving furniture—the TV and so on—but when I moved my bed, I'd be committed. It was a queen-sized canopy bed, and it would be a pain to move. I'd have to do it on a Sunday, and I'd need help to disassemble it and get it down the stairs. The box springs and the mattress would be the hardest part. Nat and Gina had helped me move them in, over a year ago.

We'd gotten them in, we could get them out. I had considered leaving the bed at the tearoom, hanging onto my suite for the occasions when I might want to crash there, but I was certain my bed was more comfortable than Tony's. It was definitely bigger—he'd told me so. Why buy a new bed if we didn't need to?

I finished my chicken with the last bite of pasta I'd been saving. Tony had scraped his plate clean. He drained his wine glass again, and the waiter reappeared to carefully divide the last of the bottle between us.

"May I interest you in dessert?" she asked.

"Not for me," I said.

Tony shook his head. The waiter nodded and withdrew.

"Shall we stop by the new place?" I asked.

Tony blinked. "Sure."

He picked up the bill, and I drove up to Artist Road. Our new home! A little ball of excitement formed in my gut. I parked in the empty driveway and Tony used his key to unlock the door.

It was cold inside; the heat was still set low. We walked through the rooms again. We'd been all through the place before with Owen and Julio, but it was ours now. I stood in the empty master bedroom, looking out at the lights of the city and the hot tub that I would be trying out very soon. Gratitude welled up in me once more for Owen's gracious gift.

"I'm going to give Angela my bed," Tony said. "She just has a twin. I can sleep on the floor for now."

"I have a sofa bed in storage. You could sleep on that until I move my bed in."

"Oh, great! Can we get it this weekend?"

"Maybe Sunday."

He nodded. I stepped across the hall to the second bedroom. It was smaller, and the windows looked out on the front yard on one wall and the space between the house and the neighboring one on another. There was a little landscaping there—a couple of trees that were bare at the moment—but no view.

Tony joined me. "Your office?"

"No. My office is at the tearoom." I turned to him. "I think you should have this room."

Surprise widened his eyes. He looked around the room as if seeing it anew. "Why?"

"You're giving up your place. You should have a room of your own."

He turned to me, and folded me into a hug, kissing my face all over until he reached my lips, where he lingered.

"Thank you," he whispered.

I smiled. "Besides, I'd rather not have a TV in the living room. This can be your man-cave."

He grinned, kissed me some more, then took my hand, pulling me toward the door. "It's late. Gotta get home."

"Want those boxes tonight? We could put them in my car and I can follow you to your place."

He hesitated briefly. "Okay."

I drove to the tearoom and we headed upstairs. The empty boxes were tucked against the wall inside the storeroom behind Kris's office. I pulled them all out, then put back the ones that were too small. That left a dozen bigger ones, of varying shapes. I collected the tape gun while Tony carried them downstairs. I also ducked into my suite and grabbed the Sachertortes, stuffing them into a container and dropping it into the pocket of my coat.

Minuit, awakened by the ruckus, mewed sleepily from the playpen in my office. I gave her a treat and left her there; I had learned not to set her loose in my suite unless I was there. She mewed a little more as I followed Tony downstairs, her pathetic calls pursuing me. I felt bad, but I knew she'd be all right.

Tony was waiting by the back door, the boxes leaning against the wall. I picked up a few of the boxes, and Tony hefted the rest, an awkward armful. We dumped them in the trunk of my car and Tony gave me a quick kiss before going to his bike.

A few flakes of snow had started to drift down. I hoped it wouldn't be a heavy storm. Most of the leftover snow had melted, except for the shady spots on the north side of the house. The lilac buds were getting big. I was ready for it to be spring.

Tony's apartment building looked even more stark at night, under coppery streetlights that lit up the falling snow. We hurried the boxes inside, and Tony stacked them against the living room wall.

"I'll get the tape gun," I said, and headed back to the car. Tony stood in the doorway watching. Guarding me.

"Brr!" I pulled the door closed behind me and handed him the gun. "Mind if I stay a bit and warm up?"

He tilted his head a little. "Sure."

He picked up a box and carried it over to the battered leather armchair, where he sat, unfolded the box, and proceeded to tape the bottom. I sat on the couch and took the Sachertortes out of my pocket. They were a little the worse for wear, but not bad. Especially if we ate them with eyes closed.

Tony set the box aside and put the tape gun on the coffee table. "What's that?"

"Dessert," I said.

"Oh."

"Sachertorte. Ever had it?"

He frowned. "If I did, I didn't know its name."

"It's a Viennese classic. Dark chocolate cake, with apricot."

He nodded. "Should I get some plates?"

I stood, setting the container on the couch, and took off my coat. Picking up the box, I said, "It would be more fun to feed them to each other by hand."

Tony's eyebrows rose.

"I've never been in your bed," I added.

He blinked. "Your bed is nicer."

"But we're here."

Tony swallowed, then stood, dropped his coat on the chair, and came to me.

The tortes, when we got to them, which took a little while, were delicious.

This time I was the one who went home at yuck o'clock, not because I was embarrassed to spend the night, but because the tearoom was already getting busy ahead of Valentine's Day and I wanted to be at work promptly. Also, the Bird Woman had a reservation that morning and I thought I should be available. Just in case there were, you know, ballerinas or something.

The snow had stopped, but the streets had frozen into black ice by the time I left Tony's apartment. I drove home gingerly, grateful that Cerrillos Road was pretty much empty at three in the morning. The Camry slipped a little going around corners, but made it home without serious incident.

Light glowed through the sheer curtains of the dining parlor, shining a welcoming path across the *portal* and into the night. I was certain I had not turned on the chandelier.

I pulled into my parking spot, shut off the engine, and got out, clutching keys in one hand and my food container in the other. I paused beside the car, listening and looking around for anything unusual, a habit I'd acquired since last fall. The night was cold and still, and smelled of snow. Confident that I was alone, I let myself in and locked the door behind me.

The house was warm and quiet. Turning to the dining parlor, I saw that the chandelier was motionless. And the light switch was in the "off" position, but here we were.

"Hello, Captain," I said, standing in the open doorway. "Thank you for the light."

A single crystal glinted softly, swinging slightly. I smiled, then turned toward the hall, heading for the stairs. The parlor light went out.

The upstairs hall light cast a faint glow down the stairwell, enough for me to see my way. That light I *had* left on, partly to keep Minuit company. She started to cry when she heard me on the stairs.

"Yes, I know, honey. I'm sorry."

I took off my coat and hung it on the hall coat rack, then took Minuit out of her playpen, cuddling her to my chest as I carried her to my suite. I fed her, then tidied both her litter boxes. I needed a shower, but I was also yawning like crazy, so I settled for washing my face and brushing my teeth before collapsing into bed. A few minutes later, just as I was drifting off, Minuit climbed up the bedspread and curled up on the spare pillow.

I had weird chocolate dreams.

Not enough hours had passed when the savory smells of baking *bastilla* pulled me out of sleep. I stayed in bed, unwilling to move. Minuit somehow knew I was awake, though. She started parading back and forth across my chest.

"Okay, okay." I rolled onto my side and caught her, subjecting her to the punishment of a cuddle. She purred loudly, so my choice of punishment wasn't so great.

"Mew," she said, then went back to purring.

"Yeah, I know." I yawned. "Okay."

I dragged myself out of bed and bumbled my way to the kitchenette, where I dished up some breakfast for the kitten. Leaving her quietly eating, I took a hurried shower, finding little smears of chocolate in odd places.

That *had* been fun.

I got dressed, choosing a heavy cotton blouse over a plaid wool skirt—Night Watch—for warmth. A lace collar and a dark green string tie completed the rather prim ensemble. I took Minuit to her playpen in my office for the day, fired up the samovar and made tea, and got through the previous day's messages by the time Kris arrived, slightly later than usual.

"How are the roads?" I asked her, helping myself to tea.

"Wretched."

"Cup of tea?"

"I'll get some in a minute. Thanks."

Seeing she was already focusing on work, I headed downstairs after drinking my tea. The kitchen was bustling, Ramon assisting Julio and Hanh. Dale was in the butler's pantry setting up trays for the first seating. The hot water urn gurgled as I greeted Dale.

"Need anything?" I asked.

"Nope. We're all good. Rosa called in—she's on her way, but she'll be late."

I nodded. "Better safe than sorry."

I toured the parlors. Dale had already laid fires in the fireplaces. We'd light them closer to opening, so it was still a little chilly downstairs, making me glad I'd dressed warmly. I checked on the gift shop, restocked a few items, then headed back up to my office.

A brand-new lavender message slip lay in my in box: Gina had called. I was a little reluctant to call back, knowing she'd assign me wedding homework, but I shook it off and compromised by texting.

> Got your message. This
> Saturday works for tea with
> Angela. What's a good time?

She fired back almost immediately:

> How about we shop for
> dresses instead and have
> dinner out after?

> Okay. I still owe you guys tea,
> though.

> Next week would be good.
> Angela's free on
> Wednesday afternoons.

> I'll reserve a spot for us at 1:30,
> then. We're booking up
> already.

> Great. I'll let Angela know.
> Pick you up at 12:30
> Saturday?

Fine.

She was not going to let me postpone the dress-shopping.

Bringing up the reservations software, I saw that Wednesday was indeed booking up. Jonquil was the only available alcove at 1:30, so I grabbed it, then went back to hunting for a wedding venue. I had no better luck than before, and gave up after half an hour of searching. Santa Fe was horridly expensive.

Well, I knew that perfectly well. Tea at the Wisteria Tearoom was not cheap, although the cream tea—just tea and a scone—was more accessible than the full afternoon tea, which was a substantial meal. I felt no remorse for our prices: they reflected the quality of our food, not to mention the elegant and cozy atmosphere I had so carefully created. Good china was not cheap either, and we inevitably lost a piece now and then to careless handling, more often by customers than by my staff, whom I had drilled on the proper care of fine porcelain. Mick had not broken a piece in months, even when we were frantically busy.

I had a good team. I paused for a moment, thinking about how far we'd come since the opening last April. We'd made lots of mistakes early on, and had recovered from them beautifully. We still made mistakes, but we had learned what worked and what didn't, and we had built strong relationships of trust among the staff. We had many regulars, whom we treated like family. The Wisteria Tearoom was more than a restaurant. It was a community.

For all this, I was deeply grateful. I closed my browser, wanting to spend a few minutes reflecting on the many blessings that had made the tearoom possible. I filled my teacup and moved to the chaise longue to drink it.

Every member of the staff was important, but there were two without whom the tearoom could not function: my chef and my business manager. Julio was doing great, and our recent conversation the night he and Owen had given us dinner had assuaged my concerns that he might be thinking about starting his own restaurant. He was, but he was in no hurry, and he would make sure the tearoom would not suffer when the time came for him to move on.

Kris concerned me more; she seemed to be struggling, and I wasn't sure how to help. I understood grief, although everyone experiences it differently. Kris was not prone to confide in me about personal issues. She kept a professional distance.

I wondered if I should take her out and invite her to talk. Sipping my tea, I realized I had assumed that her social circle was supporting her as she worked through her loss, but that might not be the case. Gabriel had, so Kris herself had told me, been romantically involved with *all* the women in that circle. And it was possible that he might not have stuck to just the women.

Deciding not to wander down that path of thought, I finished my tea and refilled the cup before returning to my desk and my duties. Gina had emailed me a dozen links to pictures of wedding dresses she wanted me to look at. They were all of the Cinderella variety.

I adore Gina, but we have vastly different taste. She must have assumed that Victorian would be my preferred style. Hoop skirts and sparkling trains and giant bows on the butt—I dutifully looked at them all, and did not like any of them.

Deciding I'd better try to redirect her enthusiasm before she loaded me into a magic pumpkin, I surfed up a few evening dresses I liked, and sent the links back to her. If we were going shopping Saturday, I did not want to have to try on the Cinderellas.

I had just hit "send" on the email when Rosa appeared in my doorway, slightly out of breath and prettily flushed from running up the stairs.

"Can you come down to the gift shop?" she said, a little wide-eyed.

"Sure."

Minuit, hearing Rosa's voice, mewed and uncurled herself, hoping to play. Rosa glanced at her, but didn't answer the call of cuteness. There must be something serious going on downstairs.

I stepped out into the hall, drawing Rosa away from Kris's doorway. "What is it?" I asked *sotto voce*.

"Mrs. Olavssen," she said.

Say no more. I headed down the stairs, with Rosa close behind.

It wasn't yet eleven, but the gift shop opened at ten-thirty. I braced myself for an interesting group of guests, but when I reached the shop, I saw that the Bird Woman was alone. She stood by the table of Valentine's Day merchandise, wearing her long fake-fur coat and a surprisingly modest purple hat, slightly larger than a pillbox, with a tasteful spray of feathers. She caught sight of me and stepped toward me, brandishing one of the black heart mugs that I disliked.

"There you are! I need three dozen of these, and you've only got six!"

"Good morning," I responded. "I believe we have more of those mugs upstairs."

"I looked in the storeroom and didn't find any," Rosa said.

"They're in the hall, front corner on the left."

Rosa darted off, and I smiled at the Bird Woman. "I know we have at least two dozen more. If you need more than that we can order them, and they should be in before Valentine's Day. Will that do?"

"Yeah," she said, and grabbed a second mug. I helped her bring the six mugs on display to the checkout counter. Glancing at the reservations, I saw that she was down for a party of four.

"Would you like to take them after your tea? I can wrap these up for you, and leave the rest in their boxes."

"Yeah, that'll be good. Thanks," she said, and wandered over to the greeting card display.

I sent Kris a text asking her to order another two dozen heart mugs, and be prepared to order more.

Rosa arrived with Dale behind her, each of them carrying a box of twelve mugs. I gestured toward the counter and they put them there. The Bird Woman insisted on inspecting them, so I opened the boxes to show her their contents. She gave a nod and a gruff "hmph" of approval, then plunked a fistful of valentine cards on the counter.

"These too. Got any more of the alligator ones?"

I glanced at Rosa, who obviously wanted to get back to preparing for guests.

"I'll check," I said. "Thank you, Rosa."

She shot me a grateful smile and left, with Dale close behind.

"Is this for Esperanza?" I asked.

The Bird Woman looked up from the greeting card display. "Yes it is, and don't you go giving me a discount again. I can afford it."

"All right."

While she continued to browse, I checked the reservations for the rest of the month. Valentine's Day had been booked solid since New Year's, but on the day before I saw "Olavssen" down for a party of twelve in the dining parlor.

"I see you have a large party on the 13th. If those are Esperanza residents, I'd like to give you a discount then."

She brought another fistful of cards to the counter and gave me a sharp look. "Okay, but make it a little one. Don't go giving me half off."

"Twenty-five percent?"

"Ten."

I kept my amusement down to a smile. "Twenty," I said. "I can deduct it."

"Okay, fine, but only if it doesn't put you in the red."

"It won't. Thanks for your concern."

"Hey, I'm selfish!" Her face lit in a sudden grin. "I want this place to stick around. It's the best place in town to dress up and bring my buddies."

I smiled. "Thank you! And we have every intention of sticking around."

I heard the bells on the front door jingle. Guests arriving for tea. The Bird Woman looked up and went to the doorway to greet the new arrivals—two women and a man, dressed in business attire. A working tea, then. That explained Mrs. Olavssen's subdued (for her) appearance. I finished entering a note about the discount on her reservation for the 13th, and stepped out from behind the counter.

"And this here's the owner, Miss Rosings," she said. She rattled off the names of her guests.

"Good morning," I said. "Welcome to the Wisteria Tearoom. May I take your coats?"

"Nah, I'll show them where to hang them," said the Bird Woman. "What flower are we in?"

"Iris."

"Gotcha. We'll find our way back."

Resisting the impulse to follow them, I stayed behind and restocked the depleted greeting cards, setting aside six more alligator cards for Mrs. Olavssen. Other guests began to arrive, and for the next half hour I was busy showing them to their alcoves and packing up the mugs. When everyone was seated and the servers were bringing out tea trays, I went upstairs to fetch more cards and do a little electronic investigating.

At my desk, I brought up the Esperanza website and looked at the names of the shelter's organizers. I was right: Mrs. Olavssen's guests were the manager and two of the board members.

Pleased with myself, I checked the teapot on the samovar, which was empty. I set a fresh pot steeping and ducked past Kris's desk to the storeroom to get more valentine cards. My attitude toward the goofy alligator cards, which Nat had insisted we order, was similar to my feelings about the heart mugs. I was happy to be proved wrong in both cases.

Kris had been on the phone, but she now hung up and gave me a questioning look as I emerged from the storeroom with the cards.

"Mrs. Olavssen," I said. "How fast can we get the mugs?"

"By Monday, if we pay for expedited shipping."

"Okay."

"Is she taking all the ones we have?"

"Yes."

"Then I should order three dozen more. They're selling," Kris added when I gave her a look.

The timer for the tea went off, excusing me from answering. Leaving the valentines on my credenza, I removed the infuser and set the lid on the pot, then picked it up.

"Tea?" I offered, glancing around the corner at Kris.

"Yes."

I filled Kris's cup, then went into my office to fill mine.

"Mew," called Minuit from her playpen.

I returned the teapot to the samovar and went to distract the kitten so she wouldn't bother Kris with crying. Also, kitten therapy.

She really was good for that, I reflected as I teased her with the feather wand. Rosa wasn't the only member of my staff who liked to take kitten breaks: Dee played with her frequently, and Dale now and then. Even Mick liked to visit her.

Minuit tired of the feathers, so I picked her up and cuddled her, scritching her head. She rewarded me with a loud purr. I carried her to my desk and petted her, and she curled up on my lap. Looking up, I saw the valentine cards I had set aside on my credenza. Oh yeah.

Well, Mrs. Olavssen would be busy with tea for a while. I stroked Minuit's fluffy fur and checked my email. No answer yet from Gina. I sipped my tea.

Trapped under a napping kitten, I surfed wedding venues some more, then surfed wedding dresses. Nothing I liked in either category. How depressing.

There were no messages in my in box. I had finished my tea. Remembering my musings earlier that morning, I sent a text to Kris:

> May I take you out to dinner sometime soon? It would give us a chance to chat without interruptions.
>
> Is there something you want to talk about?
>
> Nothing in particular. Just thought it would be nice to spend some time with you.

I waited for a response. Glancing up at my computer screen, I noticed Kris standing in the doorway beyond it, looking puzzled.

"Kitten in my lap," I said.

Her face cleared. "Oh. I thought something must be wrong."

"No, no."

We gazed at each other for a moment.

"You want me to bring you some tea?" Kris said.

"Thanks, but I should probably get back downstairs." I lifted Minuit from my lap, holding her gently as I moved her to the playpen. She complained softly, then settled into her towel bed. I zipped the playpen closed.

"Will you think about dinner?" I said, straightening. "Check your calendar?"

"Okay."

Kris sounded less than enthusiastic. I smiled and picked up the valentine cards from my credenza. She headed back to her desk.

In the gift shop, I topped up the greeting cards and added the remaining alligator cards to the Bird Woman's pile, then taped up the two boxes of mugs and made sure everything else was ready. The six extra mugs were wrapped and tucked into one of our large lavender merchandise bags. I had a small bag ready to hold the cards, once she decided which ones she was taking.

Dale breezed through with a teapot for Dahlia. "I'm going to want your help carrying boxes out for Mrs. Olavssen," I warned him.

"Right-o," he said, and disappeared through the doorway.

Caught up. I began to eye the macarons in the pastry case.

Lunch! Must not forget to eat.

Again. I'd missed breakfast. Oops.

Odd that a foodie, as I considered myself to be, would often forget to eat. It was just that the tearoom was a complex operation, and there were almost always multiple things demanding my attention. From the moment I was fully awake each morning, must-do tasks occupied my thoughts.

I glanced at the clock on the checkout station: quarter to one. Guess I'd officially missed lunch.

A party that had been in Lily wandered into the gift shop. Their server would have settled their bill, but they wanted to shop. For the next half hour, as the other parties from the seating went through, I was busy ringing up purchases.

Mental note: ask Nat if she could help all next week.

The Bird Woman came in at last, along with one of her guests, who headed for the tea display while her hostess came to the counter. Mrs. Olavssen had not yet collected her coat, which I had noticed hanging on one of the hooks in the hall. Her dress was a rich purple, and beautifully tailored. Perhaps just a trifle too close-fitting for her, but that was nitpicking. She looked quite smart. My only quibble was with her necklace of sparkling faceted gemstones—Miss Manners would tsk at their being worn before evening. When I'd first met the Bird Woman I would have assumed they were costume jewelry, but I now suspected they might actually be real.

"I hope you enjoyed your tea," I said.

"Yeah, it was great! Loved those macaroons!" She pointed to the pastry case. "Wrap up a couple dozen for me, will you?"

Macarons.

"Which flavors?" I asked, getting out a large pastry box.

"Mix 'em up."

"All right. I brought down all our stock of the alligator cards for you to look at."

"Great! I'll take 'em all!"

She reviewed her card choices while I filled the pastry box. The smell of the macarons made my stomach grumble. I would have to eat something soon.

Dale emerged from Dahlia with a tray of used china. I caught his eye and glanced toward the boxes of mugs on the counter. He nodded and whisked out to the hall.

Ringing up the Bird Woman's purchases took a while. Dale returned from the kitchen and set about helping, tucking the box of macarons in with the six mugs and the greeting cards while I tallied them up.

At last we were done. Mrs. Olavssen paid the staggering bill, then went out to the hall to fetch her coat, accompanied by Dale. Her guest from Esperanza, who had patiently waited, said as I finally rang up her two packets of tea, "The menu was delicious! I'm so glad Eugenia brought us."

Eugenia.

I had seen her name on her credit card, of course, but I couldn't convince myself it was her true name. To me she was the Bird Woman, though I had sometimes heard her friends call her Ginny.

"Thank you! I hope you'll visit us again," I said, sliding a card for a free cream tea into the bag with the guest's tea.

Dale and I each carried a box of mugs out to Mrs. Olavssen's massive Cadillac, walking behind her like sherpas down the path to the gate while she carried the large lavender shopping bag of mugs and valentines. I noticed my snowdrops pushing up by the fence, and my mood brightened. The day was sunny and crisp. Good to get outside for a minute.

Dale stepped around to the driver door to open it for the Bird Woman, a bit of gallantry that made her beam with delight. I gazed around my sleeping garden, and noticed a young woman in black jeans and a dusty black parka with patches of duct tape on the elbows standing by the corner of the fence, gazing into my yard. She looked familiar.

The Cadillac pulled away, and Dale joined me by the gate. I looked back toward the young woman, now walking away down the sidewalk.

"Was that…?"

"Margo," Dale said, nodding.

UESTIONS ROLLED THROUGH MY MIND as we went back inside. All the guests from the first seating were gone, and Dale hurried back to the task of clearing and setting up alcoves for the next seating. I went upstairs to my suite and threw together a tuna sandwich, making myself sit down to eat it at my café table.

What was Margo Foss doing here? She hadn't been to the tearoom since Halloween, and I had not expected to see her again.

I didn't *want* to see her again. She was a troubled young woman, and though I had intervened on her behalf, not wanting to see her charged with murder for Gabriel's accidental death, the fact was that she had caused his death, intentionally or not.

Remembering the events of last autumn was something I would have preferred to avoid. My interference, as Tony had seen it, had created a painful silence between us for weeks. Thanksgiving had been miserable for me, despite Gina's inviting me to dine with her large and boisterous family. I wanted to forget that time.

I looked at the half sandwich remaining on my plate. My hunger had fled. I picked up a piece of celery that had fallen out and ate it.

Maybe Margo was trying to find closure. Or maybe she was still obsessed with Gabriel. That seemed more likely. She did morose very well, which may have been what led her to become a Goth.

But why would she come here? Gabriel hadn't died here. Was she also hanging around Hidalgo Plaza? I hoped not.

One thing was certain—I didn't want Margo pestering Kris.

Dale—would he mention he'd seen her to Kris? I didn't think so, but I wanted to make sure.

I stuck the rest of my sandwich in the mini fridge in the kitchenette, and took a little bit of tuna that I had saved out for Minuit across the hall. Kris was on the phone, so I gave the kitten her treat and then headed downstairs.

The tearoom was filled with guests again, already enjoying their feasts. I stepped into the butler's pantry, where Dee was brewing tea, and glanced through to the kitchen, looking for Dale. Not there.

He was serving Dahlia and Violet that day, so I staked out the gift shop, and soon saw him coming out of the doorway to the alcoves with an empty teapot. I walked with him to the butler's pantry.

"Don't mention to Kris—"

"I won't."

"Thank you."

We went into the pantry, passing Dee on her way out with a full pot of tea. She flashed us a smile as she left.

I watched Dale rinse out his teapot and fill a fresh infuser with tea leaves. "Any idea what she was doing here?" I asked as I filled a kettle from the urn for him and set it to boil.

"No."

"I assume she hasn't been socializing with…Kris's friends."

Dale glanced at me. "I've had coffee with her a couple of times. She's going through a tough time."

Well, she wasn't the only one.

"That's kind of you," I said.

"She didn't say anything about coming here, if you're

wondering."

"I'm just a bit surprised."

"Me, too."

The kettle whistled. Dale poured boiling water over the tea leaves, sending up an aroma of jasmine. I got out of his way, going back to the gift shop, where I made the rounds of the displays, tidying and restocking.

Maybe Margo had just been passing by. She lived on the other side of town, I knew, but she might have had business in the area.

At the courthouse?

I swallowed. I hadn't kept track at all of what was happening with Margo, but I assumed she'd be facing a possible trial. It occurred to me that I might be asked to testify at such a trial. I had not witnessed the accident, but I *had* spotted the evidence that had led the police to suspect Margo, and I had also realized that Gabriel's death was accidental. Tony hadn't liked that insight.

Margo probably wanted to see me as little as I wanted to see her, really.

I decided to let it go, as there was nothing I could do about it. If Margo showed up again, I might have to be proactive.

An older couple came in, their clothes just different enough in style from Santa Fe's usual, and their manner just hesitant enough, that I deduced they were tourists. I greeted them and learned they were visiting from Pennsylvania, and had heard there was a wonderful tearoom in Santa Fe. Could they get some tea?

I explained our reservation system, gave them our brochure, and invited them to have cream tea in the dining parlor while they thought about making a reservation for afternoon tea later in their vacation. They accepted with delight, and I escorted them back to the parlor, then found Iz and told her they were there. She nodded and headed for the butler's pantry to put on a kettle. The gift shop was quiet, so I went upstairs to check on my desk and maybe have a kitten fix.

Minuit was asleep. Leaving her alone, I sat at my desk, dealt with a couple of messages, and sent an email to Nat asking if she'd come in and help next week.

I also texted Tony, inquiring if he knew what was going on with Margo's case. It took a little courage to do that since it was a sore point between us, but if Margo came back around I wanted to be up to date on her status. He didn't answer right away, so I assumed he was busy.

My stomach growled. It was getting close to four. I wanted a macaron or five, but I made myself go across the hall and finish my half-eaten tuna sandwich before permitting myself to go downstairs for sweets. The couple from Pennsylvania was in the gift shop, being checked out by Dee.

"We loved the cream tea!" said the woman. "This house is so beautiful! We made a reservation for Friday."

"We'll look forward to seeing you again," I said, smiling.

I checked the pastry case, saw that it was half-empty, and went to the kitchen for more macarons and rose almond cookies. Hanh and Ramon had left for the day, Julio was just putting on his jacket, and Mick was at the dish washing station. The kitchen smelled of soap and the ghosts of baked goods.

"Have a nice evening," I said to Julio as I opened a container of sweets and began filling a tray for the gift shop.

"You too. Oh, Owen asked me to give you this."

He took a small envelope out of his jacket pocket and handed it to me. It was fine stationery, and had my name written on it in fluid script.

"Thanks," I said.

"Night," he added, heading out the door.

"Good night."

I took the sweets to the gift shop and put them in the pastry case, saving out two macarons and a rose almond cookie for myself. I tucked them under the counter with Owen's note, waited on two shoppers, then escaped upstairs as Dale came in from Dahlia with a party of three young women whom he took to the tea display, showing them the teas featured with the current menu.

Minuit was awake and mewing. I put my sweets and the note on my desk, played with her for a couple of minutes, then gave her a treat and checked the teapot on the samovar. Half a pot left. I poured a cup for myself and looked in on Kris.

"Tea?"

She shook her head, absorbed in her computer as usual. I retired to my chaise longue with my tea, sweets, and Owen's note, which turned out to be a thank-you for the afternoon tea. His handwriting was elegant and more perfect than mine. I tended to write hurriedly, but the beauty of this note made me resolve to take my time more in future.

Setting it aside, I turned to the sweets. The chocolate hazelnut macaron was perfection. The rose almond cookie was also perfection. Anticipating a trifecta, I was about to bite into the elderflower macaron when Tony walked in and came over to me, holding out my tape gun.

"Done with this."

I put the sweet down on my saucer. "You've finished packing?"

"I've finished putting boxes together. Packing will take another day or so."

For a moment I felt chagrined. Packing was certain to take me longer. Tony really did live simply, apparently.

"Put it on the credenza, please."

He did so. "Got your text. Margo's going to trial for Man One. Should be in the next few months."

I glanced toward Kris's office, hoping she hadn't heard. "I see. Thank you."

"She's lucky. Thanks to you, she'll get off easy. Might get a little jail time and be fined a few hundred bucks if she's convicted."

I stood, wanting to divert him from the subject. "Would you like some tea? Maybe a scone?"

"No, thanks. Got a couple more errands to run, then I'm gonna start packing."

"All right. If you need emergency pizza, give me a call."

That got a grin out of him. He put his arms around me, hugging my hips to him. "Might need emergency chocolate."

I felt myself blush. He kissed me, then released me.

"Talk to you later," he said on his way out.

"Bye," I said softly as I listened to his steps descending the stairs. I stood still for a minute, then shook myself back to the present. Retrieving my teacup, I went to the samovar and filled it, then glanced casually toward Kris's desk.

She wasn't there.

Maybe she hadn't heard, then. I sat at my desk and ate the last macaron. The elderflower flavor was beautiful and haunting. I felt sad when it was gone.

Actually, I just felt sad. For Margo, for Kris, and for Gabriel. For everyone in that circle—Kris's Goths, as I thought of them—who had been traumatized in one way or another by Gabriel's death. The shape of their lives had been shattered that night, like the shards of glass surrounding a naked woman in one of Gabriel's paintings. They might put the pieces back together eventually, but it wouldn't be easy, and there would always be a gap.

I finished my tea, then took my cup and saucer across the hall and washed them. I'd had enough for today. Evening was coming on, and I went down for my final check on the parlors. A few guests lingered over their sweets; more were in the gift shop. Kris was there also, collecting the day's receipts. A couple of regular customers waylaid me before I could approach her, and she left as I stood chatting with them.

Dee was handling the register, so as soon as I was free I went upstairs. Kris was at her desk, tallying up the deposit. I did a quick check of my messages, then came and sat in her guest chair. She ignored me while I watched her do the numbers. Capable of intent focus, she was rarely flustered, and didn't seem so now. Yet she did seem tense, as she had been frequently of late.

She completed the deposit and tucked the cash and checks into the bank bag, then finally looked up at me. "You waiting for this?"

"I'm waiting to talk to you."

The faintest tinge of color came into her cheeks. "Okay."

"Did you get a chance to check your calendar?"

"Oh. No."

"Could you do it now?"

She was still for a few seconds, then picked up her phone and poked at it. "Tuesday night's free."

"Tuesday is perfect. How about Luminaria?"

She met my gaze. "Pretty fancy."

"It's comfortable. Relaxing. Seven o'clock?"

"Okay."

I watched her enter the date in her phone. "Thanks, Kris," I said. "I'm looking forward to some girl time with you."

A swift, surprised glance, then she was back to business, picking up the bank bag and locking her desk. "I'll drop this at the bank on the way home."

"See you tomorrow," I said, standing and collecting her teacup, which I carried to the samovar table. Kris breezed past me to the coat rack, swung into her coat, and was headed downstairs before I had put the teapot and her cup onto a tray.

"Mew," said a sleepy Minuit, roused by the noise of our activities.

I left the tea things and took the kitten out of her playpen. I needed a cuddle.

By Friday, the tearoom was almost as busy as it had been during December. My calves ached from going up and down the stairs all day, and I began to think seriously of installing a dumb waiter. Tony was busy packing, and I was too tired to do more than heat up some leftovers for dinner. I took a bubble bath and collapsed into bed.

On Saturday morning, Nat entered the gift shop like a ray of sunshine, in a warm gold dress with a necklace of yellow and spring-green beads. She had come in at my request so that I could take the afternoon off for shopping with Gina and Angela.

"Hi, sweetheart! Haven't seen you in a while!" She crossed the room to where I was restocking the loose leaf tea.

I put down the tea packets to accept a warm auntie hug. "Thank you so much for coming in!"

"Happy to help. How's the new arrangement doing?"

"Fabulous. Gift shop sales are up ten percent."

"Wow!"

"It's partly Valentine's." I went back to stocking the tea shelf. "I'm having trouble keeping up."

"Time to think about increasing the staff?"

"Maybe. We'll see if it falls off after mid-month."

She helped me get the gift shop stocked for the day. Once the displays were full, we went upstairs and fetched more merchandise to tuck into the cupboards, until every bit of storage space in the shop was stuffed. The boxes that I had moved to the upper hall from Kris's office were finally gone, and though new stock came in continuously, we hadn't overflowed the storeroom again.

Yet. Next week would be the challenge.

The morning was blustery and cold. The wind wasn't quite howling, but it was audible, and I could feel the cold whenever I got near a window. Iz had already made sure the fires were all lit, making the alcoves cozy.

When I unlocked the front door at ten thirty, there were six people waiting outside. They swarmed into the gift shop, shivering. Four of them had reservations, and the other two wanted cream tea. Nat took them in hand, and I darted to the butler's pantry to warn the servers.

Dale had the day off. Rosa and Iz were busy all morning, and I helped them until Dee arrived at noon, then went upstairs for a bite of lunch and a change of clothes. I wanted something that was warm and easy to get in and out of, since I'd be trying on dresses. I decided on slacks, but put on hose underneath them, and wore my old character shoes: comfortable dress shoes with one-inch heels that I'd worn a lot on stage in my theatre days.

Kris had come in for a half-day, as she usually did on Saturdays. I looked in on her before going downstairs to meet Gina. She had dressed up a bit, in a long-sleeved black dress and knee-high boots. Her hair was swept up in a French twist, unusual for her and classy-looking.

"I'm heading out soon," I said from the doorway. "Anything you need before I go?"

She glanced up with a fleeting smile. "No, thanks. Have a good time."

"Thank you. I'm hoping for a not-terrible time at least."

"If it's terrible you can have a couple of margaritas after."

I chuckled. "See you Monday."

She nodded, turning back to work. I checked on Minuit and gave her some food so she'd sleep more and cry less. Then I fetched my coat, purse, and phone and headed downstairs. It was a little before twelve thirty, and there were guests having cream tea in the dining parlor, so I hung out in the kitchen, staying out of the way and watching out the windows for Gina's red Camaro. A few flakes of snow blew around the bud-tipped bare branches of the lilacs.

Julio was preparing mini quiches. Hanh was making macarons while Ramon sprinkled powdered sugar over a freshly-baked tray of *bastilla*. The kitchen was warm and smelled delicious, making me want to snitch a bite of something despite my having eaten lunch, but I knew Hanh would scold me if I did. Earlier I had taken four macarons from the gift shop and put them into two small pastry boxes for Gina and Angela, little thank-you gifts. They were tucked in the pocket of my wool coat. I wished I had grabbed a macaron for myself.

Gina's Camaro rumbled up the driveway and stopped behind my Camry with a light toot of the horn. I slipped out the back door and hurried to the passenger side.

"Where's your hat?" Gina asked as I pulled the car door closed. She herself wore a plush furry hat and her red winter coat.

"Didn't want to keep track of hat and scarf and all while changing clothes."

"Good point. Maybe I'll leave mine in the car." She backed out, turned the Camaro, and headed for Angela's address.

I had never been there, but it turned out to be quite close to Margo's apartment building, just a couple of streets away. Angela's building was more modest than Margo's—smaller apartments, and three stories—but the landscaping was pleasant and it wasn't smack alongside a major street, so it was fairly quiet. I got out while Gina kept the heater running.

Angela must have been on the watch, because she came out to meet me, her cheeks pink from the cold, almost as rosy as her parka. She had on a dress, stockings, and heels underneath, so I hustled her to the car, thinking her legs must be cold. I hopped into the back seat before she had a chance to protest. She hesitated, but obeyed when Gina yelled "Get in!"

"Angela, this is Gina," I said, leaning forward between their seats. "Gina, Angela."

"Hi," Angela said shyly.

"Lovely to meet you," Gina said, flashing a smile as she put the car in reverse. "Let's get this show on the road!"

I fastened my seat belt.

Gina navigated out into traffic, which on Saturday afternoon was pretty heavy despite the poor weather. When she had merged into the flow, she started talking to Angela.

"Ellen says you're in college."

"Part time," Angela said. "I'm also working."

"Been there. What's your major?"

"Nursing."

"Not going for an M.D.?"

"I just want a steady job."

"Fair enough. What made nursing your first choice?"

"My grandmother complaining there weren't enough nurses when she was in the hospital a couple years ago."

Ah. And *Abuela* might be needing home care eventually. If Angela could provide that, it would save the family money.

The thought made me a little sad. Angela seemed to be sacrificing herself for the sake of her family. I wondered if she had any secret dreams.

Maria Hidalgo came to mind, and I saw the parallel. Maria had given up—or lost, rather—her own hopes, and had spent all her life with her family. She had done a lot of good, but I couldn't help thinking of how different her life would have been if she'd succeeded in eloping with Captain Dusenberry.

"Well?" Gina turned to look at me while the car was stopped at a light.

"Sorry, what?"

"Have you chosen your colors?"

"Um…not lavender or purple."

"Girl, we need to know so we can look at dresses."

"Oh, yes. Well, let me think. Not red or orange."

"I could have guessed that." Gina leaned toward Angela, pretending to whisper. "She hates red."

"I do not! I just don't look good in it."

"You will be wearing white, girl."

The light turned green. I thought my way through the rainbow while Gina drove.

Yellow wasn't high on my list. Green—I liked it, but Margo had worn green at the All Hallows masquerade. That shouldn't matter, but it did. No green.

Blue, then, since I was kind of avoiding purple hues. Blue and what? There was usually a second color, like team colors for school. I guessed I didn't *have* to have two colors, but blue alone seemed... inadequate.

Gina was headed toward downtown, not far from the tearoom, but working her way in from the southeast. She pulled onto Shelby street and parked at a meter outside an adobe building with turquoise-painted trim around the door and windows.

Turquoise. Hm.

"Turquoise and teal," I said as Gina shut off the engine.

She looked at me over her shoulder, tilting her head, then took off her hat. "Okay. Here, put this on the seat behind me."

We got out and went to the turquoise-trimmed shop. Two nebulous white figures loomed in the windows that flanked the door. The doormat read "Here Comes the Bride!"

Gina tried the door, which was locked. She knocked.

"Are they closed?" I asked.

"It's by appointment," Gina said.

A slender blonde woman in a clingy black dress came and unlocked the door. "Ms. Fiorello?" she said, opening it a few inches.

"Yes," Gina said.

"Hi, I'm Darlene. Come on in!"

The shop, like many in the older buildings of Santa Fe, was deep and narrow. The walls were painted white, and both sides were lined with racks of dresses, all white, many pouffing out from the wall making the room seem to be full of clouds.

My heart sank a little. I was not looking for pouff.

Our steps rapped hollowly on the wood floor as Darlene led us to a pair of overstuffed chairs in the middle of the room, facing a large mirror that occupied the only gap in the pouff. A second woman, a slender brunette whom Darlene introduced as Nicole, set a folding chair beside the comfy ones, and Angela claimed it, though I thought she might as well have a nice chair as I might not be sitting much.

"Coffee?" Darlene offered.

"Maybe later," Gina said.

"All right. Please make yourselves comfortable and we'll bring you some dresses to look at. Did you have any particular style in mind?" she asked Gina.

"Ellen is the bride," Gina said, gesturing to me. "She likes Victorian."

"I like other things, too," I said, wanting to avoid being offered Cinderella gowns. "I'd love something like an evening gown."

"Hmm," Darlene said. "Well, we can start with Allure, La Sposa, maybe Rosa Clara. June wedding?"

"September," I said. "Probably outdoors."

She asked my dress size, then headed for the racks. I mentally kicked myself for not noting the names of the designers whose dresses I'd looked at online—not that I'd fallen in love with any of them. Gina and I sat in the wing chairs while Darlene and Nicole started bringing dresses to show us. The first one had a plunging neckline and was encrusted with crystals that flashed and glittered in the bright overhead lights. I shook my head. The second one was

Victorian indeed, with full Cinderella pouff. Another no.

As we looked at more dresses, I found myself thinking of a line from Jane Austen: "a shocking lack of satin." There was no lack of satin here, nor (alas) of tulle.

Gradually we eliminated the pouff, the crystals, and most of the satin. "I'd like something I can dance in," I said when they brought out a plain white dress with crystal-covered spaghetti straps and a train that was longer than the gown itself. "Do you have any silk?" I added, hoping that would minimize the glitz. Silk wasn't cheap, but then none of these dresses would be cheap.

Darlene exchanged a look with her assistant. "Rosa Clara," she said, and the two of them took the dresses they were holding away. They returned with two gowns of a simpler, more elegant style: one that looked like something Ginger Rogers might wear, the other more Audrey Hepburn-ish. Both had trains, but not excessive ones. Closer.

"I like that one," I said, indicating the Ginger Rogers. "Do you have one with long sleeves, though? Maybe lace?"

"We have one Autumn Silk that might do," Darlene said, glancing at Nicole, who whisked the Hepburn dress away.

"Sorry to be so picky," I said.

"No, no! You absolutely should be picky. This is for your big day! Would you like to try this one? We could add a lace bolero jacket over it."

"All right."

Darlene carried the Ginger Rogers away through a door at the back of the shop, then brought me three lace jackets to look at. I nixed the one covered with crystals. A second one was covered with pearl beads, which might be all right although they reminded me a little of the edible pearls we sometimes used for decorating sweets at the tearoom. The third had a high collar and looked stiff, but I'd give it a try.

Darlene beckoned me into the dressing room to try on the Ginger Rogers dress. She stood by while I undressed, then offered efficient and impersonal assistance to get me into the gown, which had side zippers that tightened the bodice to my torso. It felt like a negligée, and I was grateful for the pearly jacket that Darlene held out for me to slide into. There was no mirror in the dressing room, so I had to come out and parade before Gina and Angela to get a look at myself.

"Ooohhh," Angela said as I swept by, the train ghosting at my heels.

"Nice," Gina agreed.

I looked in the mirror. I had piled my hair in a bun on top of my head to make it easier to change clothes. My reflection looked a bit unbalanced: the dress was stark and too tight at the hips, although the skirt draped beautifully. The pearl-encrusted jacket looked rather heavy over it. Darlene helped me swap it for the other, which was as stiff as it looked. The lace had been impregnated with glue or something to make it stand up around the neck, and while the effect was pretty, I could already feel it itching.

"Not quite," I said.

Nicole stepped forward with another dress. On the hanger it looked a little boring, white silk with a high, pointed waistline formed by two crossing bands that made the bodice, with lace sleeves and a sheer overskirt augmented by more lace. It didn't thrill me but it wasn't horrible, and I nodded.

Darlene took the gown and handed Nicole the pearly lace jacket. We headed back to the dressing room, and I paused to whisper to Angela, "Take the comfy chair."

Darlene carefully transferred me to the new dress. The lace of its sleeves was much softer than the lace jacket—they'd be comfortable. The skirt flowed out from the high waist, and I was pleased to find that there was only a hint of a train in the overskirt. I walked out toward the mirror.

Gina and Angela's heads turned to watch as I moved to the middle of the room, and I heard Angela—who had moved to the wing chair—catch her breath. I turned to look in the mirror, and magic happened.

The dress was perfect. The criss-cross bodice, which had looked unimpressive on the hanger, fit me beautifully. The flowing skirt had the Ginger Rogers quality I had liked in the first dress, but was loose and comfortable. It felt light, and looked lovely. Not a crystal or a pearl to be seen.

"That's gorgeous, girl," Gina said.

I stood staring at myself, looking for anything less than pleasing. I could find nothing. I turned, viewing the side and the back of the gown, then took a couple of steps and twirled, as if waltzing. The dress politely got out of the way of my feet.

"Yes," I said.

I didn't ask how much. I was a little afraid to, but as Gina would say, that's what credit cards were for.

Darlene shifted to accessories, bringing veils and tiaras and even giant bows, which apparently could be added to the behind of any gown. I banished the bows, and didn't pay much attention to Darlene's gentle patter as she decorated me with various headgear. I was mostly looking at the dress, still, and I sent away all the veils and crowns that detracted from it.

"I think I might just wear a wreath of fresh flowers," I said at last. "And that veil," I added, indicating one I'd given Angela to hold. It was the closest in style to the overskirt of the gown, sheer and soft with a modest lace edging.

Darlene brought out a couple of wreaths of silk flowers. I tried on the smaller one, and she draped the flowing veil over it, pinning the fabric to a comb that she tucked into my hair at the back of the wreath. The veil looked graceful hanging down my back. Darlene pulled the front part up and over my hair, to drape over my face and shoulders. In the mirror, I thought I looked a little like Maria Hidalgo—Tia Maria, always in white, the eternal bride.

"Beautiful," Darlene said. "Picture perfect."

I bet she said that to all the girls.

Relieved that I had found a gown I actually liked, I followed her back to the dressing room where she helped me out of it and whisked it away to pack up while I got dressed.

Well, that was one wedding chore out of the way. Only ninety zillion left to go.

Gina and Angela were chatting over coffee when I emerged from the dressing room. Angela jumped up from the wing chair, but I waved her back to it and looked for Darlene. I paid the bill, which was actually less than I'd expected, and thanked her for her expert assistance.

Darlene smiled. "You're very welcome. We'd love to have a photo of you from the wedding."

I nodded. "I'll send you one. Oh, and here—" I dug a cream tea card out of my purse. "Come by for tea and a scone some time."

Her eyes lit up. "You work at the Wisteria Tearoom?"

"Well, I'm the owner."

"Fabulous! Is that where the wedding will be?"

"No."

She looked slightly disappointed. "You do have weddings there, though, right?"

"We've done a few, yes. Smaller ones. We're better suited to bridal showers. We do a lot of those."

"People ask, you know. We're not wedding planners, but some people come in and they haven't even thought about it."

"Well, I can bring you a stack of those cards to give out," I said.

"That would be great!"

I took another card from my purse. "For Nicole."

She beamed. "Thanks."

Nicole emerged from the back of the shop with a large, white box. Angela hopped up to carry it, and Darlene thanked us for coming in, wishing me a beautiful wedding. We stepped out into the cold afternoon.

The wind had died down a bit, and the snow had stopped. Clouds scudded low over the city, occasionally parting to give a glimpse of the sun. Gina opened the trunk of the Camaro and Angela reverently set the box inside, then we all climbed into the car. This time Angela insisted on taking the back seat.

"Okay," Gina said. "Now it's our turn."

She drove to a boutique, where it was my turn to sit and watch while Gina and Angela tried on dresses. There were not many in teal, but plenty in shades of turquoise. I'd have to decide on a shade, I realized. Probably easiest to let the bridesmaid dresses influence that choice.

After an hour, they had tried on a dozen dresses between them and ended up with a couple of maybes. We moved on to another boutique and went through the same drill.

Gina was having a blast playing dress-up. Angela had gotten quieter as the afternoon progressed. She'd enjoyed it at first, but she'd kind of stopped smiling. I saw her checking the price tags as she looked through the dresses on a rack, and realized they might be more than she could afford.

Santa Fe was not cheap.

I waited until Gina was in the dressing room, then joined Angela at a rack of dresses that she was browsing rather desultorily. I spotted a pretty, pale turquoise dress that I'd seen her looking at before, and took it off the rack.

"What about this one?"

Angela shook her head. "None of these are right," she said. "Would you mind if I made one?"

"If that's what you want," I said. "But you know, I was hoping I could give you a dress as a gift."

She looked startled. "That's not the way it works."

"It's the way I'd like to do it. You've helped me a lot, especially getting to know your family. Will you let me do this for you?"

She blushed fiercely. I put the turquoise dress in her hands. "Just try it on, okay?"

Angela swallowed, then flashed me a grateful look and turned toward the dressing room. Gina passed her on the way out, wearing a dress with an asymmetrical neckline that didn't really suit her, although the color was nice.

"Mm," she said, frowning slightly at herself in the mirror.

"Mm," I said.

"This style would be great on Angela. Not so much on me."

"You don't have to wear the *same* dress."

Gina sighed. "I thought it would be nice to match, but we're such different shapes."

"The color can match. That's enough."

"Yeah. Okay, I have two more to try."

The boutique employee who had been hovering nearby followed Gina toward the dressing rooms. As they went in, Angela came out wearing the dress she'd admired.

It was simple: a floor-length, sleeveless gown with a modest V neckline. The bodice had a criss-cross of fabric rather like my bridal gown. It looked smashing on her. She smiled shyly, and I smiled back.

"You look beautiful. Like it?" I asked.

She nodded. "It's expensive, though."

"Hush. It's perfect." I hugged her. "Let's show Gina."

We moved toward the dressing room, and heard Gina say, "Aaah! No!"

"Gina?" I called. "You okay?"

"I'm fine, but this dress is not." She pulled back the curtain to reveal herself in a neon turquoise dress with gigantic puffed sleeves. She looked like an escapee from Jane Austen had collided with a jar of Day-Glo blue.

"Oh! Um."

"Yeah. Oh, Angela! That's great on you!" Gina came toward us. "Turn around!"

Angela twirled. The skirt swished around her feet. The back was rather low.

The shop employee smiled. "I think I have a similar one in your size," she said to Gina.

"Great! Let's see it!"

Gina ducked back into her dressing room and pulled the curtain closed. Angela looked at me, eyes bright with excitement. "I hope the other one looks nice on Gina."

We browsed the racks while we waited, though I was sure Angela had found the right dress. When Gina emerged from the dressing room, we both let out a cry of delight.

It was the same dress, except with a different neckline: a strapless, sweetheart line that was formed by the same criss-cross of fabric. It showed off Gina's cushy figure beautifully.

"Wow!" I said. "That's it!"

Gina spun around, grinning. The shop attendant stood by, looking pleased. She ought to—she was probably about to get a nice commission.

I collected the price tags so the attendant could ring up the dresses while Gina and Angela changed. I took a deep breath and paid for Gina's dress as well as Angela's. If she wanted to fight about it, we could do that later. It was getting late and I wanted my margarita.

The attendant boxed up the dresses, putting a heart sticker on Gina's and a daisy sticker on Angela's. Angela held her box like it was a fragile treasure. The happy look on her face was worth all the trouble and expense.

"Okay," Gina said as they set their boxes in the trunk with mine. "Shoes next."

"Or dinner," I said. "It's getting late."

"I made a reservation for seven. We've got time."

I refrained from rolling my eyes, or whining, and got into the car. It took visits to three shoe stores before Gina found what she wanted: a pair of strappy sandals in a slightly darker turquoise than the dresses. Angela meekly yielded to her on the matter of the style, but insisted on buying her own shoes. I browsed, but I was pretty sure I wanted a pair of character shoes, like the ones I had on, only white. They were comfortable for long stretches of standing, and also for dancing. I'd order them online.

At last we piled in the Camaro and Gina drove to Vanessie, a restaurant at a boutique hotel not far from the tearoom. I had been there before, and it was perfect for a girl's night out. The food was excellent, the bar was fabulous, and there was live entertainment: a brilliant pianist and singer who performed highly singable oldies interspersed with hilarious patter. The pianist knew how to play the crowd, and the room was full of happy fans, many of them apparently regulars, as now and then he called one of them by name.

Gina ordered a pitcher of margaritas to get us started, along with appetizers. I realized I was starving, and told myself not to spoil my appetite by gobbling too much guacamole while we thought about our entrees.

"This is my treat," Gina said, watching Angela peruse the menu. "I'm getting the filet mignon."

"That sounds good," I said. "And a salad."

"Save room for dessert," Gina said.

Angela shyly made it three filets, and the waiter went off to put in our order. Gina wrote a request on a napkin and tucked a ten into it, then took it up to the piano, resulting a few minutes later in the pianist calling her out.

"And for my friend Gina, here's 'Crazy Little Thing Called Love'."

We drank, and sang oldies, and discussed hats and jewelry for the wedding. Angela offered to make beaded turquoise necklaces for Gina and herself, and I was grateful to Gina for saying it would be perfect. I would wear my mother's pearls.

By the time we had coffee and shared two desserts among us (praline cheesecake and chocolate volcano cake), it was almost nine. Gina, who could drink me under the table any day of the week, had stopped after two margaritas, leaving me and Angela to finish the slightly watery but still potent dregs of the pitcher. I was tipsy and happily exhausted.

We got back in the Camaro, still singing, and Gina drove to Angela's. I walked her to her door, carrying her shoes while she carried the dress box.

"Thank you, Ellen!" she said, and kissed my cheek.

"Thank *you!* I'm so glad you're my bridesmaid!"

I hugged her, waited until she was in and I heard the door lock, then walked back to the car. Gina backed out and turned the Camaro toward the tearoom.

"Now, about the dress—"

"I talked Angela into letting me give her the dress."

"I figured. But you don't need to give *me* a dress."

"It was just easier to ring them up together."

We haggled over who would buy what while she drove me home. I pointed out she had bought dinner, and was planning to throw me a bridal shower *and* a bachelorette party.

"Which, we don't really need both," I said.

"Oh, yes we do! We are going to 10k Waves and scarfing sushi the night before your wedding, so don't argue."

"You're going to spoil me," I said as she pulled up to the front of the tearoom.

"That's the idea."

She got out with me and took her dress box out of the trunk so I could reach mine. I picked it up and turned toward the house.

"Oh, crap!"

Gina closed the trunk. "What?"

She turned to look where I was looking. "Oh, crap!"

In the yard south of the tearoom, swinging slightly in the cold breeze, a body hung from one of the big, old cottonwoods.

4

GINA HAD HER PHONE OUT before I could move. My arms were full of a dress box and my heart was sinking.

Let it be a prank. Please let it be a prank.

I walked to the gate, then thought to look around the yard and the street to see if anyone else was there. I did a slow turn and saw no one. No other cars at the curb.

Don't touch the gate. Fingerprints.

The picket fence was low enough that I could swing a leg over and cross without touching it. I did so, carefully, aware that my balance was margarita-impaired. I hurried up to the front *portal* and put my dress box on one of the café tables, then slowly approached the tree.

The body was female, dressed in black jeans and a black hoodie, dark hair hanging forward hiding her face. Looked pretty real.

My first panicked thought was of Kris, but it wasn't her. The hair was too long, and the figure too full. A Goth, though, I suspected. Might be someone I'd met.

Damn, damn, damn.

"They're coming," Gina called, and headed toward the gate.

"Wait—don't touch it," I said, hurrying toward her. "Here."

Pulling my coat sleeve over my hand, I pushed the latch open, touching as little of it as possible. Gina nudged the gate open with her foot and came into the yard.

Together we approached the tree, looking up. Gina turned on the flashlight on her phone and shone it on the body, revealing more detail with a stark blue-white light.

Under the hoodie was a scoop-necked black T-shirt. Above the neckline, over the heart, there was blood. It was smeared around a bit, and partly hidden by the hair, but I thought the wound was not just random. It looked like a deliberate cut, maybe a cross.

Even the rope was black. Definitely Goth. As I looked at it I saw a slight glimmer just above the body's head. The last couple of feet of the rope looked different from the rest. I peered at it, and realized it looked like beads—multiple strings of black beads.

Okay that was bizarre.

"Oh, girl," Gina said. "You've got another murder."

"Might be suicide," I said.

"No. Her hands are tied behind her back."

It was true. I hadn't registered that. I was not thinking very clearly, obviously.

I stepped a little closer, trying to see the face. I didn't want to get right under the body. There might be blood, and in fact, there might be other evidence.

"We shouldn't get any closer," I said, backing up to where Gina stood.

"No problem!"

A siren wailed in the distance. We stood listening to it get louder.

"You could go inside," I said.

Gina shook her head. "After they get here."

We didn't have long to wait. More sirens joined the song, becoming a painful cacophony before they stopped as two squad cars pulled up behind Gina's Camaro. Red and blue lights flashed all over the yard and the neighboring buildings.

Here we go again.

Gina and I walked toward the open gate and stood out of the way. Two police officers jumped out of the squad cars and ran in, heading for the tree. More sirens were coming.

One of the cops, a tall, lanky Hispanic guy, jogged back to us. "Either of you belong to this place?"

I raised my hand. "It's my house."

"You got a ladder?"

"In the shed. I'll show you."

The other cop, a stocky white guy with a buzz cut, started asking Gina questions as I led the lanky one toward the back of the house. A siren let out a final loud bleat and shut off, and I paused to glance back toward the street. A rescue squad had joined the cop cars.

I took out my phone, trying to remember how to turn on the flashlight, but the cop made it unnecessary by shining his own large flashlight on the shed door. I opened it and found the ladder, and he pulled it out and jogged back toward the tree.

I sighed. Standing still for a moment, I thought of all that was about to happen. I'd be up for a while, I knew. Might as well make the cops some coffee.

And get my wedding dress out of the way. Ay, yi, yi.

A third squad car had arrived. Gina was still talking with the buzz cut. I knew he'd want to talk to me, too, so I unlocked the front door of the house and put my dress in the gift shop before joining them.

Maybe I should call Tony. I took out my phone, but before I could wake it up, a short, less-loud siren wail made me look up to see a black motorcycle glide to the curb in front of Gina's car, a single red light flashing at its back. A flush of gratitude, accompanied by a slight worry that I was about to get chewed out, went through me.

Tony hopped off the bike and paused to look toward the tree, then strode through the gate and straight up to me. He stopped and gave me a long look.

"How many does this make?" he asked.

"I'm not keeping count," I said, a little shakily.

"Have you been interviewed?"

"Not yet. I was going to make coffee."

He nodded, and accompanied me into the house. "When did you get here?" he said as I walked back to the kitchen, turning on lights as we went.

"Just a few minutes ago. Gina called 911 as soon as we saw…"

"Where were you before then?"

"We dropped Angela off at her apartment. Before that we had dinner at Vanessie."

"Angela was with you the whole time?"

"All afternoon and evening."

"Good."

I pulled out Julio's coffee maker and fired it up. While it started gurgling, I turned around and leaned against the counter. The police would want to question me, but I wanted a minute first. I sighed, then covered my face with my hands.

"Ellen."

I looked up, and Tony folded me into his arms. I cried a little, and he rocked me back and forth.

"You're okay. It'll be okay."

I couldn't articulate my feelings, my concern that there was a connection to Kris and her Goth friends, that the person hanging in that tree was someone I'd met. A dark, nebulous cloud of worry clung around me.

"Can't wait to get you out of this house," Tony said.

I looked up at him. "It's not the *house's* fault!"

"Babe, there is something weird about this place."

"I have built my livelihood around this place!" I said defensively, knowing full well he was right. There was more than a little weird about my house.

"I don't mean that. I know the tearoom is your dream. I'll just be glad when you're not living here."

I frowned, feeling slightly offended, though I also saw where he was coming from. Maybe it wasn't *me*, but the house that was a corpse-magnet.

Except…

No, I wasn't going down that path right now.

"Need to get out some mugs."

I gently extracted myself from Tony's embrace and put together a tray for the coffee. Sugar, cream, a handful of spoons and a plate for the used ones. When the coffee was done I added the carafe, picked up the tray, and went out to the hall.

Gina came in the front door. "There you are! They want to talk to you."

"Can you open the door for me?" I said.

She did so. "Mind if I stay in here? It's freezing."

"Yes, get warmed up. Have some coffee if you like."

I put the tray on the nearest café table and poured mugs for Gina and myself. Gina went inside while Tony went on out into the yard and up to the buzz-cut cop. Had I seen him before? Maybe.

More emergency vehicles had arrived, including a ladder truck. There were cops and paramedics and firemen all around the tree, and a couple up in it, plus another on my ladder. Spotlights from the vehicles shone a stark light onto the scene. A stretcher stood on the ground beneath the tree, paramedics waiting to receive the body.

Tony returned with the buzz-cut, who gave me a nod and said, "ma'am."

"Would you like some coffee?" I said.

"Thanks."

He accepted a mug, shook his head when I pointed out the cream and sugar, and asked where we could talk. I led him inside, trading a glance with Tony, who remained outside.

Gina was nowhere in sight. I sat in one of the gold wing chairs from Marigold-that-was, which were near the front door. The cop took the other chair and took out a notepad.

"You're the owner of the house?"

"That's right."

He asked the usual questions: my name, where had I been, who was I with. Same as Tony had done, establishing that I had an alibi.

"I'm going to ask if you know the victim."

"I'm not sure. I couldn't see her face."

"Would you mind looking, when they get her down?"

"All right."

"Anyone you know who might have done this?"

I blinked. "I have no idea."

I hoped I had no idea.

"Anyone you know been acting strange lately?"

No more than usual. Except Kris, but she had a really good reason.

"No, not really."

"Okay."

His radio let out a burst of static and a short dialogue I couldn't quite make out. The cop responded briefly and looked at me.

"They've got her down. Come and look."

I stood, thinking I should get my coat, then realized I was still wearing it.

Deep breath.

The yard looked surreal. Across the street, neighbors had come out of their houses and stood watching. I could see Katie Hutchins on the porch of her B&B on the corner.

I followed the cop to the stretcher. The body had been strapped to it, but there was no emergency activity going on. So she was definitely dead, then.

The lights were all aimed at the tree, still. It wasn't until one of the cops shone a flashlight on her face that I recognized Margo Foss.

"Oh, God!" I cried.

I now saw the cuts on her chest more clearly. Right above the raven tattoo, which was peeking out from her neckline, was what I had thought was a cross.

It was not a cross. It was a wavy-bladed dagger. A kris.

"You know her?" the cop asked.

I nodded. "Margo Foss."

"How do you know her?"

"Um, she's a—a friend of a couple of my employees. And she, um—it's complicated."

I turned away, not wanting to look at Margo any more. I'd have nightmares as it was.

"What are the names of your employees who know her, please?"

I swallowed. "Kris Overland and Dale Whittier."

"I'll need their phone numbers."

I got out my phone, feeling numb. There were so many possibilities of who might have killed Margo. I didn't want to think about any of them.

Damn, damn, damn.

Tony came up to stand beside me. "The victim was the defendant in the Rhodes case," he said to the buzz-cut cop. The cop looked up, glanced at me, glanced at Margo, and wrote some more on his notepad.

"Well, that'll make things interesting."

"M-may I go inside?" I asked through chattering teeth. I didn't know if it was the cold or shock.

"Yeah, go ahead. Please don't leave."

"I live here," I said.

Tony put a hand on my elbow, gently nudging me toward the house. He grabbed the coffee carafe, which was empty, as we went in.

No way I could make enough coffee for all the cops and firemen outside.

"Let's make you some tea," Tony said, keeping me moving toward the kitchen.

I started crying in earnest, though I tried not to howl. Tears poured down my face and I coughed and hiccuped and shivered my way to the kitchen, where I stood and sniveled while Tony put the coffee carafe in the big industrial sink. He then came and gave me a hug, holding me tight until the tears subsided.

I needed to blow my nose. When I relaxed my grip, Tony let me go. I found a box of tissue and mopped my face.

"Where's the tea?" Tony asked.

"Pantry," I said, and led him into the butler's pantry.

The big hot water urn was shut down, so I filled one of the electric kettles from the tap and set it to boil. Tony took a teapot off the shelf. I got out an infuser and grabbed the nearest black tea canister—a berry-scented puerh that was one of our featured teas for the month. My hands shook as I measured the leaves into the infuser.

I was not all right.

"Ellen?" Gina called from out in the hall.

"In here," I answered.

Gina came into the pantry, glanced at Tony, then wrapped me in a hug. "The media are here."

Oh, crap.

"Did you talk to them?" I asked.

"No, I've been watching from the window in Lily."

I swallowed. "Don't make me talk to them."

"No, honey," Gina said. "Not now. Where's your dress?"

"In the gift shop."

"I'll take it upstairs for you."

"Thanks."

She gave me a sympathetic smile and went out.

"Dress?" Tony asked.

"My wedding gown," I said, and burst into tears again.

Tony wrapped me in his arms and held me until the kettle began to whistle. I shut it off, poured hot water into the teapot, slopping some on the counter, and set the timer. Tony grabbed a dishcloth from the sink and wiped up the spill.

"Let's sit down until the tea's done," he said.

"We can take it with us."

I got out a tray and put the teapot, the timer, and three cups and saucers on it. I added milk and sugar because I wanted comfort. Spoons, a tea cozy, and a dish to put the infuser in. Tony picked up the tray.

"Where to?"

"Violet," I said, and led the way down the hall and through the gift shop to my favorite alcove. Tony put the tray on the low table while I poked at the ashes in the fireplace. There were a couple of coals still alive. I added some kindling and a log, and plied the bel-lows until the fresh wood caught.

"You're good at that," Tony said.

"Lots of practice."

"Want to give me your coat? I'll hang it up."

"Thanks."

He helped me out of the coat and went out to hang it in the hall, returning with Gina close behind. She'd also taken off her coat, and her dress reminded me of the day we'd spent shopping. It didn't seem like this same day.

The timer had gone off while Tony and Gina were gone, and I

had already drunk half my first cup of tea, loaded with milk and sugar. I poured for them and topped up my cup.

Gina stirred two sugar lumps into her tea. "Shouldn't you be outside?" she said to Tony.

"I'm not going to be the lead on this case. I'm too closely associated."

Gina took a sip of her tea and added some milk. "Well, did you recognize the body?" she asked me.

Tony frowned. I nodded.

"Margo Foss. I don't think you met her. She's—she was—one of the Goths in Kris's social circle."

"Oh. That's not good."

"No, it isn't."

I glanced at Tony, who was watching me—not as a cop, but as my fiancé. Concerned. It comforted me to know that he was not in cop mode, or not very much, at the moment.

I wondered if he had taken note of the kris. Did he know that name for the wavy-bladed dagger?

Even if he didn't, he'd probably seen Kris's tattoo at some point. He'd remember that.

Were there cops headed to Kris's house even now? Knocking on her door, demanding to interview her? I hoped, whenever she had to deal with them, that she would happen to be wearing long sleeves. If they saw her tattoo they would assume there was a connection.

And there might be.

Could Kris have done this horrible thing?

I frowned and took a swallow of tea. Kris had been troubled lately. I had assumed it was grief over Gabriel. Now the woman who had killed him—accidentally or not, Margo had killed him—was dead. Murdered. Hanged, as Gabriel had been hanged. With a kris cut into her chest.

In her worst anger, could Kris have done this?

I didn't know.

My cup was empty. I filled it, and topped up the others. More sugar and milk. The tea might keep me awake, but I certainly didn't expect to sleep well anyway. Not after this. Not without chemical assistance.

At least the tearoom would be closed tomorrow. A work day would have been stressful on the heels of this.

Always take a day off after finding a body.

"Penny for your thoughts," Gina said.

I glanced at her, then shook my head. "Nothing important."

"You almost smiled for a second there."

"A stray bit of morbid humor."

Tony tilted his head. "Not gonna share?"

"It's not really that funny."

Gina gazed at me for a bit, then looked at Tony. "You're spending the night here, right?"

He looked at me. "Probably."

"Good. Ellen shouldn't be alone." She finished her tea and put the cup and saucer on the table. "I'm going home, but if you need me for anything, just call. Doesn't matter what time."

"Thanks, Gina." I set down my own cup and got up to see her out. Tony tagged along.

In the hall, there were still flashes of red and blue light from the emergency vehicles, and some splash from the spotlights in the yard. I helped Gina into her coat and walked with her to the door, with Tony close behind.

The squad car behind Gina's Camaro was parked pretty close. "I'll move my bike so you can get out," Tony said.

"Thanks."

Tony jogged to his bike, and I glanced toward the tree. The ladder truck and the rescue squad were gone. So was the stretcher. There were big mobile spotlights set up in the yard now, and people combing through the grass, and someone up my ladder looking at the tree branch with a flashlight. I recognized a familiar evidence tech: sandy hair and glasses. Stirred his coffee with the sugar spoon.

"You take care of yourself, honey," Gina said to me. "Take a hot bath. Get some rest."

"Thanks, Gina. And thanks for today. It was great."

She hugged me. "I hope that's what you remember about today, and not this."

"Yeah."

I managed a smile as she let me go and headed for her car. It was cold, so I went in for my coat, then moved to the end of the portal, a little closer to the tree but still out of the way. Tony joined me as Gina drove away.

"Let's go back inside," he said.

"That technician—what's his name? Phillips?"

"Yeah."

"Is he the one who could lend me a metal detector?"

"Um, yeah, he might be able to."

"I'd like to talk to him when he isn't busy."

"He's gonna be busy for a while, babe."

"I know."

Tony glanced toward the tree. "I'll let him know you'd like to talk to him, okay?"

"Okay."

He strolled off to join the group at the tree, and stood with Phillips and a police officer—not one of the two who'd arrived first —for a few minutes. The energy level of the people working the scene had shifted, now that the body was gone. The sense of urgency was diminished, or it had shifted into quiet intensity. They were looking minutely at every square inch of the area in the lights. Carefully, not hurriedly.

Tony came back. "Let's go in."

I nodded, and picked up the tray that I'd used to bring out coffee. The spoons were scattered on it, and there was one used mug. The other mugs were probably all over the yard.

"Should I make more coffee?"

"You don't have to, babe. It's nice of you, but it isn't necessary. I'm going to move my bike around to your driveway."

I nodded, and he jogged off toward the street. I was feeling rather tired, and a little numb still, so I conceded on the issue of coffee. I carried the tray to the kitchen and left it, hung my coat in the hall again, and went to the back door to let Tony in. He parked his bike next to my car, and we returned to Violet.

The fire crackled gently, dying down again. I debated adding more wood as I lifted the cozy from the teapot and filled my cup. The tea was almost gone. I poured the last of it into Tony's cup, then added sugar and the last of the milk to mine.

"They found the knife under the tree," Tony said. "A utility knife."

I frowned. "Like a box cutter?"

"Sort of. Smaller, though, and wicked sharp."

"Maybe they'll get prints off it."

"It had been wiped."

I sipped tea, thinking. "Were those beads, at the end of the rope?"

"You noticed that. Yeah, three long strings of black beads. One would have broken, but three together were strong enough to—well, strong enough."

"I hope her neck broke, and she didn't suffer," I said.

"It did."

I wondered if the beads were jet. Maybe Phillips would tell me, if I asked.

This was so Goth, all the way through. The kris, the beads. Hanging Margo as Gabriel had been hanged. It had to be tangled up with his death. Which meant I probably knew the killer, or had met them, at least.

If it wasn't Kris, and I hoped with all my heart that it wasn't, then whoever had done this had tried to frame her. Because the combination of the kris and the jet beads sure seemed to point to her.

I closed my eyes. I did not want to start thinking through all of the Goths, many of whom I liked, trying to decide which one had killed Margo. A lot of them—maybe all of them—had been furious with her when Gabriel died. I hadn't been pleased with her myself, but I couldn't help pitying her. She had been an unhappy person.

I sighed, finished my tea, and looked at Tony. "So how was *your* day?"

He smiled. "I packed boxes."

"Sounds blissfully boring."

"How about you? Your day, not this." He waved a hand toward the yard.

"Well, I found a dress I like. And then we found dresses for Gina and Angela. And then shoes. We had dinner at Vanessie and had a really great time."

"Thanks for taking Angela."

"Thank Gina. She picked up dinner."

"I meant thanks for having her as your bridesmaid."

I looked up at him. "I like her."

Tony smiled.

"I'd better tidy up. Unless you want more tea?"

He shook his head. "Thanks. I'm good."

I collected our cups onto the tea tray and made sure the fireplace was safe. Tony came with me to the pantry and then the kitchen, where I washed up the tea and coffee things. I'd search the yard for coffee mugs in the morning, when I wouldn't be getting in the way. Gina's mug might be in Lily, though. I went to look for it, and paused to look out the front window at the yard, still full of lights.

Why here?

Again, it seemed to point to Kris, but in an odd way. An unrealistic way, if there was anything realistic about the whole thing. Assuming for the moment that Kris was angry enough to wreak fatal vengeance on Margo, still I couldn't believe that she would do it here, at the tearoom. It made no sense. And Kris, though she could come on like a steam roller if she chose to, was usually more subtle than that.

Gina's mug sat on the low table in Lily. I picked it up, checked that the front door was locked, retrieved my purse from Violet and returned to the kitchen, where Tony was leaning against the counter, poking at his phone.

"Got a text from Phillips," he said as I came in. "He says he'll call you tomorrow."

"Okay." I washed the mug and put it to dry in the rack with the other dishes, then glanced at the clock hanging by the window. "Oh, jeez!"

It was almost eleven.

Tony followed my gaze. "Yeah. Let's go up."

As we climbed the stairs, I realized how tired I was. I wanted to crawl straight into bed, but I really ought to take a shower at least, if not the bubble bath Gina had recommended. I unlocked my suite and put my purse on my dresser, then turned to Tony.

"I'm going to shower."

"Scrub your back?" he offered.

I paused. That *did* sound good.

"Yes."

"Got any whiskey?"

"Um, no. I have brandy."

"That'll do."

He put his arms around my waist and pulled me to him. "How

about some of that chocolate cake?"

"Sachertorte?"

"Yeah, that."

"I don't know. If we have any left it would be down in the kitchen."

"Want me to look?"

"I'd better do it, if you want chocolate."

"What do you want, babe?"

I sighed and leaned my head on his chest. "Honestly, I'm just tired."

"Then forget the chocolate. Where's the brandy?"

"In the kitchenette. Cupboard on the right."

He gave me a lingering kiss, then released me and went to the cupboard. I watched him find the brandy, then take out a couple of sturdy glasses, ignoring the snifters. He poured a finger into each glass and brought me one.

"Cheers."

I took a sip of brandy and rolled it around on my tongue. Tasted good, and I relaxed a little. Tony took my hand and gently led me to the bathroom.

5

I WAS TOO TIRED to do a sexy strip-tease. I pulled off my clothes and dropped them on the floor. Tony turned on the shower to let it heat up, and did the same.

I had never taken a shower with a drink before. We stepped into the steamy water and perched our glasses on the shampoo shelf. Tony grabbed my hinoki-scented soap and a washcloth and proceeded to rub my aching shoulders while I leaned against the wall. Under the influence of brandy, hot water, evergreen steam and Tony's massage, I gradually relaxed.

When the brandy was gone, he turned the water off, slicked soapsuds all over me and then himself, and then gave me a full body hug that turned into a different kind of massage. I was tipsy again and in sensory overload, and I let go of the worry and just focused on Tony: the feel of our soapy flesh sliding together, the warmth of his kisses, the way his arms supported me so that I could just let go of everything and enjoy him completely.

It was just what I needed.

A while later, Tony turned on the water and we rinsed off, then stepped out and wrapped ourselves in my two big bath sheets.

"Bed now," Tony said, opening the door.

"Uh-huh."

I started toward the bedroom, but stopped when I saw Minuit's dish and her kitty bed.

"Minuit! Oh, poor kitty!"

I found my robe and put it on, leaving my towel draped on the foot of the bed as I hurried across the hall to rescue Minuit from her playpen. It needed attention; I'd deal with it in the morning. Minuit mewed at me in a tone of slight accusation as I carried her back to my suite.

"I'm sorry, honey. Come on, let's get you some food."

Tony, still wrapped in a towel, watched from the doorway to the bedroom while I fed the kitten and made sure she was set for the night. The warmth of the shower was fading, and my bare feet were getting cold. I put a hand on the chimney, which was slightly warm from the fire downstairs, but that would also fade.

"You want a T-shirt?" I asked Tony.

He shook his head. "We'll be warm enough."

He was right. I usually put on a nightshirt, but having Tony in my bed was like having my own personal furnace. I curled up in his arms and thought about how grateful I was for him as I finally drifted to sleep.

In the morning, I woke to find Minuit curled up on the pillow beside Tony's head. I was glad neither of us had rolled on top of her in our sleep. She lifted her head.

"Mew."

Tony jerked awake.

"Kitten," I said. "It's okay."

He groaned and rolled over. I reached a hand out to pet Minuit's fluffy head, and she purred.

Wanting to let Tony sleep, I got up and fed Minuit to quiet her, then threw Tony's clothes in the washer so he wouldn't have to put them on dirty. I made us a breakfast of waffles and berries, which we enjoyed in bed. Manny was meeting us at my storage locker at eleven, to move my parents' sofa to the new place. When Tony's clothes were dry we both got dressed and went out to look at the yard in daylight.

There was still crime scene tape around the tree, but apart from the somewhat trampled condition of the dry grass, the yard looked normal. No cop cars at the curb. Three coffee mugs had been placed on one of the café tables on the *portal*. I walked over to the tree and peered at the ground under the branch from outside the tape, but didn't see any blood.

An SUV with Santa Fe Police markings pulled up to the curb, and Phillips got out. His smile as he joined me and Tony was cheery as sunshine.

"Morning!" he said. "Came to check if we missed anything."

Tony gave him a nod and we watched while he went inside the tape and slowly examined the ground, then peered up at the tree branch.

"That ladder still around?" Phillips asked.

I looked toward the shed and noticed the ladder propped against the side of the house.

"I'll get it," Tony said, and jogged off.

Phillips straightened and smiled at me. "So you want to borrow a metal detector?"

"Actually I'd like you to do the detecting if you have time. I don't know how to use one." I explained about Captain Dusenberry's murder and my hope of finding the bullets in the adobe wall of my dining parlor.

"Oh, yeah, sure," he said. "Have to be after work, but yeah, I can help."

"After business hours, for me. We close at six."

We took out our phones and compared calendars, deciding on

Wednesday evening. Meanwhile Tony had propped the ladder against the tree. Phillips stood gazing at the lawn.

"See, we didn't find any marks except the ones we made with this ladder last night," Phillips said.

"So how did she get up in the tree?" Tony asked.

"Right." Phillips nodded, circled the trunk of the tree slowly, peering at it, then went up the ladder.

Another SUV pulled up to the curb. I glanced at it, thinking it was more police, but the logo on the side was from channel 4.

"Crap," I said, as Carla Algodones—a reporter I'd talked to before—and a camera person hopped out and started toward us.

It was too late to escape into the house. Here I was, in T-shirt and jeans under my parka, no makeup. At least I'd brushed my hair.

"Ms. Rosings?" called Algodones, coming up to us. She had on a beige raincoat and a red scarf.

I put on a small, tolerant smile. The camera operator, who looked like a gangster at first glance with shades and his ball cap on backwards, pointed his camera at Phillips up in the tree.

"Would you mind answering a few questions?" Algodones said.

"A few, okay," I said.

Tony stood nearby, exuding guard-dog vibes, while Algodones called the cameraman over and moved me to stand in front of the tearoom. Gina would love it, I reminded myself while he set up. Free publicity. We might get a cancellation or two, but from past experience we'd probably get twice as many new ones. People were ghoulish.

I wondered if the Goths would be attracted, or if they'd stay away this time.

"Okay, we're rolling," said the cameraman.

"Ms. Rosings, how did you find out about the hanging?" Algodones asked me.

Ugh.

"I was out to dinner with a friend, and when we got back here, we saw the body hanging in the tree."

"Did you know the victim?"

I repressed a grimace. "I was slightly acquainted with her, yes."

"From the Gabriel Rhodes hanging last fall?"

"Yes."

"Did you know her before then?"

"Not really. We'd met, but that was all."

"She was at a party here the night Rhodes died, correct?"

"Yes."

"How did you feel when you found her hanging in your yard?"

"Horrified."

"What did you do?"

"My friend called the police immediately."

Algodones paused, looking toward the tree, where Phillips was starting to climb down. Apparently he was a more attractive subject than me, because she said, "Let's cut it there," and started toward Phillips. "Thanks," she added, tossing me a smile over her shoulder while the cameraman hastily followed her.

"Not too bad," Tony said, watching them.

"Could have been worse," I agreed. "Let's go inside."

We picked up the mugs and took them in. We'd had coffee with breakfast, but I wanted tea so I made a pot and we shared it in Violet, which had a good view of the tree. Phillips was giving Algodones rather a long interview, with the tree and the crime scene tape behind him. Good-natured of him.

When the news people finally left, Phillips moved the ladder back to the house and started taking down the crime scene tape. Tony and I went out to talk to him.

"Who's the lead on the case?" Tony asked.

"Zeke."

Tony nodded. I put the ladder away in the shed while they

chatted, then came back in time to say goodbye to Phillips.

"See you Wednesday," he said. "Oh, and thanks for the coffee! Best coffee in town."

"You're welcome," I said, thinking I'd have to serve him tea some time. Best coffee in town was not the endorsement I needed for the tearoom.

It was time to meet Manny, so we locked up the house and drove to the storage place in my car. Tony and Manny did the macho moving while I got boxes out of the way. The shed was looking less full. Maybe I'd actually get it emptied out this year. It would be nice not to have to pay the storage bill.

The sofa had been in my dad's study. It was dark brown leather, and opened up into a bed. Not quite the style I would have chosen, but it would do for now, and it would give Tony a place to sleep.

Sheets! Tony's bed was a double—if he had a spare set of sheets, they'd be too big for the sleeper sofa. I looked for a box of linens in the shed, and found it under two boxes of books. I carried it to the car and put it in the trunk.

I took a final look-around before closing the shed, and decided to grab a box of "kitchen stuff" for the new place. I didn't remember what was in it, except that I thought it had some extra pots and pans that might be useful. I had brought the bare minimum to the tea-room for the kitchenette in my suite.

I picked up the box, and saw that the box behind it was marked "china." Memory zinged and I stood still for a moment, thinking of Mom's dinner parties with the good china and crystal.

I would come back for that box. Later, after I moved. Before I invited Owen and Julio to dinner.

"Ellen?" Tony called from outside.

"Coming."

I emerged from the shed, and Tony took the box out of my arms. "Trunk?" he said.

"Yes."

"Anything else?"

"Not today."

I locked the shed and followed him to the car, where he stowed the box beside the linens. Manny followed us to the new place in his truck.

I unlocked the front door of the townhome while Tony brought in the kitchen box. Manny came in behind him, looking around with curiosity.

"Nice!" he said, nodding approval.

"You want the tour?"

"Sure!"

I showed him the living room while Tony disappeared into the kitchen with the box. He caught up with us as I was showing Manny the bedrooms.

"This is a really great place," Manny said. "Expensive?"

"Not as expensive as it should be," Tony said.

"It's owned by a friend, and he gave us a deal on the rent," I added.

"All right!" Manny said, grinning. "Good for you, *hija!* Now where do you want the couch?"

I turned to Tony. "Living room or the man cave?"

He glanced toward the living room. "Man cave. Living room will have too much light in the morning, with those windows."

"Good point."

Tony and Manny moved the couch into Tony's room while I fetched in the box of linens. I took it to the laundry room and extracted the sheets that went with the sleeper sofa: cream with brown and green stripes (ay yi yi). They should be washed, I thought. I'd have to bring some laundry soap over.

I went to the kitchen and opened the other box. There were indeed several good pots, including Mom's Dutch oven. I stowed them all in the cupboards, along with a few utensils that were also in the box, and Mom's canister set. I smiled as I put those on the counter, thinking of filling them with sugar and flour, and actually getting to bake in the beautiful ovens. I was excited to try the narrow one that was perfect for a pizza or a sheet of cookies.

Or scones, of course.

Manny and Tony came in, talking football. "Okay, *hija*," Manny said, "if you don't need anything else moved today, I'm gonna go catch a game."

I hugged him. "Thank you, *Tío*. That's all for today."

"You two stay out of trouble, you hear?"

"Do our best," Tony said.

I saw him out, then went to look at the sofa in Tony's room. He had placed it along the outer wall, beneath the window. I showed him the sheets.

"They should be washed—they've been in that dusty shed for a year. I can bring some soap."

"I'll just bring mine over," Tony said. "Might as well start doing my laundry here."

"Oh, okay."

"Are you going to bring your TV?"

I hesitated. I'd loved the fact that Owen and Julio's living room did not have a television, and had been thinking of doing the same. My TV wasn't terribly fancy, but it was bigger and newer than Tony's.

"You want it in the man cave?" I asked.

"If you don't mind. I'll give mine to Angela."

I smiled. "Well, only if you invite me in to watch movies."

"You make the popcorn. I always burn it."

"Deal. Shall we bring it over here today?"

"That would be great. Can we bring some boxes from my place, too?"

"Sure. Oh, and I emptied the kitchen box, if you want it."

"Might come in handy."

The doorbell rang. We traded a look.

"Expecting anyone?" Tony asked.

"No."

We went to answer it together and found Owen outside, wearing a dark gray wool coat over black jeans. His hair was tied back, which made him look a bit stark.

"I saw you bringing in furniture," he said. "Thought I'd come say hello. And I wanted to say I'm sorry, Ellen. About Margo."

I drew a sharp breath. "You heard."

"The police came and talked to me."

"Why?" Tony asked.

Owen met his gaze. "Probably because I hired a lawyer for Margo," he said. "But they're talking to everyone who…"

"Was at Gabriel's party," I said.

"Yes."

We were all silent for a moment.

"Why did you hire a lawyer?" Tony asked.

"Because I knew she couldn't afford one, and I didn't want her to have to use a public defender."

"That was kind of you," I said.

"You friends with her?" Tony asked.

"Not close friends, but she was part of our community. And she was troubled. Gabriel's death—well, before that. When Gabriel dropped her it really knocked her off balance. She never really got back on track, and now…"

"It's cold," I said. "Let's go inside and talk."

Owen nodded, and we all went into Tony's room, since the couch was the only furniture in the house. It was big enough for the three of us. Tony placed himself in the middle.

I wished I could offer tea or coffee. Instead, I asked Owen, "Do you know of anyone in your community with a grudge against Kris?"

He smiled wryly. "You mean besides all of Gabriel's exes?"

"Well...."

"I don't. Kris doesn't let many people close to her, but she's a pillar of our community, really."

Tony was listening, and I knew anything we said might be passed along to Zeke. I looked at him. "Can I share details?"

He gave a one-shoulder shrug. "Whatever you observed belongs to you, babe. Maybe don't share it with the media."

I looked at Owen. "I think someone killed Margo and tried to frame Kris."

Owen frowned. "I can't think of anyone who would do that."

"It's the only thing that makes sense. Kris—well, if she *was* angry enough to kill Margo, and I don't think she was—she wouldn't do it like this. She wouldn't use mourning beads to hang her, and she wouldn't carve a kris into her chest."

Owen's mouth dropped open and his eyes went wide. He recovered a second later. "They did that?"

I nodded.

Tony shifted. "A lot of killers leave signatures."

"Kris wouldn't," I said. "She's smarter than that."

"I have to agree," Owen said slowly. "It's not Kris's style."

"People make mistakes when they're enraged," Tony said.

Owen looked at him. "If Kris had been enraged by Gabriel's death, she would have acted immediately, not waited for months."

"Unless she heard something recently that enraged her," Tony said.

I frowned. "What are you getting at?"

He gave me a troubled look. "Remember I told you Margo might get off lightly? Kris was in the next room, wasn't she?"

I thought back, and remembered my worry that Kris had overheard. I shook my head. "She might not have been. And even if she was, I don't think that's enough to make her…make her—"

"People make mistakes."

"When was this conversation?" Owen asked.

"Friday," Tony said.

"The day before the murder," Owen said.

"Yeah."

No. No, it can't have been Kris. It can't.

"I'd better go," Owen said after a moment. "Let me know if I can help with anything, Ellen."

"Thanks."

"Same to you, Tony. Good luck with the move."

Owen stood, and we went with him to the door. I watched him walk down the path to the sidewalk, feeling depressed. Tony closed the door and gathered me into his arms.

"Let it go, babe. Zeke will sort it out."

"But what if he decides Kris did it?"

"He's OCD. He won't go for the easy answer, not without checking every other possibility. It's why he's a good detective."

I swallowed. "I'm *sure* it wasn't Kris."

"Let's go get some lunch."

We grabbed burgers and fries and chocolate malts and consumed them at Tony's apartment, then filled my car with boxes and drove back to the townhome. A second trip took care of the rest of the boxes, plus a suitcase into which Tony tossed clothes and a shaving kit.

"Laundry soap?" I said.

"Thanks."

Tony put soap and fabric softener into his laundry basket, thought for a minute and added a carton of milk from the fridge and a box of cereal, and stuffed a blanket and pillow from his bed on top of it all.

Guess he was really moving in.

By the time we got the second load into the townhome, it was mid-afternoon and I was getting tired. Tony asked if we could bring my TV over.

"Okay, but that'll be it for me," I said.

"Fine, babe. I'll carry it."

As I pulled the Camry up my driveway, I saw movement in the front yard. At first I thought the evidence techs were back, then I realized it was another news team.

"Crap," I said, shutting off the engine.

Tony's eyes narrowed. "Maybe they won't see us."

We hurried into the house and upstairs. I peeked out the window from my suite and saw a different reporter standing under the tree, talking to a camera.

We unplugged the TV and wrapped it in a blanket to protect it, and Tony carried it downstairs. The day had warmed up, so I left my parka and put on a sweater instead. Keys in hand, I opened the back door, hoping we'd escape the notice of the news team.

No such luck.

"Ms. Rosings? Ms. Rosings!" called a voice from the yard.

It was *another* reporter, from a different channel, frantically waving to a cameraman who was taking a long shot of the house from the far corner of the yard. Tony came out with the TV and I locked the back door, then opened the trunk of my car. The reporter, wearing a jacket with his channel's logo, hurried up to me.

"Rick Marconi, News Thirteen," he said, slightly out of breath. "Mind if I ask a few questions?"

"I'm busy," I said, closing the trunk.

The cameraman jogged up, camera on his shoulder aimed at me.

"I understand you knew the woman found hanged in your yard," Marconi said.

Tony stepped between us. "She said no."

"Sorry, this isn't a good time," I added.

The reporter stepped to one side and leaned toward me. "Did you—"

"You're trespassing," Tony said. "Better leave now."

"What are you, a cop?" said the reporter, annoyed.

Tony took his badge out of his pocket and flashed it. The reporter deflated.

"Sorry, ma'am," he said, stepping back.

The cameraman took the camera off his shoulder. Tony stood like a bulldog, watching until they both slunk out of sight beyond the front of the house.

"Thanks," I said, opening my car door.

"Best part of having a badge," Tony said as he got in. "You get to tell assholes to stuff it."

I decided to hang out at the new place for an hour or so.

While Tony emptied a couple of boxes and set up the TV on top of them, I quietly rescued his milk from the laundry basket and put it in the fridge, which was empty. The cereal went into a likewise empty cupboard, then I laundered my dad's sheets and Tony's blanket and pillowcase and put them in the dryer.

Tony had noticed a cable connection in the man cave. He wired up my TV to it, discovered the service was live, and found an old movie that was just starting. We curled up together on the sofa to watch it while the laundry dried. We had turned up the heat when we brought in the first load of boxes, but the house was still a little chilly. I snuggled against Tony and he wrapped his arms around me.

"You might want some firewood," I said during a commercial break. "We could bring some from the tearoom."

"Not today. I'll be fine."

"You going to sleep here tonight?"

"Yeah, I think I will. How about you?"

I shook my head. "Lots to do tomorrow."

"I thought you were closed Mondays."

"We are, but that doesn't mean I don't work."

"Isn't it your day off, though? Weekend day two?"

"Sort of, but this month is busy. And this week will be really busy."

Valentine's Day was fast approaching. I had less than a week to get ready for next Sunday, the actual day, and there were flowers to order—

"Sure I can't tempt you?" Tony said, sliding a hand under my sweater.

"Um."

My phone rang. I took it out and glanced at the screen.

"It's Kris."

6

$\mathcal{I}$ disentangled myself from Tony, then hopped up and went out in the hall to get away from the noise of the TV.

"Kris! I'm glad you called."

"Just wanted to let you know I won't be in tomorrow," she said in a tired voice. "I'm taking a sick day."

"Are you all right?" I asked as I walked down the hall toward the living room.

"Not really."

"The police came to talk to you."

"They came last night," she said. "Now I've got reporters ringing the bell."

Crap.

"I'm so sorry," I said. "Is there anything I can do? Bring you food?"

"Thanks, but I'm just going to hole up, I think. I didn't sleep well last night."

"Well, don't hesitate to call. Doesn't matter what time," I added, reminding myself of Gina.

"Thanks."

Searching for something more to say, I stepped into the living room and caught my breath. The sun was setting, well to the south still, and visible at the edge of the picture windows, sinking beneath the horizon. Streamers of cloud glowed golden-orange in the slanting light. In the city, lights were beginning to twinkle.

"Ellen? You okay?"

"Fine. Listen, don't be alone if you don't want to. Call me, or call someone else, but don't be alone."

She was silent for a moment. "Thanks, Ellen. It's good of you to care."

"Of course I care! And if you want to talk before Tuesday, I can come over." I would even brave the reporters, armed with Tony's "no trespassing" threat, though I didn't have a badge to back it up.

"I'll be okay," Kris said.

"All right. See you Tuesday."

"Good night," she said, and hung up.

I frowned at the phone. I'd have been much happier if she had confirmed my last statement.

I stood gazing at the glorious sunset, wishing Kris was here with me and could see it. I was worried about her. Had Zeke bullied her? It must have been late when he went to talk to her.

Kris would never hurt herself.

I hoped.

She was so strong, but she was also brittle at times. I hoped this awful murder wouldn't break her.

Tony joined me. "Wow," he said, looking at the sunset. The clouds were getting reddish now, and the sun was down. "Everything all right?" he added, putting his arms around me from behind.

"I don't know. I hope so. Kris said the police came to talk to her last night."

"Yeah. I would have, if it was my case."

"Because of the kris."

"Afraid so. Makes her a top suspect."

I shook my head. "She wouldn't have done that. I'm positive."

Tony kissed my cheek. "Let it go," he whispered.

He coaxed me back to the sofa, but I'd lost interest in the movie. With the sun setting, I began to feel I should be home. Poor Minuit had been alone most of the day—again—though I'd checked on her when we fetched the TV.

I folded the dry laundry and put Tony's pillow back in its case while he watched the end of the movie. Bringing the sheets, blanket, and pillow into the room, I set them on the end of the sofa.

"I'd better get home," I said.

"Hungry? We could order a pizza. Get it delivered."

I shook my head. Lunch had been late, and high-calorie. "I'm just tired."

Tony shut off the TV, stood up, and stretched. "Okay, babe. If the media jerks are still there I'll run interference."

That made me smile. "Thanks."

We made up the sofa bed, then drove back to the tearoom. As it turned out, the media jerks had apparently given up when the sun went down. The house was quiet, and what I could see of the curb out front from the driveway was occupied only by a battered yellow VW Beetle. Tony got out of the car and came around to meet me for another hug.

"Coming in?" I asked.

"Nah. I think I'll unpack some boxes."

"Okay." I kissed him. "Have a good night."

"You, too. Want me to check for trespassers?"

I smiled. "Maybe just cruise by the front?"

"You got it. Love you, babe."

One more hug. "Love you."

I watched him get on his bike, then went inside. The house was quiet and dim, fading light coming in through the windows, just enough for me to see my way. I left the lights off and went upstairs, listening to the little creaks of the old house.

I might miss being here alone at night. I did love this place, and despite its quirks, it had been home for over a year.

A very eventful, often stressful year. A year of finding dead bodies: some of them here, others elsewhere.

I sighed as I reached the top of the stairs. The sound of a motorcycle driving past made me smile, and I hurried to the front window in time to see Tony's bike disappear up the street.

Minuit mewed from her playpen in my office. I took her out and cuddled her as I returned to the window, sitting on the couch and watching the last of the sunset fade into a deepening indigo sky. Magical time of the evening.

So much change in the past year. I was busier than I'd ever been. I'd met many new people, made a lot of friends, and learned so much. And now I was preparing to get married. How different would my life be a year from now, I wondered?

I loved this view, looking west over the rooftops of my neighborhood, though it was nowhere near as spectacular as the view from the townhome. Buildings blocked the horizon from sight here, but when there were clouds, the sunsets were lovely, and at night the stars were magical.

My thoughts returned to Kris. I hoped she had some kind of solace like this view. I had never been to her place, so I didn't know what it was like. Owen was right—she didn't let people near her. I wondered about that.

Why the kris tattoo? Yes, it was her name, but the knife was such a dark thing. Was it just a part of her Goth life, or was there something more to it?

Whoever had killed Margo had known about that tattoo. That meant it was almost certainly one of the Goths. A Goth who was willing not only to kill, but to add the cruelty of cutting an image into Margo's chest. I hoped that had been done after the death, but actually, it was almost certainly before. Difficult to carve things on a hanging body.

Ugh. I needed to think about something else.

I gazed at the sky outside the window, looking for the first star, trying to let go of my thoughts. A new idea bubbled up into the space: a Goth who (in my limited knowledge) had cut flesh. Her own flesh. Cherie.

Could Cherie have killed Margo?

Although I thought it possible she would want to, I wasn't sure she was physically capable. Margo had been sturdily built, and probably outweighed Cherie. Unless Cherie was a martial artist, which I doubted, she would have had a hard time overpowering Margo.

But if she'd had a weapon with which to threaten her? Maybe a knife? I doubted Cherie had a gun, but who knew? There was a lot I didn't know about that crowd.

Another possibility was that more than one person had been involved in Margo's murder. Were there two Goths who would be willing to kill her, and want to frame Kris? It almost made more sense—two people would have an easier time hanging Margo from a tree than just one—but the only couple that came to mind was Roberto and Gwyneth. They had less motivation than others for the murder, and as far as I knew they were friends with Kris and wouldn't try to frame her.

There were so many other Goths in that circle, though. Many that I didn't know at all. It could be any of them. I felt a little sorry for Zeke, having to talk to the fifty or so people who had been at the Halloween party. Selfishly, I hoped he'd find the killer among those I didn't know.

"Mew."

I scritched Minuit's head. "You're right. It's suppertime."

I carried her into my suite and fed her, then cleaned up her litter boxes. It was getting late and I was actually hungry now as well. I looked in the fridge, but there were only a couple of eggs and a zucchini.

Zucchini fritter, maybe? It didn't inspire me.

If only there was some pizza or something. I could check downstairs for tearoom leftovers from yesterday—if there were any they would just be thrown out come Tuesday.

Minuit was in her kitty bed, washing her face after her meal. I shut her in the suite and went down to the kitchen to raid the fridge there, but the pickings were slim: two endive salads and a strawberry puff. I put them on a plate and poked my nose in the freezer to see if there was anything there I could turn into dinner. A foil-wrapped package on the top shelf caught my eye. I took it down and saw it was labeled "Ellen" in my handwriting. It was long and slightly triangular. A calzone!

I took it upstairs along with the tea goodies, and ate the endive salads while the calzone was heating up in my toaster oven. Since the endives lasted maybe forty-five seconds, there was still plenty of time to throw together a simple marinara sauce from a can of stewed tomatoes I had in the cupboard. I opened a bottle of Cabernet and poured a glass, then set my café table for one. I even lit a candle and placed it in the center of the table.

I was missing Tony, I realized. Had he ordered that pizza? Thinking of him in the townhome, unpacking boxes and channel surfing, made me feel I was close to a strange, new life. It wouldn't be long before I was living over there, too.

Couple weeks, maybe. *After* Valentine's.

The calzone was ready. I put it on a plate and poured marinara all over it, then took it to the table and seated myself. Minuit came over to investigate. I picked her up and let her sniff my dinner. She was interested in the smells, but apparently didn't find them appetizing. She hopped down off my lap and returned to her bed.

Marinara sauce had to be one of mankind's better inventions. Tomatoes and garlic, a little salt and pepper. Simple, easy, and so good. The calzone was a golden-crusted marvel of onions, cheese, mushrooms and pepperoni. I savored the meal, sipping the wine between bites and thinking about the week ahead.

Monday would be busy, because I'd have to cover the phones, which Kris usually did. I winced at the thought. It was quite possible that the media would call the tearoom number looking for me. I'd have to evoke my secretarial voice, and take messages for myself, because I sure didn't want to get into any conversations about the murder over the phone.

I'd need to put in the orders for the week, also. Extra flowers for Valentine's Day. I'd check with Julio during our morning meeting, to make sure we'd have everything we needed for Sunday. I should look over the staff schedule, too.

I put down my fork. I'd slipped into working mode, and that was not good. I took a swallow of wine, fetched a notepad and pen, and made a list of all the to-do things I'd just thought of, so I could let them go until morning. Then I put it aside and finished my meal, thinking about all the things I was grateful for.

The tearoom. My friends and family. Tony.

Marinara sauce.

Little black kittens.

The overhead light flicked off and on, so fast I almost wasn't sure it had really happened. I froze, listening. The house was silent.

"Okay, you too," I said. "I'm grateful for you, Captain."

The light blinked again, longer in darkness. What was the captain trying to tell me? He didn't mess with the lights that often, and when he blinked them he was usually trying to get my attention.

Another blink. I put down my fork and sat listening. Only the wind whispering at the window.

Then the lights went off and stayed off, but there was still a flickering somewhere. I looked toward the window, where the shadows of bare tree branches swayed gently. Looked around the room, and saw that there was light under the door—the chandelier was on out in the hall. Had I left it on?

It blinked off and came on again.

"Okay, all right," I said, standing and leaving my napkin beside my plate.

I went out into the hall, closing the door of my suite so Minuit wouldn't get loose. The light promptly went out, and the stairwell light came on. The captain wanted me downstairs. I went down, expecting the light in the dining parlor to be on, but instead the stairwell went dark and I saw a faint light coming from the gift shop.

He was getting good at this.

I went into the shop and saw that the light was coming from the adjacent alcoves—looked like from Violet. I followed it through the curtained passage. It was the spotlight on Vi's portrait. I looked at the painting, wondering what the captain was trying to tell me, then the light went out.

Standing in semi-darkness, I became aware of a different flickering light. Outside the window there was a small flame at the base of the cottonwood tree where Margo had been hanged.

A chill went through me. Was someone trying to set fire to the tree?

I hurried out through the gift shop and the front door, then stopped at the end of the *portal*. A dark figure stood by the tree. I hesitated. The flame was small and not growing. The figure stood still, looking up at the tree's crown. It looked like a male. Dark coat, hands stuffed in pockets. Curly hair, not as dark. The hair looked familiar.

I walked slowly toward the tree, keeping a few feet between

myself and the visitor in case I'd have to run. As I got closer, my worries diminished. The flame was a candle: a tall glass votive like the ones that were always burning in the cathedral, green. It was tucked between two roots of the tree, and a bouquet of flowers—the kind you could get at a grocery store—lay next to it.

I came even with the visitor and looked at his profile. He had the collar of his coat turned up, and an elaborately carved black gauge earring in the ear that I could see, which was unusual. At work, he always wore a modest stud.

"Dale?"

He turned his head to me, a frown of dismay on his brow. "I just heard. I was away all weekend."

He looked down at the candle. I waited a moment, then said, "Would you like to come in and have a cup of tea?"

He let out a sigh. "Yeah. Thanks."

We went in together and I locked the door behind us, then turned on the hall light. We walked to the butler's pantry and I filled a kettle.

"You choose the tea," I said.

He gazed at the canisters on the shelf, then took down the one labeled "Iron Goddess of Mercy." It was an oolong, one I had recently added to our collection.

Dale selected a teapot with gold and blue designs in an art deco style, probably the least flowery one on the shelf. If we'd had a black pot I'm sure he'd have picked that. He put an infuser in the pot and added leaf tea, then got out a small tray and began loading it with cups, spoons, sugar, and milk. Usually he drank his tea black, but he was on autopilot, doing tasks he did every day at work.

"Are you hungry?" I asked while we waited for the kettle to boil. "I could pop in a couple of scones."

He swallowed. "That would be great. I was going to get dinner after I got back, but then...."

I nodded. "Be right back," I said.

In the kitchen I turned on an oven, got out a small baking sheet and put four frozen scones on it, then added a *bastilla*, thinking Dale could probably use a bit of protein. I set a timer and took it with me back to the pantry. He had added clotted cream and lemon curd to the tray. The timer for the tea went off as I joined him. He removed the infuser and put the teapot on the tray, then picked it up.

"Where shall we sit?" he asked.

"You choose."

He was still for a moment, thinking, then led the way out to the hall. I followed him back to the gift shop, turning on lights since his hands were full. I thought he was heading for Violet, but instead he stepped past the curtain into Dahlia.

"This okay?"

"Sure," I said.

Dale set the tray on the table, sat in one of the wing chairs, and poured tea for us both. I set the timer for the scones on the table and picked up my cup, taking a sip to refresh my memory of the tea before deciding whether to add anything. It was earthy and soft, mellow but with caffeine lurking in the background. Oolongs required attention to fully appreciate, and I took my time, knowing it would also help Dale.

"This is the best tea," Dale said after savoring a mouthful. "I'm so glad you added it."

"Me too."

He sipped again, then met my gaze. "What happened? All I saw was a teaser for the news."

"Oh. Heaven knows what they're saying."

I told him about finding the body and the police-filled evening. A small part of me, influenced by Tony no doubt, warned me to withhold the details about the kris and the beads. They would only upset Dale further, anyway.

The timer went off, and I hurried to the kitchen to fetch the scones and *bastilla*. I piled them all on a small plate and rejoined Dale in Dahlia. He had taken off his coat and draped it over the chair. Underneath, he had on a black and gray striped long-sleeved shirt with a large skull-and-crossbones design on the front. He was wearing dark eyeliner, too. Much more Goth than usual. Like Kris, he really toned it down for work.

I set the plate on the table between us. Dale refilled our cups, then took a scone and slathered curd on it.

"Thanks," he said after swallowing the first bite. "Starving."

I put curd and cream on a scone for myself, and ate it between sips of tea while Dale devoured the rest of his scone and the *bastilla*. He then looked at me.

"Do they know who did it?"

"They're looking at Kris," I said, watching for his reaction.

He looked confused, then frowned. "Because of Gabriel."

"That, and a couple of other things."

"Kris wouldn't kill Margo," he said. "Even if she was pissed as hell, and she was, back in November."

"I agree."

"So who did it?"

I shrugged. I had no good speculations, but I was glad to hear Dale asking these questions. It meant he was probably not the murderer. I hadn't thought he was, but you never knew.

"You were friends with Margo, right?" I asked.

He sighed, gazing toward the dark fireplace. "You never saw her at her best. She was really fun, until Gabriel got hold of her."

Having no response to that, I took a sip of tea.

"He really messed her up," Dale said bitterly. "If he'd just left her alone, they'd both still be alive."

"I'm so sorry," I said after a moment.

Dale looked up at me. "Thanks."

"Do you know of anyone who was angry at Margo?"

"Hell, a *lot* of people were mad at her, but not mad enough to—no, I don't know anyone who would kill her. No."

He shook his head and drank more tea, then put down his cup and took another scone, pulling it apart.

"What does your detective think?" he said.

My detective? Okay.

"He's leaning toward Kris. But it isn't his case."

Dale looked surprised. "Not his case?"

"He's too close to me, and I'd be a suspect if I didn't have an alibi," I added. "Speaking of which, I hope you were with other people Saturday night."

"I went up to Los Alamos. Saw some friends, then spent the night with my parents."

"Good."

Los Alamos was only an hour's drive away, but if he'd been with his parents he was fine. And anyway, Dale was the last person I'd suspect. He'd been kind to Margo, even after Gabriel's death.

"She was super depressed," he said, glancing toward the south wall. "She always hid it by being rude. I tried to cheer her up, but when the trial was scheduled, she kind of crashed."

"Crashed?"

He turned his head, meeting my gaze sidelong. "She knew she'd go to jail. She was terrified of that. Kept saying her life was ruined."

"Oh."

"I tried to talk her out of it. Said it wouldn't be that long in jail, but to her one day was too long." He shook his head.

Someone had saved her from that fate, at least. I frowned. This did not have the hallmarks of a mercy killing, though. It was more an accusation, aimed at Kris. Why?

Gabriel.

Kill Margo, who had killed Gabriel. Accuse Kris, who had been

Gabriel's last lover.

And who had inherited his estate.

This was vengeance. Double vengeance. I was even more certain of it now, but no closer to a solution.

I picked up my cup, which had only a little tea left in the bottom. Dale was eating his third scone, so I refreshed both our cups. A sip of tea, and I closed my eyes to savor it.

The Iron Goddess of Mercy was Kwan Yin. My mother had owned a little statuette of her, standing, white robe draped around her as if blown by a breeze. I'd have to find that, I decided. Maybe it was in the storage shed.

Memories of Margo bubbled up in my mind. She had been rude, and I'd rather disliked her for it. How sad that she'd been so off-balance. Clearly, she'd had a better side, the side that Dale had tried to support.

I opened my eyes and drank more tea. Dale gave me a sheepish look.

"I think I ate one of your scones."

The plate was empty, even of crumbs.

"It's okay," I said. "I had dinner. Would you like something more?"

He shook his head. "I'd better go. Thanks, this was a big help. Thank you for talking with me."

"Of course."

Dale insisted on helping me tidy up the alcove. When we had brought all the dishes to the kitchen, I turned to him.

"I'll wash up. You go home and get some rest."

"Thanks, Ellen. You're the best." He gave me a swift, patchouli-scented hug, shrugged into his coat, and went out the back door. I watched him walk behind the kitchen to the south, back toward the tree. When he was out of sight, I washed the dishes and went upstairs.

Minuit was asleep. I put the remains of my calzone in the fridge, took a shower, and decided to go to bed myself. Monday would be a long day.

I put on comfy pajamas and glanced out the window before climbing into bed. I could see the candle at the foot of the tree, its light flickering as the branches waved above it.

"Rest in peace, Margo," I whispered.

The phone calls started early, before nine o'clock. I had been up and working since seven-thirty. Minuit was happily rattling her ring toy in the playpen when the first call came in. Since we weren't open to the public on Mondays, I let it go to voicemail, then listened to the message.

It was a cancellation. I updated the reservation software, telling myself not to worry. We were booked solid all week, and had a waiting list. Kris handled that, and since I wasn't sure how she preferred to do it I left it for her to deal with on Tuesday.

Three more cancellations came in before I went down to meet with Julio, and one call from a news reporter. I made a note of that one before deleting it, but I didn't intend to return the call.

I emptied the tea from the samovar pot into a thermos and took it downstairs with me, picking up a teacup from the butler's pantry on my way to the kitchen. Julio smiled when I came in, and reached to turn down the music. His chef's cap and matching pants were black with pink and red hearts, rather like the mugs I disliked from the gift shop.

"Morning, boss," he said. "Ready for a good week?"

"I could use one," I answered.

"Sorry about the body," he said sincerely.

"Thanks."

We spoke no more about Margo, but instead sat at the break

table with our tea and coffee and went over plans for the week. Julio had decided to double the output of macarons—we'd sold them out all the previous week—and would need additional almond flour, elderflower essence, and raspberries. These were all expensive, but since the macarons sold for a dollar a pop we'd still make a tidy profit.

"Kris coming in today?" Julio asked, glancing toward the clock.

"No, she's taking the day off."

"Okay, but we should get these orders in this morning."

"I'll do it."

"Can we schedule Ramon for some extra hours?"

I nodded. "Try to keep him under forty, and remember he's playing guitar on Sunday." I had talked to him about playing the guitar every evening that week, but it looked like he'd be needed in the kitchen.

"Okay. Might need a little overtime somewhere, though, either from him or Hanh."

"Make it Hanh if you have to."

Hanh had a higher pay rate, but Ramon was already putting in extra time and I didn't want to overload him. Anyway, Hanh could make macarons, and Ramon hadn't mastered them yet. While we were looking at the schedule I decided to give Dee and Iz some extra hours, too—more coverage in the afternoons, when we'd probably have more shoppers. Nat was coming in mornings, so the gift shop would be covered all day.

I'd better look over the inventory, in case I needed to replenish any. Those orders would also have to go in today if the merchandise was to arrive before the weekend.

My tea was gone by the time we wrapped up. I washed the cup and left it in the rack, then put away the dry things from my visit with Dale the night before. Julio finalized his order and gave me a copy of the list. He glanced toward the window. Gray skies outside.

"Think I'll make a frittata for lunch, if it's okay with you. Saves time."

"As long as you make enough for me," I said.

"Deal. Come down at eleven."

"Will do."

I gathered my notes and the thermos, and headed back up to my office. Seven more calls had come in, five of them cancellations. One was a new reservation request, which cheered me up a bit. I added it to Kris's waiting list. The seventh was a message from my neighbor Katie, expressing concern about the murder and offering support. I made a note to call her back.

Wanting more tea, I set a fresh pot steeping on the samovar, then strolled to the front window and looked down at the street. A familiar figure in a long, white coat came into view walking down the sidewalk from the north. Gwyneth, and she wasn't alone. Cherie was with her, dressed in black.

They came in the front gate of my property and headed for the tree. I went into my suite to watch them from that window. They stood talking briefly, looking up into the branches, then placed two more votives at the foot of the tree. Gwyneth's was white, and Cherie's was red.

Well, that was interesting. I watched Gwyneth add a large bouquet of white lilies in a vase—*not* from the grocery store—and stand quietly with Cherie for a minute.

Great. My tree was turning into a shrine.

The timer at the samovar went off and I hurried out to rescue my tea. I returned to the south window, but Gwyneth and Cherie had left. Looking out the west window again, I saw no sign of them on the street.

I poured myself a cup of tea and returned to my desk to tackle the orders. The kitchen orders were easy, but for the gift shop I had to check what was in the storeroom and what was downstairs. This took over an hour, by which time it was almost eleven. We were low on the little ceramic heart boxes and I couldn't figure out which vendor to order them from, so I texted Kris, glad of the excuse to touch base with her. To my relief, she responded promptly. I placed the orders, gritting my teeth at the cost of expedited shipping. Just as I was about to go downstairs I remembered the extra order for flowers, and hastily put it in.

Arriving at the foot of the stairs a little breathless, I found the regular flower delivery standing in white buckets in the hall by the back door. Lots of roses—pink and red—with alstroemeria and baby's breath for accents. I picked up two of the buckets and carried them through the short hall to the kitchen.

"Sorry, I didn't have time to put them in the fridge," Julio said, up to his elbows in flour.

Hanh was there also, and we exchanged nods. All the work surfaces were covered with trays of macarons in various stages of completion. Their sweet smell mingled with something savory, making my mouth water.

"It's okay," I told Julio, and opened the walk-in refrigerator.

By the time I'd moved in all the buckets the fridge was pretty full. I'd be arranging the flowers in the afternoon, so they wouldn't be in Julio's way for long. I closed the door and looked around for something to do.

A timer went off. Julio looked up. "That's lunch. Ellen could you get it? The small oven."

"Right."

I grabbed a couple of towels and opened the oven, releasing a burst of savory aroma and revealing a golden-brown cloud of frittata in a cast-iron skillet. I moved it to the range top, which was about the only place not covered in macarons, and turned off the oven.

Hanh thew together a salad with swift efficiency while I set the break table for three, and we sat down together to enjoy the frittata, which turned out to be mushroom and spinach, with sour cream, onions, and cheese. Fabulous. I had to concentrate on each bite to keep from gobbling my share.

I was on my last bite of frittata when the back doorbell rang. Julio stood and went to the window.

"It's Gina," he said, returning to the table.

I hopped up and went out to the hall to let her in. She was wearing her red coat and had a newspaper in her hand.

"Thought you'd better see this," she said, handing it to me. "I know you don't get the paper."

I opened it and regarded it for a moment. "Front page," I said, swallowing my dismay. "Good publicity, right?"

Margo's picture was front and center under a large headline: MURDER SUSPECT HANGED AT SITE OF SATANIC PARTY.

ina gave me a sympathetic look. "Brace yourself for some blowback, honey."

"It's already started. We're getting cancellations."

A photo of the tree accompanied the story, and a third photo showed the front of the tearoom. Damn.

"It was *not* a satanic party," I grumbled.

"How about some tea?" Gina said.

"Sure. Let's go upstairs."

"And she was not charged with murder," I said as we climbed the stairs. "It was manslaughter."

"Not quite bad enough for a libel complaint, but I think you should consider giving some interviews to correct these—misconceptions," Gina said.

"Yeah." I sighed. Talking to the press was one of my least favorite activities, even under cheerful circumstances, which these were not. "Thanks for the heads-up."

"You're welcome."

I made a pot of tea for us—raspberry chocolate truffle, Gina's favorite—and we sat by the front window to discuss damage control and plan talking points. I studiously ignored the occasional ringing of the office phone.

The timing of the newspaper story was bad, especially since I'd just placed expensive orders for the week. But none of it would be wasted, even if we lost business. There were plenty of people who didn't care about sensational news stories. Plenty who still wanted their tea, regardless.

And in a weird way, this *was* good publicity. My tearoom's business on the front page. We'd been here before, and survived, and in fact sometimes thrived.

"Did you see the candles by the tree?" I asked Gina.

"No, I parked in back."

"I honestly didn't expect anyone to mourn for Margo, but some of the Goths are leaving candles and flowers. It's turning into a memorial."

"Great!" Gina said. "That's where you give your interviews! Can you get a TV spot or two?"

"I'm sure I can."

Did I want to? No. But I'd do it, for the sake of the tearoom. Maybe Carla Algodones would appreciate being offered a scoop.

Gina helped herself to more tea and added sugar and milk. She tilted her head, regarding me as she stirred it. "Let me be your publicist for this one. Give you a little cachet."

"Fine with me. I don't love talking to reporters." Especially when asking for favors.

"When are you free for an interview? This afternoon?"

"Really busy day."

"How about offering them a live spot on the evening news?"

I raised my brows. "Think they'd go for it?"

"They might. And the candles will look great at dusk."

"Okay."

"You'll have to be available between five and seven. That work?"

"I'll have a late dinner."

"We'll have a late dinner. I'm going to be with you for this one. I'll wear my publicist costume."

"Gina, you're a peach!"

She smiled, pleased with herself. "You're going to look *so* important, and *so* gracious. Do you have something angelic to wear?"

"I'll channel Gwyneth."

"Who?"

"One of the Goths. She always wears white."

"Ooh, that'll look great with the candles! Too bad you can't wear your wedding gown."

"That would be overkill, don't you think?"

I chuckled as I refilled my teacup. Gina held out hers for more, and I obliged. She had managed to put me in a good mood, and even make me look forward to giving an interview.

"I've got plenty of lace dresses," I said. "I'll find one that works."

"Hair and makeup, too. Do you want help?"

"I can manage."

"All right." Gina made some notes in her pocket notebook, then looked at me. "Which station gets offered this gem of human interest?"

"Channel four. Carla Algodones did a story Sunday. She might like to do a follow-up."

"Perfect. I'll call her and let you know what time." Gina glanced at her watch and swallowed the rest of her tea. "And now I have to get back to work. Got a few things I need to get done, but I'll hop on this in the next hour."

"Thanks, Gina. I'm glad you've got my back."

She hugged me. "We'll fix it."

I escorted her to the back door, poked my nose in the kitchen and apologized for abandoning lunch, then returned to the upper hall to gather our tea things and wash them up in my suite. I needed to get the flowers done, but first I checked the phone messages.

Eleven more cancellations. I bit my lip. This could get bad.

Going through my closet and choosing a dress for the interview made me feel a little better. I decided on a cream-colored linen overlaid with lace, with long sleeves and a high collar. It would be warmer than some of the others, and was a close match for a shawl I would keep handy just in case the evening got cold. I laid them out on my bed and got out stockings and shoes as well, so I'd be able to dress quickly.

It was almost one o'clock. I took my phone downstairs with me and put the working tablecloth on the table in the dining parlor, then hauled all the buckets of flowers into that room and collected the vases from all over the tearoom. Some of last week's flowers, which had been predominantly pink and white, were still nice. I trimmed their stems and collected them into a plain glass vase, thinking I'd add it to the memorial.

Working with the flowers soothed my feelings considerably. I stuck my face into every arrangement I completed, inhaling the roses' heady fragrance and the sweet, light scent of the baby's breath.

When I'd done about half of the vases, my phone rang. I picked it up, expecting Gina, but it was Tony.

"Hi, babe. How about that pizza tonight?"

"Oh, I can't, sorry. I'm going to be doing an interview."

"Tomorrow?"

"I have a dinner date with Kris tomorrow."

"Dang. Wednesday?"

"If we have it here. Phillips is coming with the metal detector."

A brief silence followed. "When can you spend a night at the new place? The sofa bed is pretty comfortable."

I sighed. "I think this week's a wash. It's already nuts and it's only Monday."

"Try to fit me in sometime, okay?"

"I will. Want to have pizza here Wednesday?"

"Maybe."

"Okay. Let me know."

"Talk later, babe."

"Bye," I said, though I knew he was already gone.

I picked up a pink rose and smelled it, closing my eyes. We hadn't discussed Valentine's Day, I realized. It was probably already too late to get a dinner reservation, and I would certainly be too exhausted to cook an elaborate meal Sunday evening.

Damn.

Things felt like they were slipping out of control. I had a couple too many balls in the air, but they were not things I could delegate to others. I had to deal with it myself.

When in doubt, drink tea.

It was time for a break anyway. The table was full of vases and lidless teapots stuffed with roses. I put a kettle on in the pantry, then carried the finished arrangements to their places in the alcoves and elsewhere around the tearoom, making room on the dining table for a second round. This task always improved my mood, and as I moved through the tearoom, I gave silent thanks for each beautiful alcove, for the roses, for all my blessings.

I made myself a pot of Wisteria White and sipped it while I continued arranging the flowers. The sweet smell of macarons—chocolate ones, now—had pervaded the ground floor, and I began to have serious cravings.

"They're not done yet," I reminded myself. They'd have to cool, and be filled.

Of course, there might be some in the pastry case. Those might be getting a little stale. It would be a shame to waste them….

My phone rang again: Gina this time.

"You're on for the six o'clock news!" she said.

"Wow!"

"Algodones is *very* interested in following up with you. They'll arrive at five forty-five to set up. I'll come at five-fifteen. You'll be ready?"

"Yes."

"Make sure the Goths didn't leave any black candles."

"I'll check. Thanks so much, Gina! I'll buy dinner."

"You bet you will! See you soon."

I put down the phone and finished the last few floral arrangements. As I was placing them around the tearoom, I glanced casually at the pastry case, but some industrious person had cleaned it out. Sighing, I went through to Dahlia where I placed a teapot full of roses, then on into Violet. There I set a tall bud vase with three pink roses and a burst of baby's breath on one end of the mantel under Vi's portrait. Pausing to look out the window, I saw that the memorial was growing: more floral bouquets lay haphazardly on the ground, and more candles stood here and there.

That needed tidying up. I felt a little badly about messing with people's offerings, except that the candles were a bit of a concern. It would not be good if the tree caught fire.

The only vase left was the pink and white roses I'd culled from last week's arrangements. I topped it up a bit with water and carried it out to the tree, placing it opposite Gwyneth's gorgeous white lilies. I thought about collecting the bouquets into a couple of other vases (they'd last longer in water), but decided it was better to leave them as they were, and settled for pulling them all to the center and laying them out a little more tidily. Two of them were tied with black ribbons.

The candles were all the tall, glass votive type that lasted seven days, so they were fairly safe for now. If one fell over it would go out. I moved a couple of precarious ones to more level spots, and tucked one purple one (which might look black on television) behind the pink and white roses.

Standing back, I assessed my handiwork. Much more tidy, yet still spontaneous-looking. I nodded with satisfaction and went back to the dining parlor to clean up the floral arrangement mess. By the time that was done it was after three, so I looked in on the kitchen.

Julio and Hanh were filling macarons. Trays of finished ones rested on the counter, and the work tables were less crowded. I resisted nabbing a macaron, though the temptation was great. I'd better eat something before five, since dinner would be late.

Dinner! I should make a reservation. On Mondays many restaurants were closed, so the choices were limited.

Julio glanced up at me. "When are the staples coming in? We're almost out of almond flour."

"Should be here by Wednesday morning. If you need more tomorrow I can run to the grocery store."

"We should be okay. Got enough macarons for a couple of days now, even if we sell a lot."

"Thank you both," I said, nodding to Hanh. "I'll be upstairs if you need anything before you go."

"Night, boss," Julio said, sounding just a tad weary.

Minuit greeted me with a slightly plaintive mew. I played with her a little, fed her, and left her in the playpen.

There were twenty-six messages waiting on the phone. I worked my way through them, thinking about rewarding myself with a margarita. That reminded me about dinner and I paused to call La Choza and request a table for two at seven o'clock. I asked about Sunday night while I had them on the phone, but they were booked solid.

Back to the messages. Final tally: fifteen cancellations, three new reservations, seven calls from reporters, and one from Willow Lane, expressing sympathy and offering to stop by. I made a note to call her back—tomorrow.

Almost four o'clock. Tea time. The pot on the samovar, left over from morning, was too tired by now. I shut it down for the night. I didn't want a whole pot of tea, so I made myself a mug of Darjeeling in my suite and baked up a couple of frozen scones to go with it. Ate them by the window in my suite, looking down at the candles. It looked like there were a couple more bouquets down there.

Either Margo had more friends than I'd realized, or the Goth community had decided to forgive her after being contacted by Detective Zeke. Surprising, and comforting in a way. There was a lot about Goth culture that I didn't understand, but the one thing I'd learned was that there were good-hearted people among them, at least in Kris's circle.

I cleaned up, swallowed the last of my tea, and hopped into the shower. When the hot water hit my shoulders I realized they were aching. Stress and flower-arranging. I scrubbed myself all over, emerging into a steam-filled bathroom. Leaving the door open so the mirror would clear, I went to my bedroom to dress.

The sun was westering, light slanting through the tree branches down in the yard. I dressed, then returned to the bathroom to do my hair and makeup. I was just finishing when the back doorbell rang.

Grabbing my shawl, I hurried downstairs. Gina was there in a tailored suit of camel-colored wool.

"You look snappy," I said as I let her in.

"And you look like Miss Manners herself. Perfect!"

I put on a brave smile, bracing myself for the ordeal. We sat in the dining parlor and went over our plan. Gina rehearsed me a little, asking a couple of questions in the persona of Carla Algodones. I replied calmly.

"Good," she said. "You're ready. Let's check the candles."

A few clouds had moved in, and a chilly breeze made me resort to the shawl. The sun wasn't quite down but the buildings to the west blocked it, so the candles were beginning to make a glow. As we came around the corner of the house, two young women in black jeans and leather with bits of silver chain here and there were standing in front of the tree.

I put a hand on Gina's arm and slowed my pace. I didn't know these Goths, though one of them looked slightly familiar. Maybe they'd been at the All Hallows party.

"—had this many friends," one was saying. "You'da thought she was a damn cheerleader."

"Dude, she *was* a cheerleader," replied the familiar-looking one.

"You missed the 'sarcasm' light."

The second one noticed our approach and shushed the other. I put on a smile as they looked in our direction.

"Good evening," I said when we joined them.

They stared back.

"I'm Ellen Rosings. I'm the owner of this property." I nodded toward the house, then met the gaze of the familiar one. "You've been here before, I think?"

Her shoulders rose. "A long time ago."

"Yeah," said her friend. "Not last weekend."

The familiar one shot her a look. "Dude."

"Did I hear you say Margo was a cheerleader?" I asked. "Was that in high school?"

"Yeah," said the familiar one.

"That's...surprising," I said.

"They didn't want her on the squad," said the unfamiliar Goth in a sullen tone. "They only took her 'cause she could do the splits better than anyone else."

"And back bends and grab her ankles," added the other.

"Oh," I said. "My."

"The other cheerleaders hated her," said the sullen Goth.

"How sad."

Why had she wanted to be a cheerleader, I wondered? She was so not the type. Desperate to fit in? To be liked?

I gazed at the flowers, feeling pity for Margo. So much unhappiness in a short life.

"Come on," said the sullen Goth, breaking my reverie. I glanced up to see them leaving, shooting final looks over their shoulders as they walked across the lawn to the front gate.

"Okay, let's set you up," Gina said.

She positioned me in front of the tree and the candles, a little to one side to leave room for the reporter, then stepped back and gazed at me with a critical frown.

"Stay there," she said, and moved a couple of the candles while I stood. One bouquet was separate from the central group. Gina brought it in, and adjusted the vase of pink and white roses.

The last of the sunlight broke through the evening clouds and slanted through the tree branches above as the sun went down. Where I stood was already in shadow. I looked up at the golden light on the bare branches. Someone had tied a large, black bow on the branch where Margo had died.

The Goths? Either they'd used a ladder or they'd climbed the tree. I frowned. It might not look good in the interview, but it was too late to do anything about it. The channel four van pulled up in front of the house and Carla Algodones got out, followed by a cameraman. No, a camerawoman: petite and agile, with the obligatory ball cap on backwards and large plug-style earrings. Cameraperson?

Gina went to meet them and stood talking with them both for a minute, gesturing toward the tree. After a minute Algodones nodded and they all came toward me. I silently called down the mantle of Miss Manners to assist me, and smiled graciously.

"Good evening," I said.

"Hi," Algodones said. "Yeah, this is great! Did you set this up?"

"No. These were left by others." Mostly.

"Love the bow."

I winced inwardly. The cameraperson set up and peered through the lens, then moved the camera to a different spot, aiming it from the side rather than where Gina had stood. So much for careful positioning of the flowers.

Gina hovered in the background while Algodones stood beside me and we both stepped this way or that way until the cameraperson was satisfied. The light was fading fast and the air was getting cold. The cameraperson went back to the van and returned with a spotlight which she set up a few feet from us. It would probably wash out the candle glow.

Ah, well. I just wanted to get this done.

The cameraperson muttered to herself a lot. I finally realized she was talking to someone remotely when I spotted the earbud in her ear, similar to the one Algodones wore.

"We're live in six," the cameraperson said, and Algodones nodded.

"You lived in Santa Fe long?" she asked me.

"All my life."

"How'd you end up with this place?"

"I bought it." Sank my inheritance into it, actually, but that was too much information.

Not the stuff of exciting interviews, but Algodones would probably use it to research the tearoom, if she hadn't already done that. She gave a nod and glanced at the cameraperson, who held up five fingers.

I swallowed and straightened my spine, then fussed with my shawl. Gina stepped forward to help. "Do you want me to hold it? Are you warm enough?"

I took the shawl off. The breeze was cold, but I could stand it for a few minutes. "Yes," I said, and handed it to her.

I felt strangely vulnerable without the shawl, but that might be good. Gina wanted me to look sweet and vulnerable, for maximum sympathy. Rather calculated, but not inaccurate, I supposed.

"Live in thirty seconds," said the cameraperson, who bent to look through the lens.

I rearranged my smile. Algodones faced the camera holding her mic in front of her and nodded.

"Yes, I'm at the Wisteria Tearoom, where Margo Foss was brutally hanged from the tree behind me on Saturday. Since then mourners have been leaving flowers and candles in a memorial to the victim. With me is Ellen Rosings, the owner of the tearoom." She turned to me. "Do you think this murder had anything to do with the death of Gabriel Rhodes last October?"

"It's possible. I don't know."

"Margo Foss was at a party here with Rhodes on Halloween, the night he was killed."

"That's correct."

"And she was scheduled to be tried for manslaughter in connection with his death."

"Yes."

"Did that party include a satanic ritual?"

"Certainly not! It was a literary-themed party, based on a story by Edgar Allen Poe."

"But were there any satanic costumes?"

"I'm not sure what that would be, but there were plenty of costumes. It was Halloween."

Algodones seemed dissatisfied with that answer, but continued. "Both Margo Foss and Gabriel Rhodes were Goths, right?"

"Yes."

"Are you a Goth, Ellen?"

"Me? No."

"You were at the party, though, right? In a Goth costume?"

"Yes, I was helping to manage the party, since they had rented the tearoom. I wore a borrowed costume."

"Is it true there was going to be a ritual at midnight?"

How had she found out about that? I took a careful breath.

"There was going to be an unmasking at midnight, and a toast. That's all."

"So everyone at the party was going to drink something at midnight?"

"Yes. A cocktail made with cinnamon vodka. That didn't happen, though."

"Could there have been something more than vodka in that cocktail?"

"It was prepared by my staff, according to Gabriel Rhodes's instructions. I can give you the recipe."

"What if someone slipped something into the drinks?" Algodones insisted.

"We were concerned about pranks," I said calmly, "so the cocktails were kept secure in the kitchen. After the accident, we turned them over to the police. I'm sure they can verify that there was nothing added to the drinks."

"Do you think Margo Foss got what she deserved?"

I blinked, surprised by the abrupt change of subject. "No one deserves to die like that," I said calmly. "I think it's quite tragic, and apparently so do a lot of other people," I added, gesturing to the flowers and candles.

Algodones faced the camera again. "Margo Foss's murder remains a mystery," she said. "We'll continue to bring you the latest on this developing story. Reporting live from Santa Fe, I'm Carla Algodones."

The light went out, leaving us in darkness. I blinked, standing still to let my eyes adjust. The candles flickered as Gina brought me my shawl.

"Thanks," I said, hugging it around me. My hands were cold.

"OK, that's a wrap," said the cameraperson.

I glanced at her, wondering if she was being funny. Algodones was doing something with her mic. She looked up at me.

"Thanks," she said briefly.

I nodded. She headed for the van, leaving the cameraperson to break down her gear.

"Let's go inside," Gina said, shepherding me toward the back of the tearoom. I glanced over my shoulder to see the cameraperson taking a shot of the black bow in the tree.

"You did great!" Gina said when we were safely inside.

"Thank you," I said, sighing with relief that we were done. "I think I'd like to change before dinner. What time is it?"

"Six-twelve," Gina said. "You must have been the lead story!"

"Yay. I made us a reservation for seven."

She came upstairs with me while I changed into a warmer dress. I'd have preferred jeans, but since Gina was in a dress I picked a comfortable, long-sleeved green knit that was so warm I could only wear it in winter. I did take my hair down, clipping it back with a barrette, since I'd prefer not to be recognized by anyone who had seen the news.

I checked on Minuit, who was sleeping in the playpen. Collecting coat, scarf, purse and phone, I saw that I had messages. *Lots* of messages.

Gina drove while I scrolled through, looking for Tony's number among the calls and texts. It wasn't there. The texts were mostly from other reporters—I had added their numbers to my contacts so I'd be forewarned if they called. There were several voicemails from reporters as well. I left those for later.

"It would be a good idea to give a couple more interviews," Gina said over dinner at La Choza. "Just so you don't look like you're playing favorites."

I took a long pull at my margarita. "I'll think about it. Not the 'satanic party' reporter, though."

"No."

"It's a busy week."

Gina raised her glass. "Here's to the waiting list."

I joined the toast. "Thanks again, Gina. I sure hope this helps."

"It will, honey. Promise. You looked like the sweetest angel. Nobody would accuse you of being satanic."

"Good thing they couldn't read my thoughts."

That was too cynical, really. I was more sad than angry about the whole thing. Also, I was genuinely grateful for the opportunity to counter the "satanic party" story.

"I set my TV to record the news," Gina said. "Want to come over to my place and watch it?"

"Sure."

We ordered takeout flan and took it to Gina's apartment, where she made coffee to go with it. I settled into her voluminous couch and glanced around the living room, thinking she'd redecorated since I'd last been here. The drapes were new—dark red, and they'd been white before. Accent cushions on the furniture were a match- ing red.

Gina brought in the coffee and our takeout dessert, set them on the coffee table, and turned on the TV. I picked up my flan and cut off a small bite with my spoon while she ran the recording back to just before six o'clock.

Right after the opening music and "News 4" logo, a picture of the tearoom filled the screen. Gina let out a whoop. The anchor at the station gave a brief summary of the Margo Foss story, then introduced Carla Algodones.

Boy, was I glad I'd worn makeup! The light washed everything out, making me look ghostly pale, but at least I didn't look dead. As Algodones interviewed me, the tree trunk behind us was stark white, and the light reflected off the plastic wrappers on some of the flower bouquets leaning against it. I was grateful to see that the black bow on the tree branch did not show in the picture—it must have been up too high.

Not only did I look vulnerable, I looked positively fragile in my pale lace. A little tired, also. I was glad that my voice didn't waver, and that I didn't appear dismayed by Algodones's curve ball question about whether Margo had gotten what she deserved.

When the anchor segued into the next story, Gina hit the pause. "That was fantastic, girl! Want to watch it again?"

"No, thanks. I looked pretty anemic."

"Always go a little heavy on the makeup for TV."

I took a bite of flan and washed it down with coffee, savoring the aftertaste of the caramelized custard. If I had my preference, I wouldn't need that advice about the makeup, because I'd never give another TV interview. Gina was right, though. It was promotional gold, and didn't cost a penny. I disliked doing it, but the benefits were too good to pass up.

Gina had finished her flan. She put the plate on the table and picked up her coffee mug. "Want to stay for the ten o'clock news? I bet they'll replay it."

"No, thanks. I'd better get home."

"Well, you can watch it there."

"Um, actually I can't. We moved my TV over to the townhome."

"Oh! Moving in already?"

"Tony is. I'm too busy this week."

I carried our plates into Gina's kitchen and helped her clean up the coffee things, then she drove me home. We hugged in the car in my driveway.

"Thanks for everything, Gina. You're the best."

"Well, you deserve the best, honey. Get some rest. See you Wednesday."

Wednesday? Wednesday—oh yeah—tea with Gina and Angela. Why had I not put that off until next week?

"Right," I said with a smile I hoped wasn't too weary.

"I'll call you," Gina said.

And prod me to give more interviews, no doubt. I went into the house, waving from the door, and heard her pull away as I locked it behind me.

I stood for a moment in the darkness, thinking about the day. A hint of rose scent reached me from the dining parlor, and I relaxed, smiling with gratitude to be home. I went upstairs and into my office, where I gritted my teeth and sorted through thirty-odd messages on the business line. I didn't want Kris to have to deal with them first thing in the morning.

There were a few cancellations, but many more reservation requests. Hurrah! Several calls from reporters. Also, three calls requesting the recipe for Gabriel's cinnamon vodka cocktail.

Hmm. That might make a good special feature for next October. If people remembered Gabriel's death by then—and I suspected they would—they'd probably love to drink his cocktail at Halloween time. It would be a way of honoring his memory and his creativeness, but I'd talk to Kris about it first. If she didn't like the idea I wouldn't do it.

Kris. A flash of worry went through me. I hoped her day off had helped her recover her balance. I was tempted to call her, but didn't want to intrude. I glanced at the time and decided to send her a text.

Hope you had a restful day. Been thinking of you.

My phone buzzed before I had finished—Tony, texting me. I sent the text to Kris and checked Tony's message.

You gave good answers.

He must have seen the news interview. I called him.

"Babe."

"Hi," I said. "So you saw it."

"Yeah. You looked cold."

"I was freezing. Gina wanted me to look vulnerable."

"Well, that worked."

"I'm just glad they didn't ask about Kris."

"Zeke is keeping the details about the body under wraps," Tony said. "Don't mention them."

"I haven't."

"He's going to want to talk to you, by the way."

"Are you helping him?"

"It's his case, but it ties in with the Rhodes case, so yeah. I'm filling him in on that."

"Did you have pizza for dinner?" I asked, tired of talking about the murder.

"No, I cooked some pasta and unpacked a couple more boxes."

Tony cooks! Bachelor cooking, at least.

"We'll have to get that hot tub set up," I said wistfully.

"It's running," Tony said. "Owen came over and showed me how to treat the water."

"Oh! Have you been in it?"

"Not yet. Want to come try it?"

It was late. I should go to bed, but it sounded too good.

"Yes," I said.

I threw some clothes and my travel kit into my overnight bag, tended to Minuit and left her in the playpen with some kibble. Downstairs, I went into the kitchen and stole two brand new Sachertortes from the fridge, leaving Julio an apologetic note of confession.

It was cold outside, and the clouds had settled, muffling the sounds of the city. Tony's bike was in the driveway of the townhome and the front porch light was on, its crescent moon beaming warm light onto the path. I parked at the curb and walked up feeling tired, and to my surprise, happy. Tony must have been watching for me, because he opened the door as I approached.

"Welcome home," he said, smiling as he slid an arm around my waist.

8

HE HOT TUB WAS DIVINE. I sighed as I slid into the hot water, shivering a little at the shock of the transition from the cold night air. Every aching muscle in my body sang out in joy. I found a jet and leaned my shoulders into it.

The adobe wall around the yard hid all but a thin line of the city lights. Overhead the sky was leaden. I looked forward to being here on a clear night with a view of the stars, but for now I was just grateful for the soak.

Tony sat beside me and slid his arm around my waist. I thought I was too tired, but I was mistaken. We spent a long time in the tub and I enjoyed every minute.

By the time we emerged, prune-fingered and thoroughly relaxed, it was almost eleven. I yawned, clutching the skimpy bath towel that Tony had given me around myself. I'd have to bring over some bath sheets.

"Want dessert?" I said. "I brought chocolate."

Tony pulled me against him and kissed me. "Mmm. Chocolate."

"I take it that's a yes."

We refrained from smearing the Sachertorte all over each other, and ate it in a civilized fashion, mostly. There was some licking of fingers involved. I insisted on following this with hand-washing since we'd be sharing the sofa-bed.

It was smaller than my bed by a long shot. We had no choice but to cuddle together. Tony didn't seem to mind, and I was too tired to care. I yawned and snuggled against him. But this was definitely no substitute for my queen-sized bed.

After Valentine's, I thought as I sank into sleep.

Sunlight woke me, though it was dimmed by the window shade. I lay blinking sleepily, wondering what was wrong.

No baking smells, I realized. No scones, no macarons.

No tearoom.

I started fully awake, which roused Tony. His arm tightened around me as I fumbled for my phone to check the time.

7:52. Yikes!

"I'm late," I said, disentangling myself from the sheet. Tony restrained me for a second, then let go.

I grabbed my overnight bag and went into the bathroom, where I took a quick shower and got dressed. When I emerged, I smelled coffee and followed the aroma to the kitchen. Tony was leaning against the counter, eating cereal.

"Want some?" he offered.

"I'll take some coffee, thanks," I said, opening a cupboard to look for a mug. "No cereal. I've got to get going."

Tony opened a different cupboard and took down a plain white mug. I filled it halfway from the carafe and took a sip.

Not bad. Strong, but not bad. I added a splash of milk from the carton on the counter.

"Thanks."

Tony set down his bowl and collected me into his arms, kissing my neck. "Glad you came over."

"Me too, but I really have to go. Thank you."

I finished the coffee, collected my dirty clothes into my overnight bag, and put on my coat. Tony walked me to the door.

"Come again tonight," he said.

"We'll see."

A long, tingle-inducing kiss, then I hurried down the path to my car. It had snowed a little overnight—just a dusting, like powdered sugar on *bastilla*. Tony watched from the doorway as I drove away.

My arrival at the tearoom aroused curious looks, much as Tony's departure had done on other occasions. I ignored them, tossed "Good morning"s hither and yon, and took a deep breath of baking aromas from the kitchen: *bastilla* and scones. The world was right again.

Minuit greeted me with an indignant yowl from the playpen as I reached the top of the stairs. I extracted her and took her across to my suite, where I fed her. While she was eating I cleaned up both litter boxes and made sure she had fresh water. I shut her in the suite, not wanting to confine her to the playpen again so soon. With a prayer for the safety of my drapes, I returned to the business side, and glanced into Kris's office.

She was at her desk, on the phone, to my great relief. Probably managing cancellations and new reservations. She had on a black turtleneck over a broomstick skirt, with the mourning beads. She glanced up at me and I gave her a smile and a wave, to which she nodded in response.

The samovar was up and running with a pot of Lapsang souchong on top. I poured myself a cup and added a large dollop of milk and a spoonful of sugar. Between that and the coffee, I'd be buzzing.

A pile of message slips waited in my in box. There must have been more calls after I left, and/or this morning. I looked through them, sorted all the reporters into a pile for later, and worked my way through the rest, returning calls. By the time I finished, my teacup was empty and my stomach was rumbling.

Oh, yes. Food.

Returning to my suite, I opened the door cautiously, looking for the kitten. A thumping of tiny feet began in the bedroom and Minuit came galloping toward me. I closed the door and picked her up, nuzzled her and was rewarded with a big purr, then put her down.

Breakfast. I turned on the toaster oven and got out some frozen scones. Fruit? There was one tired orange in the fridge. I cut it into slices while the scones baked, and made myself a pot of Keemun. While I waited, I made a virtuous grocery-shopping list, including lettuce and three kinds of fruit. Maybe I'd make a fruit salad and nosh off it for a couple of days.

The smell of the scones made my stomach growl even more. They were Julio's scones, the tearoom's standard cream scones with currants. It had been a long time since I'd had time to actually make scones myself. Months ago I had asked Julio to add a dozen scones for me to his weekly total, and I dutifully reported them as inventory removed for personal use on the tearoom's sales tax returns.

I supposed I should add the Sachertortes this month. Leftovers were fair game after business hours, but those had not been leftovers.

I put the scones, orange, and my tea on a tray to take out to the sitting area in the hall. As I started for the door Minuit trotted along with me.

That would not do. I put the tray down, caught the kitten, and took her across to the playpen. She gave one disappointed mew, then settled into her towel bed, apparently worn out by her explorations in the suite. Triumphant, I fetched the tea tray and took it to the sofa by the front window.

The day was sunny. The snow had already melted, I saw as I paused to look down at the front yard. A light breeze stirred the branches of the trees. A young woman I didn't recognize came in the front gate, carrying a plastic-wrapped bouquet. She headed for the tree.

I'd have to check on those candles again, but later. Food first.

Keemun and oranges go beautifully together. I savored them slowly, knowing I might not get a lunch break. This would do, since Kris and I were dining out tonight.

"Morning, ma'am," said a masculine voice behind me.

I turned, but the speaker had not been addressing me. I caught a glimpse of a sheepskin coat at the doorway to the offices: Zeke Walters. Drat.

Kris said something I couldn't make out.

"Well, I just wondered if you remembered anything more about Saturday night," Zeke said.

I'd better intervene. I stood and walked over to the detective, even as Kris answered him rather sharply.

"As I told you, I was home by seven-thirty and didn't go out again. I didn't talk to anyone on the phone. I didn't text anyone."

"Yes, well," Zeke drawled. "Mind telling me where you got that necklace?"

"Good morning, Detective," I said brightly.

He turned to me. I gave his cowboy hat an arched eyebrow, and he hastily removed it.

"Morning, ma'am," he said, looking rather like a ranch hand as he held the hat in front of him with both hands.

Kris came toward us, looking pissed as hell. "The necklace was a gift. And by the way, I'm not stupid," she said. "If I wanted to kill someone and get away with it, I wouldn't do it on Ellen's lawn!"

There was a moment's silence.

"Quite right," I said, turning to Zeke. "Tony mentioned you wanted to talk to me. Is that why you're here?"

"Uh—"

"This is a very busy week for us, but I have a few minutes now. Would you like some tea?"

"S-sure," he said.

I had knocked him off balance a little. Good.

I poured him a cup of Lapsang souchong and led him to the sitting area by the window, gesturing to a chair and setting his tea in front of it. He put his hat on a side table, took off his coat and draped it over the back of the chair, and sat, looking uncomfortable. He picked up the cup, sipped, and coughed slightly.

"I hope you're making progress on your investigation," I said, sipping my Keemun.

Zeke set his cup and saucer down carefully. "We've talked to everyone who was at that Halloween party," he said.

Again, I thought.

"Most of 'em have alibis, but not all. What we don't have is any solid evidence of a motive. Other than, you know, the cuts," he added, glancing toward Kris's office. "I wondered if you might have thought of something we didn't."

He was paying me a high compliment, asking that. He was no fool, though, and those lazy eyes were more watchful than they appeared.

The cuts. I swallowed, not liking what I felt obligated to suggest.

"Have you talked to Cherie Legrand?" I asked in a quiet voice, hoping Kris wouldn't overhear.

"We did. She was at an AA meeting Saturday night. Dozens of confirmations."

"Ah." I sipped my tea, relieved. Cherie had enough troubles. "Well, I can't think of anything else that's likely to help you, I'm afraid. I will say that I'm surprised at how many people are leaving flowers by the tree. I was under the impression that Margo didn't have that many friends."

"I guess people saw you on TV last night," Zeke said with a

sidelong glance at me. "Sometimes folks like to join in on something like that even if they didn't know the person."

I nodded, thinking back to the interview and the flowers and candles. "Have you talked to the people she knew in high school? I heard she was a cheerleader."

Zeke's brows rose, and he took out his phone. "Where'd you hear that?"

"A couple of people who were here leaving flowers mentioned it."

"Wouldn't have thought of her as a cheerleader," Zeke said.

"Neither would I."

Zeke punched his phone and quietly dictated: "Check Foss's high school friends. She was a cheerleader." He put the phone away and said, "All right, thanks. Don't suppose you have any thoughts about that knife with the wiggly blade?"

"The only thought I had about it was that someone might be trying to frame Kris," I said quietly. "She *isn't* stupid, Detective. She wouldn't leave such a damning mark, if she had done this. I am convinced that she's innocent."

He gazed at me, blinked once, and nodded. "Thanks, ma'am."

"You're welcome," I said as we both stood. Zeke shrugged into his coat and picked up his hat.

"And thanks for the...." He waved the hat at his teacup. I smiled, then followed him to the stairs, watching him descend. When he was gone, I went into Kris's office.

"Thanks," she said, looking up at me. "Sorry I lost my temper."

"Entirely understandable, but do be careful, Kris."

She nodded. "I hate this," she muttered under her breath.

"We'll talk this evening."

I returned to my belated breakfast, finished it while thinking about the detective's visit and all the things I had to do that day, then cleaned up the dishes, pouring out Zeke's Lapsang souchong.

That had been a little petty of me. I could have at least offered him some milk to soften it. I was annoyed at him for pestering Kris, though.

Check messages, check kitten, go downstairs. It was ten-thirty, and the gift shop was now open. I found Nat there, cheerfully packaging macarons for an early shopper.

"Thanks for coming in," I said when the customer had left.

"Oh, I'm happy to help," Nat said.

"It's going to be a nutty week."

She smiled.

"You looked great on TV, dear," Nat said.

"Thanks. That reminds me, I'd better go check to make sure those candles are safe."

She nodded. "I'll hold the fort."

I went out the front door and around the south side to the tree.

"Oh my God!"

There were *dozens* more bouquets and at least twenty candles surrounding the tree. Ay yi yi! The flowers lay everywhere, haphazardly surrounding the tree, piled up against the trunk and scattered among the candles. A cold wind made me wish for my coat, but I hadn't wanted to go upstairs.

Who was leaving all this? I wondered as I moved teetery candles to better locations and gathered stray bouquets into the pile. This would be a big mess when the flowers started fading. I'd have to keep on top of it. I didn't have the heart to just throw them all away.

As I was finishing the tidying, Mick came walking up from behind the tearoom, his long blond hair streaming out behind him. "Hi, Ellen! Wow, you could open a flower store!"

"Morning," I said, moving a lone candle nearer to a bunch of others that were on a flat spot.

"Want me to help keep it organized?"

"Would you? That would be wonderful. I'm concerned about the fire hazard."

He smiled, which made him look even more like Dee. "Sure. I'll check it when I come in and when I leave, and on my breaks."

"Bless you."

"You looked good on the news," he added as we walked back toward the kitchen together.

"Oh, thanks."

"They came and talked to me about the hanging."

"I'm sorry."

"Nah, not a problem. Sorry for you, having to deal with it."

I spent a lot of that day saying thank you to customers who had seen me on the news. My refuge was my office upstairs, something of a reversal from usual. Normally I'd go downstairs to escape the messages and business tasks, but now I needed breaks from the customers, many of whom were curious about the murder. I turned aside questions about Margo as graciously as I could, often falling back on saying that I mustn't discuss it because of the ongoing investigation. By five-thirty I was thinking wistfully about the wine I intended to order with dinner. I collected the receipts from the gift shop and took them up to Kris's office, leaving Nat to handle the shoppers for the last half hour.

"Here you are," I said, depositing the bank bag on Kris's desk.

"Thanks," she said.

"Shall I drive us to dinner?"

"That would be great. I'll do the deposit and we can drop it at the bank."

"Okay."

I went to my desk and worked through the latest messages, then shut down the samovar and rinsed out the teapot. Minuit was getting restless so I took a kitten break in my suite, letting her run free and giving her an early supper while I tidied my hair and makeup for dinner. I was ready at five minutes to six.

Looking out the window down at the tree, I saw the multitude of candles flickering in the twilight breeze. A couple had blown out. Should I relight them?

No, I didn't feel obligated to do that. They were enough of a hazard as it was—if some went out, so much the better. Mick had done a good job keeping the memorial under control—there were more flowers and candles than there had been in the morning, but they were not a mess.

Gathering my purse and a scarf, I crossed to the office side and collected my coat from the coat rack in the hall, leaving Minuit sleeping off her supper in the suite. Kris shut down her computer and joined me, bank bag in hand.

"Did we get a lot more cancellations?" I asked.

"A few more, but we got a *bunch* of new reservations. We're back up to solid this week, and solid most of next week, too."

"Wow! Thanks for managing all that."

"It's my pleasure, believe me. Was it your idea to give the interview? I didn't see it, but I heard about it all day."

"Gina and I agreed it would be a good move. She recorded it, if you want to watch it."

"Maybe later."

I put on my coat. "Shall we? I'm starving."

"Me, too."

I looked in on the kitchen as we headed out. Mick was alone, and smiled as he removed his earbuds.

"Thank you for keeping the flowers and candles under control," I told him.

He grinned. "No problem. People are leaving little notes, too. I'm weighing them down with the candles."

"Okay, thanks."

Notes? Ai. Zeke would probably want to look at them.

That reminded me of something I'd wanted to ask Kris. I turned to her once we were in my car.

"Kris, who was it who gave you that necklace?"

She sighed. "Cherie. She has one just like it."

"The police might have told you—"

"That the same kind of beads were used to hang Margo? Yeah, I know. The killer probably got them at Krampus. They sell a lot of jet jewelry. That's where I got the urn."

"Urn?"

Kris lifted the pendant on her necklace. "It's got some of Gabriel's ashes in it."

Now that I looked closer, I saw that it had a tiny screw-top. And yes, it was urn-shaped, although flat rather than round.

"Oh, Kris. I'm so sorry. This must have brought up a lot of painful feelings."

She smiled slightly. "I can cope."

"Let's go get some wine."

I drove us to the Inn at Loretto, home of Luminaria and one of the nicer lobby bars in town, if you could get a comfortable chair. Not all of them were comfortable.

We walked past the bar and down the long hall to the restaurant. No outside seating this time of year, but we were given a cozy booth with a view of the large corner fireplace. I looked at the wine list, chose a bottle of Cabernet, and ordered some guacamole and *chile con queso* to go with it. I was grateful that the wine arrived quickly.

"Mm," Kris said after her first sip. "Nice. Thank you."

"My pleasure. It feels like it's been a week, and it's only Tuesday."

"It'll go fast."

"Here's to Valentine's," I said, lifting my glass.

Kris grimaced.

"Sorry," I said. "I was thinking of the tearoom, not the holiday."

"It's not Gabriel, if that's what you're thinking," Kris said. "I'm just not crazy about Valentine's Day."

"Oh. Any particular reason?"

She took a larger sip of wine. "The fourteenth is my birthday. It always got preempted by Valentine's. I got to where I hated heart-shaped cakes."

Now that she mentioned it, I remembered taking note that her birthday coincided with a holiday when I hired her. "Oh, I'm sorry, Kris. That's a drag."

"It sucks. I feel sorry for people born in December. They've got it even worse."

"Christmas birthdays? Yeah."

"It's not fair to get one present when other people get two."

"Very true."

Kris glanced up at me. "Sorry. It's one of my rants."

"Totally fine. I do understand."

Our appetizer arrived, and we both dug in, suspending conversation in favor of calories. When the edge was off my hunger, I took a mouthful of wine and rolled it around on my tongue, appreciating the interaction of its flavors with the chile in the *con queso*. Watching Kris in that quiet moment, I saw that she looked tired and a little stressed. The frown line between her brows was in danger of becoming permanent.

"I hope Detective Walters stops bothering you," I said.

She rolled her eyes. "He texts me three or four times a day. Latest one was about the beads."

"Tell you what. Don't answer it. Let me tell him about—was it Krampus?"

"Yeah. On Galisteo."

"I'll mention it to him. Feel free to send any other inquiries from him my way."

"He's doing it to intimidate me."

"Probably."

She gave a huff of bitter laughter. "I'm not very intimidate-able."

"Good."

"He's hung up on the kris, though. The knife."

I scooped up some guacamole on a blue corn tortilla chip. "Oh?"

"You saw—you saw Margo, right?"

"Yes. Did Walters give you details?"

"About the kris cut into her chest? Yeah. He was trying to shock me. Dropped it like a bombshell. Bastard."

"It didn't work, I hope."

"No. But he insisted on taking my letter opener to test it, even though it's as dull as a butter knife."

We both drank more wine. I topped up our glasses.

"What I can't figure out," Kris said, running a fingertip around the rim of her glass, "is who hates me enough to frame me. And also hated Margo enough to kill her."

I'd been wondering the same thing, of course. If Kris, who knew the local Goths far better than I did, had no idea, it appeared hope-less.

I sighed. "I seem to have underestimated how many Goths there are in Santa Fe."

She glanced up at me. "You mean the flowers? They're coming from Albuquerque, too. And I know some have come down from Taos."

"People you know?"

She shrugged. "Some of them. Word's gone out through the community. People are coming from all over the state."

"Just to leave flowers for Margo?"

"Yeah. It's a sign of solidarity." She sipped her wine. "There are a couple of conspiracy theories floating around. Some people think it was an anti-Goth outsider, just trying to disrupt us. So they've kind of come together. I've been getting flowers, too, at home."

I regarded her thoughtfully. "That's a good deal more tenderness than I expected from the Goths."

"There are a lot of good people in the community. Think of Gwyneth. She externalizes it, but lots of people share her feelings even though they dress dark."

"Forgive me. I'm pretty naïve about Goth culture."

"Well, there are a lot of different kinds of Goth culture. The most common misunderstanding is when people assume we're a violent group. We're not. It's more like we're wearing our sorrow for humanity on our sleeves, if that makes any sense."

In that moment, my heart went out to Kris. To think that her entire lifestyle was devoted to such a sentiment changed my perception of her manner—which could be terse and sometimes cynical.

"I think I'm guilty of that mistake," I said slowly. "Maybe I'm confusing Goth with BDSM."

"Forgivable. There's a certain amount of crossover."

"Was Gabriel…?"

"No!" she said, almost a snarl.

"Sorry!"

"I would *never* go with a sadist."

Clearly I had struck a nerve. "I'm sorry, Kris. Gabriel was—there was something about him that made me wonder, that's all."

"He was autocratic and full of himself. But he was never cruel." She took a deep swallow of wine.

Our dinners arrived. The waiter divided the remainder of the wine between our glasses, then silently withdrew with the empty bottle. I let the conversation drop and addressed my shrimp and pasta, glancing at Kris now and then. Gradually her frown softened as she ate.

"Sorry," she said after a few minutes. "Didn't mean to snap at you.”

“It’s okay. I know I can’t understand everything you’re feeling, but I do care.”

“Thanks,” she said, and sighed. Her gaze was distant, as if at memory. I had a feeling it went back farther than Gabriel. There was a note of pain there, of emotional hurt, that had nothing to do with grieving for a lost love. It was more like grieving for a wound to the soul. Wherever her thoughts had gone, I couldn’t follow her.

Finally she straightened, coming out of her reverie, and reached for her wine. “How’s the wedding stuff going?” she asked after taking a sip.

“Oh. Well, we found dresses. I actually found one I really like, which surprised me. I thought I’d have to resort to hiring a dress-maker to avoid looking like a fairy-tale princess.”

Kris smirked. “Most brides *want* to look like a fairy-tale princess.”

“Not me. I want a dress I can wear to the opera. I’ll have to remove the demi-train, but that’s not a problem.”

“I know a good seamstress if you need one.”

“Thanks.” I smiled. “Hems are hard to do by yourself.”

She nodded. “I don’t sew, but I’ve heard Gwyneth complain about that kind of thing.”

“Does she sew?”

“Yeah. She makes a lot of her own outfits.”

“Wow! She must be good, then. She always looks...great.” Belatedly, I remembered that Gwyneth had also been Gabriel’s lover. Maybe it wasn’t necessary to tiptoe around that, but I wasn’t sure.

Kris was watching me with a bemused expression. “I’m not jealous of Gwyneth. We’ve known each other a lot longer than we knew Gabriel. He only moved to New Mexico a couple of years ago.”

“You’ve been here longer?” I knew she had come from the Midwest, originally.

"I got here in 2004."

"Wow. You must have been…young."

"Fifteen."

"So your family moved here?"

"No. I ran away from home."

Whoops. Too nosy, Ellen.

"I'm sorry. I didn't know."

She shrugged. "I didn't tell you."

"That must have taken great courage," I said after a moment. "To leave home, and come so far away."

"I don't know about courage. I did it because I had to. I did it for survival." She finished her wine in one long pull, then looked at me. "My stepfather abused me, starting when I was nine. It was getting worse, and I knew he'd eventually kill me."

My heart sank. "God!"

"It was the Goth community that saved me," she said, fingering her beads. "They helped me plan, helped me run. Gave me shelter here, and helped me change my name when I was finally old enough."

"I'm so sorry, Kris. What a nightmare!"

"Yeah. It was. But I was lucky. I broke out. Couldn't have done it without help." She picked up her empty wine glass, then set it down again.

"Another bottle?" I offered.

"Might be too much."

"There's corkage. We can take the leftovers home. And I'll drop you at your place if you're not good to drive."

She gazed at the table, suddenly looking vulnerable, then met my gaze. "Yeah, if you don't mind."

I looked for our waiter and spotted him standing near the bar. I didn't even have to raise my hand—when he saw me look at him, he started over.

"We'd like another bottle of the Cabernet," I said, smiling slightly.

"I'll bring it right out."

There was a little wine left in my glass. I pushed it toward Kris, but she shook her head, so I finished it myself.

Her story made me even more determined to protect her from Detective Walters. He'd have to get through me to bother her again. With all that she'd been through, the last thing Kris needed was to be harassed by the police.

Strangely, knowing her background made me feel less concerned about the possibility of her committing suicide. She'd survived so much, it would be uncharacteristic of her to give up now.

The waiter returned with the wine, which he had already opened, and silently filled our glasses, then left without a word. He had picked up on our mood, apparently. He was definitely getting a nice tip.

I raised my glass. "To survival," I said.

Kris nodded and drank deeply. I picked up my fork and took a bite of my neglected pasta. I had offered Kris what sympathy I thought she'd accept; to continue in the same vein would probably just annoy her. Instead, I held space for her, wishing her well, silently giving her what comfort I could by my presence.

After a minute, she ate a few more bites of her own dinner. Relieved, I sipped my wine. This would be my last glass—I had to drive back to the tearoom, and I didn't want to drive drunk. Kris could drink as much as she liked.

In fact, I should probably not finish this glass. I couldn't resist sipping it, but I slowed down while I ate my pasta. When my plate was empty, I folded my hands in my lap to keep them away from the wine glass. Our attentive waiter came over a moment later and removed my plate.

"You can take mine, too," Kris said, pushing her plate away.

The waiter nodded and cleared her place. Kris picked up her wine and drank.

"Thanks, Ellen. I don't usually drink this much, but...."

"No problem. I asked you nosy questions. I apologize."

"Not necessary. It's good that you know. With all the stuff about Margo, you probably wondered."

"I was a little concerned about you, yes."

"See, I always get cranky this time of year. It's just the whole Valentine's thing. Don't worry, I'll get over it."

"How do you like to celebrate your birthday?" I asked. "Do you have anything special you like to do?"

"Stay the hell away from restaurants," she said. "They're full-on Valentine's this time of year. And flowers are super expensive, so I don't buy myself any until March." She drank more wine. "Sometimes I'll book a day at a spa and just chill. But not this year. Figured you might need me to work."

"Oh, Kris! We can manage without you," I said. "You don't want to be at the tearoom. It's as bad as all the restaurants."

She chuckled. "I don't mind when it's not aimed at me. And right now it's better for me to keep busy. And be with other people, in case...."

"In case the killer strikes again."

She nodded. It hadn't occurred to me, but that was a possibility. Who would be next, in that case? Who was a threat to the killer?

Maybe Kris, if she was exonerated. But right now, with the police still focused on her, she was more useful alive.

I shook my head. No use puzzling at that. I didn't have enough information for more than vague speculation. I looked at Kris, who was back to gazing at the table.

The waiter approached, holding two half-sheets of paper. Dessert menus. I nodded, and he set them before us and left.

"Would you like some dessert?" I said. "We could share one. Or just have coffee."

Kris looked at the menu and smirked. "Death by chocolate."

"That caught my eye, too. Want your own?"

"No, let's share. I would like some coffee, though."

"You've got it."

The waiter responded to my glance and took our order. Kris still had wine in her glass, as did I. She was slowing down on it, though. She took a sip, then set the glass down.

"Thanks for this, Ellen. I guess I needed to talk it out some."

"You are absolutely welcome any time. Please consider me a sounding board if you ever need to vent."

She smiled. "Thanks. You know, I don't think I've thanked you for hiring me. I mean, for taking a chance on a Goth."

"Well, you don't need to thank me, but you're welcome. I totally understand non-traditional lifestyle choices. I've made some myself."

"Yeah, but you're non-traditional by being uber-traditional. Good trick."

I laughed. "I'm less Victorian than I appear."

"You're more Goth than you know." She grinned, which I was glad to see, though I wasn't sure I understood the comment.

One more sip of wine. I savored it, then looked at Kris. She still seemed tired, but her face was not as tense.

"Kris, would you be willing to be my bridesmaid?"

9

KRIS LOOKED ASTONISHED. I'd surprised myself, too, by ask-ing, but I truly wanted her to stand with me at the wedding.

"What color are the dresses?" she asked warily.

"Turquoise. Or you could go teal, it's darker." I got out my phone and showed her a picture I'd taken of Gina and Angela wearing their dresses in the shop where we'd found them. "It doesn't have to be the same dress," I added. "Just something that doesn't clash."

She gazed at the photo a long time, then looked at me.

"Would you mind purple?" she asked softly. "I have a dress that would go."

"Purple's fine."

I hadn't ordered any decorations in the theme colors yet—I could adjust. I'd avoided purple because I didn't want the wedding to be associated with the tearoom, but for Kris I'd be willing to go with it.

Kris smiled. "Thanks, Ellen. I've never been a bridesmaid."

I wanted to hug her, but our coffee was arriving. I settled for squeezing her hand as she gave back my phone.

"Thank *you*," I said. "Gina's been bugging me to have more attendants. She'd like it to be a parade, I think."

Kris actually laughed at that. I laughed too.

"I could get you a new dress, if you like. I bought Angela's."

"No, let me show you the purple. If you don't like it I can find something else."

I added a dollop of cream to my coffee. "We're having tea tomorrow afternoon to talk about the wedding. Will you join us?"

She smirked. "If my boss will let me."

"I think that can be arranged."

Our dessert arrived: a slice of flourless chocolate cake topped with ganache, on a plate swiped with crème fraîche and adorned with fresh raspberries. Quite a lot of berries, actually. I wondered if the waiter had given us extra.

We ate the chocolate and berries (fabulous), drank the coffee, and avoided talking about Margo or Valentine's Day. I asked Kris if we could afford to hire musicians for St. Patrick's Day. I didn't expect it to be anywhere near as busy as Valentine's, but we'd had a couple of inquiries about whether there would be a special event.

"Why don't you ask Owen?" Kris said. "He'd do it for trade, I bet."

Remembering the evening when Owen had played the harp for me and Tony by firelight in his home, I caught my breath. "He'd be perfect! Kris, you're brilliant!"

"He's plays with some other folk musicians, too, sometimes. Ask him about it."

"I will."

It was getting late, and the chocolate was gone. The waiter brought our check and packaged the leftover wine for us. I added a fat tip and paid the bill, then drove Kris to her place, a small, older duplex on a quiet street on the east side of town. The porch light revealed a couple of plastic-wrapped bouquets by the door.

"Want me to walk you in?" I asked.

"Nah, I'm fine. Thanks."

"Take this." I handed her the leftover wine.

She looked at me. "Thanks, Ellen. This was great. I'm really glad we talked."

"Me too."

"And dinner was fab. Next time it's my treat."

"Okay."

She smiled, then got out and walked up to her door. I waited until she was inside and had turned on a light, then drove back to the tearoom.

Kris's car stood alone in the parking lot by the back door. I pulled in beside it, debating whether to text and offer her a ride in the morning, but decided to let her sort that out for herself.

Before going in, I stepped around the back of the kitchen to make sure the tree hadn't burned down. It hadn't, but the glow from the candles was bright enough to read by. I hoped it wouldn't keep me awake.

As I wearily climbed the stairs to my suite, I realized I hadn't been in touch with Tony all day. I pulled out my phone, looking for a text or a message, but there was none. Well, he'd known I was busy. And while a soak in the hot tub would be nice, it was really too late to go over to the townhome. Tony might be in bed already.

Minuit was asleep, but roused when I came in. I fed her and then got ready for bed, thinking over my conversation with Kris. Despite the coffee and chocolate, I yawned my way through washing off my makeup and brushing my teeth. When my head hit the pillow, I knew no more.

I had weird wine and coffee dreams, something to do with putting together a band for the tearoom, but it involved running all over

Santa Fe on foot, and I kept having to change shoes, because they either hurt my feet or didn't go with my dress. When the smell of baking roused me, I gratefully abandoned that scenario and rolled out of bed.

Feed cat, get dressed, put cat in playpen, make tea. My fridge was barren of edibles. I popped two frozen scones in the toaster oven and hoped I'd find time to run to the store that day. Might be difficult, since I was already taking time off to have tea with my bridesmaids.

Better tell Gina about Kris joining the party. I sent her a text while waiting for my scones.

What else? Candle patrol: I glanced out my window. There was now a ring of candles all the way around the tree, and heaps of bouquets piled against the trunk. It was getting untidy again; I'd better check it. Mick didn't come in until eleven.

I ate my scones at my desk, going through the voicemails from overnight. Kris had not yet arrived. I hoped she was sleeping in. When I'd cleared all the messages I went downstairs to deal with the candles. Two more had tipped over, one spilling red wax onto the grass. Ugh. Have to clean that up later. I picked up the offending votive glass, and several others that had gone out, and carried them to the trash bin.

Dale was arriving as I went back inside, looking grand in a brocade vest in shades of peach and gold, with a peach-colored bow tie to match.

"Good morning," I said. "Nice outfit."

"Thanks." He managed a smile, though he looked rather sad, still.

"Would you do me a favor, Dale? If Detective Walters comes in, please tell him that neither Kris nor I are available today, and ask him to call me tomorrow."

"Sure," Dale said, looking slightly surprised.

"If he tries to come upstairs, fend him off, would you?"

Dale's eyes narrowed and he drew himself up a bit. "With pleasure."

"Thank you. Oh, and are you serving in Violet and Dahlia today?"

"Yes."

"I'm adding one to my 1:30 party, so we'll be four. I'll tell Julio."

I went to the kitchen to do that, and found Julio on the phone. Hanh and Ramon were assembling tea sandwiches, and I could smell quiches in the oven. I drifted over toward the break table.

"What you need, boss?" Hanh asked, looking up at me.

"I just wanted to let you know I've increased my party by one."

Hanh stepped away from the work table to the bulletin board, where the day's totals were posted, and picked up a pencil. "For one-thirty?"

"Yes."

She made a mark on the sheet. "Okay."

"Thanks, Hanh."

Next: check on the gift shop. Nat had left it in good order the previous evening. Nothing needed restocking except for the pastry case, which would be filled closer to opening. Heading for the stairs, I met Iz coming in, taking off her coat and revealing her pretty lavender server's dress beneath.

"Good morning, Iz."

"Morning."

She smiled, then went into the pantry. I continued upstairs to my office, where Minuit was rattling her ring toy. My phone showed a text from Tony, asking me to call. First I fetched myself a cup of tea and made myself comfortable on the chaise longue. Deep breath, then I pressed "call,"

"Babe. Missed you last night."

"Oh, me too," I said, "but I got in late."

"Good dinner?"

"Yes."

A pause. I drank some tea.

"Did you give Zeke Lapsang souchong?" Tony asked.

I swallowed a laugh. "Yes. He was pestering Kris."

"Be careful, babe."

"You tell Zeke to be careful, or I'll file a complaint for harassment! He's texting Kris multiple times a day."

"Whoa, hey, calm down!"

"I will *not* let him bully my staff."

"He's just doing his job."

"It's not his job to hassle Kris!"

"Well, it kind of is," Tony said.

"Then he'd better do it elsewhere than at the tearoom," I said, exasperated. "He's interfering with her work."

"Um, okay, I'll ask him to back it down."

"And he's not welcome here until he returns her letter opener. You can tell him that, too."

"Letter opener?"

"From her desk. It's shaped like a kris. He claimed he needed to test it, but it was here in the office all along, and it's dull as dry toast. It was *not* used during the murder. He just took it to annoy her."

I heard Tony sigh. "Okay, I'll ask him to return it."

"Thank you," I said primly.

"Don't be mad at me, babe."

"I'm not mad at you."

Silence.

"Right," Tony said. "I'll call you later."

"Tony—"

Too late. He'd hung up.

I supposed I could have handled that better, I thought as I put down the phone. My annoyance had been growing overnight, and the stress of the week was making me touchy, but I hadn't meant to take it out on Tony. I had intended to ask him if he still planned to come over for pizza that evening. Maybe he'd changed his mind.

Well, I could always take a bubble bath. With wine.

I finished my tea and went back to my desk. It was almost ten by the time Kris arrived. When I heard her coming up the stairs, I stood and carried my teacup to the samovar.

"Good morning," I said as she reached the hall and took off her coat.

She was looking better: her black dress had long lace sleeves, quite pretty, and she had her hair up in a French twist. A choker of black lace with a purple ribbon threaded through it completed the ensemble. She seemed calmer, too. She had brought a black shopping bag, which she carried into her office.

"Morning," she said, going in to her desk. "Sorry I'm late."

"It's okay. I pulled the messages from overnight. Want tea?"

"Please."

I poured for us both, and sat in her guest chair. "How did you sleep?"

"Like a dead thing. You?"

"I had weird dreams."

"Weird dreams are fine, as long as they're not nightmares."

"Amen."

We chatted a little about the day ahead, then I went downstairs to the gift shop, where Nat was loading the pastry case. I greeted her with a hug and resisted snagging a macaron. I'd have plenty of sugar at tea.

"I see Mrs. Olavssen is coming in today," Nat said.

"Is she? I thought she had a reservation for Saturday."

"She does, for a big group. Today it's just her and a guest."

I looked at the reservations list, which confirmed what Nat had said but told me little more. The Bird Woman was coming for the

1:30 seating, same time as my tea, and was scheduled to be in the Jonquil alcove. I was silently grateful she would not be in Dahlia, next to my party in Violet. She was a dear, but highly distracting. And she eavesdropped.

For the next couple of hours I was up and down the stairs a lot. A steady stream of shoppers was making big inroads on the Valentine's Day cards, and I had to go up twice for more, plus more of the dreaded black heart mugs. Kris made no comment as she watched me come and go from the storage room behind her desk.

"Last box of these," I said, hefting a case of the black mugs, "except for the ones for Mrs. Olavssen."

"She's picking those up today. She called to increase her order. We have three more cases arriving tomorrow."

"Good."

I took the mugs down to the gift shop, restocked the display, and found room for the extras in the cupboards beneath. I noticed Nat had made a little heart-shaped sign and taped it to one of the mugs, showing the price. They were selling so fast we didn't have time to tag them.

On my next trip upstairs, I met Kris on the landing carrying her shopping bag. "It's one twenty-five," she said.

"Oh! Thanks. I'll be right down."

I darted up and got my phone, glancing at it in case Tony had called. He hadn't.

Kris had waited for me on the landing. Uncharacteristically shy of her, but maybe she felt a little awkward about the bridesmaid thing. We went down together, arriving at the gift shop as Gina came in the front door wearing a white dress with hot pink poppies all over and a matching pink fascinator with a little net veil and white feathers. The first thing she did was gather Kris into a hug.

"I'm so glad you're going to be in the party," she said, smiling.

"Thanks," Kris said.

I gestured toward the alcoves. "Let's go in."

Violet was usually set up for two, but could accommodate four (or five in a pinch) with a bit of furniture rearranging. Dale had taken care of this earlier: the two armchairs had been turned to face the center of the room, the table moved to stand between the chairs and the love seat upholstered in deep purple crushed velvet that normally hid in the shadows against the back wall. A standing lamp of violet brocade with amethyst bead fringe had been turned on, illuminating the love seat and bringing it into the grouping. I moved to sit there, and invited Kris to join me. As we sat, I glanced up at Vi's portrait over the fireplace. She seemed to be smiling down at us.

Outside the window, the Margo memorial was a mass of bouquets ringed by a wall of candles three or four deep. Bless Mick for keeping it in order. I turned my back to it and set about pouring tea from the pot that waited beneath a cozy on the table.

"Ellen, have you found a venue for the wedding?" Gina asked, adding two lumps of sugar to her cup.

"Not yet. This week's too busy," I said.

"You want me to make you a short list?"

"No, no. You're doing plenty, and I'm going to be pretty picky about the location. Let me do the footwork."

"All right."

Dale came in, escorting Angela, who looked charming and sweet in pale pink. "Here you are," he said. "I'll bring your tray right in, ladies."

"Am I late?" Angela asked, stepping to the armchair at Kris's right.

"No, we were early," I told her as Kris held her cup for me to fill.

Angela paused, gazing wide-eyed out the window at the memorial, then sat. Kris handed her the filled teacup.

"You've met Kris Overland, haven't you, Angela?" I said. "She's the office manager here at the tearoom."

Angela smiled shyly. "Hello. I know I've seen you, but I don't think we've ever talked."

"Kris is going to be a bridesmaid," I added.

"Oh, how nice! Too bad you didn't get to go with us to Vanessie."

"We'll just have to go again," Gina said.

Dale came in, but instead of our food he carried a tray with four flutes and a bottle of champagne. He set this on the table and proceeded to pour.

"What's this?" I asked.

"Compliments of Mrs. Olavssen," he said. "She arrived just after you did. She sends you her congratulations."

Again.

"Well, please give her my thanks, and box up a half-dozen macarons for her, will you?"

"Gladly," Dale said, and whisked away with the empty tray.

"Cheers!" Gina said, picking up her flute. "Here's to the best wedding Santa Fe has ever seen."

I smiled wistfully, thinking of the wedding Santa Fe had never seen: Captain Dusenberry's. Why that had popped into my head I didn't know. Maybe it was because Phillips was coming that evening with the metal detector. Shaking it off, I drank the toast while Gina launched into planning mode.

"Kris, did Ellen show you our dresses?"

"Yes," Kris said. "I have one that may go with them. I brought it to show you."

She set down her glass and reached into her shopping bag, producing a double handful of silk that was such a dark purple it almost looked black. She stood, letting it fall as she held it by two narrow straps. The fabric had a subtle sheen to it—like shot, gleaming a brighter violet on the outside of the folds—and it looked familiar. The bodice had a sweetheart neckline and was formed by a criss-cross of fabric very similar to Gina's and Angela's dresses.

"Ooh!" Angela said. "That's beautiful!"

"The only thing is, my tattoo will show since it's sleeveless," Kris said, holding out her forearm. I could just see the kris on it through her lace sleeve.

"I have no problem with your tattoo," I said. We hadn't talked about it, but in light of last night's conversation, I was pretty sure she'd gotten the tattoo to commemorate her escape from her family.

"Want me to try it on?" she offered.

"That's not—"

"Yes!" Gina said. "Show us!"

"I'd love to see it," Angela agreed.

I yielded. Kris ran upstairs to change. Dale came in with the tea tray, and we busied ourselves with the savories while waiting for Kris to return. I went straight for my bastilla, since it was best warm, followed by the mini quiche. This was only the second time I'd had the February menu, other than random leftovers. It might just be the best menu Julio had created so far. I'd have to have it again to make sure.

Kris returned wearing the purple dress.

"Wow!" we all said in chorus.

Her tattoo was indeed rather striking on her bare forearm, but far more noticeable was the black lace and purple ribbon choker, which looked stunning above the sweetheart neckline of the dress. Kris's upswept hair completed the look: the ensemble was incredibly classy. Maybe I could talk her into some simple shoes instead of the black knee-high boots.

"Kris, that's fabulous!" I said. "I love it!"

She smiled gratefully. "It's okay, then?"

"More than okay!" Gina said. "Damn, maybe we should all go purple!"

"Oh, but I love my turquoise dress," Angela said.

"Let's not mess with perfection," I agreed. "The turquoise dresses are great. We can have both colors in the bouquets."

"May I take your picture, Kris?" Angela said, getting out her phone.

"Sure," Kris said. She stepped to one side, away from the chair. The curtain that separated Violet from Dahlia was behind her, and Vi's portrait was over her shoulder. Angela snapped two pictures, then thanked Kris and put away her phone.

"Text me a copy of that," Gina said, and Angela nodded.

Kris took her seat and helped herself to savories. I filled her teacup, and we chatted about how to incorporate the purple and turquoise into the décor and other wedding details. I listened, mostly. Gina could run wild with ideas all she wanted. I would make note of any that I liked, and follow up on them later. There was time.

I did, however, have to decide on a venue pretty soon. Maybe I should let Gina give me a short list after all. Nothing I'd looked at so far had filled me with joy.

"Kris, have I seen that dress before?" I asked in a quiet moment. "The fabric looks familiar."

"You've seen the fabric, not the dress. In *Ophelia*."

I caught my breath. "Gabriel's painting."

Kris nodded. "He bought a whole bolt of the fabric. Gwyneth made me the dress from it."

"Ah. Well, she did a fantastic job."

"Thanks. I haven't worn it yet. To a party, I mean."

"Well, you have now," Gina said, picking up her champagne flute. "May it be the first of many!"

We all drank to that sentiment. Moments later Dale came in and filled our glasses with the remainder of the champagne. Gina made him take our picture with her phone. He then put the sweets plate on the table and took away the three-tiered tray and the empty bottle.

Gina took her notebook out and referred to it. "You've got Julio catering," she said. "And doing the cake?"

"Ah—I still need to talk to him about that," I said, taking an elderflower macaron from the plate.

"Photographer?"

"Owen Hughes has agreed to do it."

Gina looked up at me. "It'll be outside, right? Does he have a drone?"

I blinked. "A drone?"

"For aerial shots," Gina said. "It makes great video."

"I'm not sure we need a video..."

"Oh, but you'll love watching it down the years!"

Ay, yi, yi. I reached for the teapot. "I'll think about it."

"Okay. How about the music?"

I blinked. "Haven't started on that," I said.

"Talk with Tony. Oh, and ask him what flavor he wants for the groom's cake."

"I'm not sure we'll need that much cake," I said.

"It doesn't have to be big," Gina said, "but get him a groom's cake. He'll love it, trust me. And it's an easy way to have more than one flavor."

"I'll think about that," I said. I had a lot of thinking to do.

"Flowers—Tony pays for them, but you get to pick them."

"I can talk to my florist," I said. She would give us a good deal, I thought, since I was a regular customer.

Gina nodded. "Angela, text Ellen that photo of Kris, too, so she has the color of the dress."

"I'll do it right now," Angela said, taking out her phone.

I sipped my tea. Was there such a thing as a bridesmaid-zilla, I wondered?

That wasn't fair. Gina was doing her best to help make the

wedding wonderful. I was grateful—really, I was. I was just getting a little overwhelmed.

My phone vibrated with Angela's text. I glanced at it, and saw that it was after three-thirty. Gina picked up the last Sachertorte even as I was mentally composing my farewell.

"I'd better get back to work," Kris said, saving me the trouble. "Thanks, Ellen, this has been great!"

A leisurely flurry of goodbyes and thank-yous followed. Kris went upstairs while I saw Gina and Angela out. I checked in with Nat, who was ringing up sales in the gift shop, then stepped into the main parlor to thank the Bird Woman for the champagne. As I reached Jonquil, I paused, taking in Mrs. Olavssen's guest.

It was Mr. Quentin, the reenactor who had given talks about Captain Dusenberry during the ghost tea tours in October.

I STOOD STILL, CAUGHT OFF GUARD, and the Bird Woman and Mr. Quentin both turned their heads to look at me. I stepped up to their chairs so they wouldn't have to twist to see me.

Mr. Quentin was dressed in a dark gray suit with a brocade vest in shades of burgundy and silver, and had on a burgundy satin tie. He could give Dale a run for his money, I thought.

The Bird Woman grinned beneath her hat—a red pillbox that was so covered with pink and purple silk geraniums that it almost resembled a flower pot. "Hi, Ellen! Thanks for the macaroons!"

Macarons.

"You're very welcome. Thank you for the champagne. Good afternoon, Mr. Quentin."

"Good afternoon," he said with a smiling nod.

"I hope you've enjoyed your tea." There was a Gruet bottle and two flutes on their table, I noted.

"Oh, yeah!" the Bird Woman said, chortling a little. "Everything was great! Perfect for a first date."

I smiled at them both, unable to think of an appropriate comment. I settled for saying, "I'm glad," and wished them a pleasant afternoon, then made my escape.

First date? Wow. As I climbed the stairs, I struggled to fit the idea of the Bird Woman and Mr. Quentin as a potential couple into my reality. Not a combination I would ever have expected. Kudos to the Bird Woman for her persistence.

Minuit greeted me with a mew as I entered my office. First I sat at my desk and made a list of all the things Gina wanted me to do, then I took the kitten out of her playpen and cuddled her on the chaise longue, thinking about the bridesmaids tea. Kris had gotten along great with Gina and Angela, which made me happy. The tea seemed to have lightened her mood a bit more. That alone was enough to make me grateful to Gina.

I took out my phone and looked at the photo of Kris in her dress. She was actually smiling a little, and looked simply stunning. I'd have to send it to Gwyneth.

No texts from Tony. I sighed. I'd call him a bit later, after I caught up on the office messages.

While I scritched the kitten's head, my thoughts drifted back to the Bird Woman and Mr. Quentin. Perhaps he had found her number in his pocket and followed up on it after all. He had seemed to be enjoying her company, but of course, he was a gentleman so he would not have allowed himself to appear dissatisfied even if he was. How kind of him to indulge her.

Dale came up the stairs and went into Kris's office. I put Minuit back in her playpen and went to join them. They were bringing Mrs. Olavssen's mugs out of the storage room. It looked as though she'd increased her order significantly—we had ordered an extra six mugs for her at first. Now there were apparently two more cases as well.

"Can I help?" I asked.

"You could carry a box downstairs," Kris said. She had changed back into her work dress, I noted.

"Sure."

We made a small parade down to the gift shop, where the Bird

Woman was waiting with Mr. Quentin in attendance. He immediately relieved me of my box, then instructed Kris to place hers on top of it.

"Thanks, Ellen," said the Bird Woman as Mr. Quentin and Dale carried the mugs out the front door. "See you Saturday!"

I watched her follow them out, then Kris and I went back up to our offices. I paused to examine the samovar. Its teapot was almost empty.

"I suppose you're teaed out?" I asked Kris.

"Actually, I'd love some Assam."

"Me too. I'll make it."

Filling the kettle, rinsing the pot, adding tea to the infuser: making tea was a soothing activity. While I waited for the water to boil I stepped to the window in my suite and looked down at the tree. Mick was there, tidying the bouquets. He had pulled out a couple that were faded. I'd have to make sure to thank him. He picked up the tired flowers and carried them away just as my kettle boiled.

I served Kris some Assam, then took my own cup to my desk and went through messages. None from Tony, but Gina had texted to remind me about giving more interviews and offer to be my publicist again.

Ugh. But all right. I sent her the list of reporters who had contacted me—minus the most obnoxious ones—and told her she could set up no more than two interviews.

Still nothing from Tony. I called him, hoping I wouldn't have to leave a voicemail.

"Hey Babe," he said. "Can't talk long, what do you need?"

"I just wanted to ask if you're planning on coming over for pizza tonight."

"Uh, I can't. Gotta work late. Sorry."

"Okay."

"Let me know how the metal detector goes," he added.

"I will. Thanks."

Silence. Sighing, I put down the phone. Then I picked it up again and ordered a pizza to be delivered at 6:30. Extra pepperoni. Extra large, in case Phillips would like some. I could always freeze the leftovers.

I wondered if I had any beer. Probably not, but I had wine. I'd get out a bottle. If Phillips didn't drink wine, there was always tea or coffee. I knew he'd drink coffee.

Thinking ahead, I planned to go downstairs at six sharp and clear the table in the dining parlor. Pizza first, then hunting bullets. I'd take the wine and a couple of glasses down with me. The pantry had only aperitif glasses and champagne flutes.

As I visualized the evening, I became aware of an omission: I didn't know Phillips's first name. Well, Miss Manners had ways for me to get around that.

I made a last pass through my messages, then went downstairs to see if Nat needed help. It was 5:35 and there was a line of customers in the gift shop. I wrapped mugs in tissue, bagged Valentine cards, and packed macarons into boxes and pastry bags until we closed.

"Thanks, Ellen," Nat said as she took the last few items out of the mostly-empty pastry case. "Wow, the last hour was solid shoppers! We could have stayed open serving cream tea until seven!"

"We had that many requests?"

"Yes! They settled for scones and sweets to take home, but a lot of them asked for tea." She picked up the plate of leftovers: three rose almond cookies and a raspberry macaron.

"I'll take that," I said.

Nat smiled. "Treat for Ellen?"

"I've got a guest coming."

"Treat for Tony!"

"No," I said, laughing as we went out into the hall. "It's one of his colleagues, bringing a metal detector. We're finally going to see if we can find…those bullets." I lowered my voice as we passed Dee leading some late guests to the front door. She unlocked it to let them out.

"How exciting!" Nat said, putting on her coat and scarf. "Let me know what you find."

I walked with her to the back door, then went into the dining parlor. The table had been cleared of dishes from the cream tea customers. I put the plate of sweets on the sideboard and moved the centerpiece there as well, then removed the lace tablecloth and replaced it with a plain one more appropriate for pizza.

Hurrying upstairs for the wine, I passed Kris on her way down, bank bag tucked beneath her arm. "See you tomorrow," she said, with an actual smile.

I smiled back. "Thanks, Kris!"

I fed Minuit, then grabbed a bottle of zinfandel from my wine cooler and picked up a corkscrew and two red wine glasses. The kitten had been surprisingly well-behaved lately, so I left her in my suite and went back downstairs.

Hearing voices from the kitchen, I left the wine and glasses in the dining parlor and went to see who was still here. It turned out to be Dee, who had changed out of her server's dress and into jeans and a sweater, leaning against the counter and chatting with her brother while he finished washing the dishes.

"Hi, Ellen," she said.

I nodded. "Mick, thank you again for taking care of the flowers and the candles. I'm afraid it's becoming quite a chore."

"Dee's been helping when I'm working through rushes," Mick said. "She just went out and did a pass."

"Then thank you as well," I said to Dee.

"I'm glad to help." She gave a wry smile. "Some of those candles are black."

"Well, I gather a lot of them are being left by the Goth community," I said.

"Oh. Interesting."

She showed no sign of leaving, so I left them to their chat and returned to the dining parlor to take out some paper plates and napkins from the sideboard. After opening the wine to let it breathe, I went to stand by the French doors, thinking about Captain Dusenberry as I gazed out at the back yard.

Willow had told me he was probably stuck, kept on Earth by his own emotions, either from the trauma of being murdered or from his desire to be near Maria Hidalgo—maybe both. "Earthbound," she called it. She'd said spirits who were earthbound couldn't see their friends who wanted to help them cross over into the world of spirit.

Maria was long gone, though. Could being stuck here have become a habit for the captain? Or was he obsessed with finding out who had killed him?

It was all speculation, but I hoped that finding the bullets, if we *did* find them, would help resolve the murder both for the captain and for me.

Mick came out the kitchen's back door and got into his piebald Mustang. It roared to life and he drove away. I'd expected to see Dee with him, but instead I heard her footsteps in the hall.

"I hope you don't mind," she said, coming into the dining parlor. "I wanted to stay and watch Phillips work the metal detector."

"Oh! No, I don't mind," I said. I knew she was studying forensics.

Good thing I'd ordered a large pizza. Speaking of which, a car was coming up the driveway, and the driver wasn't Phillips. I accepted the pizza at the back door, gave the driver a nice tip, and carried the box into the dining parlor.

"Would you like some?" I asked Dee as I set the pizza on the table. "I ordered extra."

"Um, sure!" she said. "It smells fantastic!"

"Help yourself. I'll grab another wine glass. Be right back."

I went up to my suite and paused by the window to look down at the candles. The sun was down and they were beginning to make a big glow. I saw an SUV pull up to the curb and winced, thinking it was a news crew, but on looking closer I realized the markings on the side were for SFPD, not a TV station. Phillips got out and went to the back of the vehicle, where he extracted the metal detector. I grabbed a wine glass and hurried back downstairs.

Dee was letting Phillips in the back door as I arrived. He had on a down jacket over jeans and a denim shirt, and smiled at me.

"Thanks for coming," I said, and waved the wine glass. "I ordered pizza."

"Wow, thanks," he said. "Smells great! Where can I put this?"

"You can leave it out here for now." I gestured to a runner beneath a row of empty coat hooks on the wall.

Phillips set the metal detector down carefully, then hung his coat on one of the hooks and followed me and Dee into the parlor. A half-eaten slice of pizza lay on a plate on the table. I offered wine, and they both accepted, so I filled all three glasses and got out another paper plate.

I hadn't thought I'd be terribly hungry after having tea, but apparently I had done enough stair-laps to work it off. The pepperoni tasted salty and greasy and wonderful, and the wine lit up all those flavors.

"So, it's this room, right?" Phillips asked after he'd inhaled a slice of pizza.

I nodded. "I've always visualized that corner," I said, pointing to the northeast corner of the room where I had found Maria's letters under the floorboards, "but of course I don't know where the captain had his desk. The French doors weren't here then. It was just a single door."

"Hm. Bad luck if the bullets were in the part of the wall that got removed."

"Yes. I'll hope they weren't."

Dee frowned. "He was shot in the back, right?"

"Yes," I said. "Twice."

"Then either he had his desk with his back to the door, or someone shot him through one of the windows." Dee gestured to the two windows in the north wall of the room.

Frowning, I tried to visualize the captain's desk there. If he was at all like Tony, he would have wanted his back to a solid wall, but it wasn't easy in this room. There were three doors—to the hall, the front parlor, and the back yard—plus the two windows. The fireplace was in the middle of the longest wall. Which door would the killer have most likely used, assuming they had come in the house?

"Since this room was his study," I said, "and the house was also his home, it would make sense to have business visitors use the outside door, rather than coming through the front door and down the hall."

Dee frowned, looking toward the French doors. "Wasn't there another officer's house behind this, though? Might have made more sense to have visitors come to the front door." She gestured to the south wall. "If he'd had his back to the fireplace, he could have seen both the outside door and the hall door.

"Then the killer would have had to come through the parlor door," I said, "but the parlor was probably a private room. Unless the killer was a trusted intimate, they wouldn't have had easy access to that room."

"Which means Dee's right," Phillips said, "the desk probably faced south, and his back was to that wall." He nodded toward the north. "He was shot through a window."

In which case there was a chance the bullets had gone through the wall where the French doors now stood. Damn.

"Well, there could have been a confrontation," I said. "The captain could have been standing anywhere in the room."

"But that would have made it unlikely for him to be shot in the back," Dee said. "I think the killer snuck up on him. If he shot through a window, he wouldn't even have to come inside."

Phillips nodded. "Good theory, Dee."

She smiled back, and their gazes held for a moment. Interesting. Come to think of it, I hadn't introduced them, but he seemed comfortable calling her by name.

Of course, Dee had met Phillips before, during investigations. She'd had to talk to him a lot the night of Gabriel's death, when she had been dressed as the Red Death for the finale that had never happened. When she'd stayed this evening to watch him use the metal detector I had assumed it was professional curiosity, since she was a forensics student. But there was something more going on here, a stronger connection.

I took another piece of pizza. My *last* piece, I told myself firmly.

"We'll just check everywhere," Phillips said. "Might as well. Better than making assumptions."

Dee nodded, chewing. I sipped my wine.

Phillips ate one more slice. There were two pieces left in the box, and I suspected Phillips had accounted for half the pie. He wasn't a beefcake, but he was tall. Sometimes tall, slender guys could burn a lot of calories.

"Last call," I said, standing and lifting the pizza box.

Dee shook her head. "I'm stuffed. Thanks, Ellen, it was great!"

"Yeah," Phillips said. "We were going to grab a bite after, but this was perfect."

Aha. They were better acquainted than I'd realized. I glanced at Dee, who gave me a shy grin.

Okay, then. Looked like they were a couple. "I'll just put this away. Be right back," I said.

As I took the leftovers to the kitchen, wrapped them and labeled them with my name and stuck them in the freezer, I mused about what appeared to be a new romance. Probably it had started with Dee pestering Phillips with questions about investigative techniques. They made a cute couple: both blonde, both wearing glasses, both full of curiosity.

When I returned, making sure to make some noise out in the hall, I found that Phillips had brought in the metal detector and was showing Dee how to operate it. I watched, curious myself, as she swept it along the floor of the north wall.

"Right. Now aim it at the wall," Phillips said.

Dee did so, stepping back and adjusting her grip to point the base of the detector toward the adobe wall. She swung it up and down, a little awkwardly.

"Smaller strokes. Pretend you're painting the wall and don't want to leave any bare spots. Yeah, that's good."

The machine emitted little clicks, but nothing more exciting until Dee accidentally swept it over the window hardware, at which point it rattled. "Oops," she said apologetically, and offered the detector to Phillips.

"Takes practice," he said.

Dee and I watched him sweep the north wall slowly, carefully. He moved on to the east wall, paying close attention to the area around the French doors. To my disappointment, the machine stayed fairly quiet. On the south wall, some stronger clicking happened when he worked around the door to the hall, and the same at the parlor door beside it. My hopes diminished as he moved on to the west wall. The machine went berserk when he reached the fireplace, with its iron grate. He moved past it and continued to the corner with no results, then went over the north wall.

That was the whole room. Damn.

Frowning, Phillips went back over the west wall from the other direction, lifting the detector high to sweep up to the ceiling. He paused, taking a step back.

"Can we take the grate out of the fireplace?" he asked.

"It'll be hot. There are still coals," I said, holding my hand out toward it. I could feel the warmth left over from the day's fire.

"I'll get the gloves," Dee said. "We can put the grate out on the driveway."

While she was fetching the welder's gloves that we used for tending the fires, I picked up the coal shovel and moved the coals into the back corner of the fireplace, then swept off the grate with the fireplace broom. Glancing up at Phillips, who seemed lost in thought, I decided I'd like to get better acquainted with him. Maybe invite him and Dee to dinner, after I had moved into the new place?

Dee picked up the grate and carried it out to the French doors, which I opened for her. She deposited the grate on the gravel driveway, well away from the house and my car. We returned to the dining parlor, where Phillips was waiting politely. He lifted the metal detector and swept it over the hearth, then started working his way up the fireplace, sweeping back and forth. About two feet up the south side, the clicks intensified.

"Oh!" I blurted.

Phillips knelt and turned the metal detector to aim its base flat at the fireplace wall. The clicks were strongest on the left side, near the top. He aimed the detector at the adobe wall just to the left of the fireplace, and the clicks became a buzz. He peered at the display panel on the detector.

"About two inches deep."

He put the detector down and took a small tool out of his

pocket, shaped like a diminutive butane lighter, but all black. He pointed this at the wall by the fireplace and it buzzed. As he moved it back and forth the buzzing changed, until he had pinpointed where it was strongest.

"There. Mind if I mark it?"

I shook my head. Phillips took a marker out of his pocket. "This can be cleaned off," he said, and made a dot on the wall, then picked up the metal detector and aimed it at the dot. It responded with enthusiastic buzzing.

"Yep. It went into the adobe. Lucky it missed the brick."

The fireplaces and the chimneys were made of fired brick, which would have been imported to the Territory at great expense, while the walls of the house were adobe which was made locally. Adobe bricks were basically sun-dried mud, with some straw to hold it together. Much softer than fired brick.

I stepped to the wall, touching the dot Phillips had made, then looking back toward the windows, visualizing the line of fire. The eastern window, then, if the captain had been sitting between them.

"It's a bullet?" I asked.

"They would have called it a ball," Phillips said. "Yeah, probably, unless it's a nail, but they didn't usually put nails into adobe. They used gringo blocks to hang things."

"Gringo blocks?" Dee asked.

"Yeah, chunks of wood, like the beams above the windows." He gestured to the heavy wooden beams over the windows in the north wall. "Sometimes they'd put smaller ones in random places in the wall, just to hang things from. Easier to put nails into wood than adobe. There might be one behind the plaster there," he gestured to the dot, "but they wouldn't usually be that low."

"They're called gringo blocks because it was the the Americans coming in that wanted to hang things on the wall," I told Dee. "The natives didn't do that."

"I didn't know. Thanks," she said.

Phillips raised the detector again and continued sweeping the wall to the left of the fireplace, but didn't find another hot spot. He went all the way to the parlor door, then checked to the right of the fireplace as well.

"Looks like just one."

"I wonder where the other bullet—ball—went," I said.

"It could have bounced off, or hit the brick and shattered, right?" Dee said, looking at Phillips.

"More likely flattened. Lead's pretty soft. Or it might have stayed in his body."

I brushed my fingers over the dot. "How do we get it out?"

"I could dig it out, but that would damage your wall," Phillips said.

"It can be repaired, right?"

"Yeah, but I'm afraid I don't know how to repair adobe."

"My uncle knows a guy who can, I think," I said.

Phillips took a step back and gazed at the wall, frowning. "I'd want to do a core, to make sure I don't damage the ball with the drill. It'll be a pretty big hole—maybe three inches. We'll want to do it on a day you're closed."

"You're right," I said reluctantly.

Part of me wanted to do it right away, but a gaping hole in the parlor wall would not be good on Valentine's Day. Also, it was getting on into the evening, and Phillips had already spent a lot of time on this.

"This weekend isn't good," I said. "Can we look at the weekend after?"

"Sure," Phillips said. "You can text me."

"Thanks. It's awfully kind of you to help with this."

He grinned. "Hey, I'm hot to find the ball that killed Captain D.!"

I picked up the plate of leftover sweets off the sideboard and offered it to him. "Well, here's a small reward."

He took a cookie and ate half in one bite. Dee took one, too. While they shared the sweets and bickered adorably over the macaron, I gathered the paper plates and napkins and disposed of them. When I got back, Dee was putting on the welder's gloves. I went with her to open the door. It was dark out, and getting cold. Dee brought the grate back inside and returned it to the fireplace.

"Thanks," I said. "I can clean up the rest. Mr. Phillips, thank you for doing this. And by the way, I don't know your first name?"

Dee laughed softly. Phillips shot her a glance, then turned to me. "It's Xavier. You can just call me Phillips, though, or Phil. Everyone does."

"Okay," I said, marveling at the cruelty, or simple thoughtlessness, of some parents. Maybe it was a family name.

I saw them out and locked up, then cleared the table and put the lace tablecloth and the centerpiece back on it. The cookie plate went to the kitchen, where I washed it and left it in the dish rack. The wine glasses and bottle I carried back up to my suite. There was a little wine left. I polished it off while I washed up, thinking about Dee and Phillips. How sweet they were together, I thought, smiling. Early days for them.

Minuit trotted up to me, mewing. I gave her a treat while I dried the wine glasses, then picked her up and sat in my wing chair. It was getting toward bedtime, but I wanted a little kitten cuddling first. Minuit obliged by purring loudly as she curled up on my chest.

So we *had* found a bullet. A ball. Maybe. I wanted to dig it out as soon as possible. I'd better ask Manny about his friend who did adobe fireplaces, and see if I could line him up to repair the wall.

I wondered what Captain Dusenberry thought about this discovery, or if he was even aware of it. He had not made his presence known while Phillips was working, but then, we'd been focused on the metal detector. What did ghosts think of metal detectors, I wondered? Did the machine somehow disrupt the etheric field or whatever it was? I'd have to ask Willow.

Yawning, I gave Minuit a final scritch and put her on the floor while I got up to brush my teeth. I'd left my phone on my desk, so I went across the hall and fetched it before climbing into bed. There was a text from Phillips, thanking me for the pizza and wine. Dee must have given him my number. Nothing from Tony. Sighing, I set aside the phone and turned out the light.

A faint glow lit the edges of the window curtains. I watched it for a while, wondering if the candles were all right. The light wavered slightly.

Okay, I'd better check it, or I'd lie in bed worrying. I got up and padded over to the window, pulling back the curtain.

The candles looked safe, but there were a *lot* of them. They made a glow as big as a bonfire, lighting up the whole tree. Against that light, a dark shape among the bare branches caught my attention. At first I thought it was a raccoon or some other critter, then after a minute I figured out that it was the giant black bow tied on the branch where Margo had been hanged.

Argh. I'd be glad when this was over, and the memorial could be cleared away. Pulling the curtains tightly closed, I went back to bed.

I had pizza dreams. Mr. Quentin and Phillips were staging how the captain's murder had happened in the dining parlor. The table was gone and there was a big, old-fashioned desk in front of the north wall, between the windows. Mr. Quentin, dressed in his Civil War uniform, sat at the desk while Phillips, dressed in a frock coat and top hat, looking like a blonde, bespectacled, clean-shaven Lincoln, stood outside the windows and pointed a laser through them at Mr. Quentin's back, moving around to try various angles.

In the three doorways of the room stood Dee in her lavender server's dress, Kris in her amazing purple dress, and the Bird Woman in a hot pink Victorian gown complete with a bustle (1870's —too late for Captain Dusenberry, more like the photo of Maria Hidalgo, except screaming pink). I had on my wedding dress and was using the metal detector, waving it at the wall wherever Phillips's red laser dot hit it. I had to pick my way among the dozens of tall votive candles that stood all over the floor of the room, being careful not to set my train on fire. Mr. Quentin watched me silently as he polished a Colt Navy pistol.

That was the most normal of the dreams. They got weirder as the night went on, and I tossed and turned a bit. Minuit finally protested with a cranky mew and jumped off the bed, making a thump much louder than her tiny weight seemed capable of producing.

Toward dawn, I finally gave up and got out of bed. It was early, but I was beginning to smell something wafting up from the kitchen downstairs: the rose almond cookies, I thought. I took a long, hot shower and ate some oatmeal, then put on an elegant dress—sage green with lace accents—in case Gina had set up an interview for the day.

I got Minuit settled in her playpen, fired up the samovar and made tea, then carried a cup to my desk along with my phone. Nothing from Tony, but Gina had set up two interviews for that day, morning and afternoon.

Well, the sooner the better. It was Thursday and from now on through Sunday, things were officially crazy busy. The first interview was scheduled for ten o'clock—before we opened, for which I was grateful. It was with a reporter from The New Mexican. Maybe I'd talk to them in the upper hall, by the front window, out of the way of my staff who'd be getting ready for business.

The second interview was at two-thirty, with another TV

station. Almost certainly they'd want to do it by the tree. I hoped the day would be warm, but just in case I hung a pretty scarf with my long wool coat on the coat rack, ready to grab if needed.

The morning was now far enough advanced that it would not be rude to call Manny. I dialed his number and he answered.

"*¡Buenas dias, hija!*"

"*Buenas dias,*" I replied. "I have a favor to ask. Can I get the number of your friend who builds adobe fireplaces?"

"Why, you gonna add on to the house?"

"No." I explained about the search for the pistol ball in the dining parlor wall, and Manny gave me the number for his friend, Louie Cordova. I called, got voicemail, and left a message.

Kris came in and dove into the phone messages. I went downstairs to check on the kitchen and the gift shop. Julio, Hanh, and Ramon were hard at work, and after saying hello I got out of their way. The gift shop was stocked and ready. Nat would be in at nine. As I was about to leave the shop, Dale came in with a sling full of firewood for the fireplaces in the shop and the alcoves behind it.

"Morning," I said. "We match!"

As it happened, Dale had worn a dark green vest and a sage-colored bow tie. He smiled. "Great minds," he said as he went to work on the fires.

He was the first of the servers to arrive. Since it would be a busy day, I went to the butler's pantry to start up the big urn that kept water hot-ish for tea. We filled kettles from it, which saved time because they came to a boil faster, enabling us to brew tea quickly. As I filled it, I glanced out the window toward the tree.

It was breezy, and the wind had tossed the bouquets around a bit. Hard to tell in daylight, but I thought some of the candles had also gone out. I'd better go out and tidy it up in case I had to give an interview out there before Mick arrived. I finished filling the urn and set it heating, then ran upstairs for my coat and scarf.

As I stepped out the back door, a gust of wind hit me. I put the scarf over my hair to protect it, and pulled my gloves out of my coat pocket, putting them on as I walked around to the tree. My first impression of it was not favorable: with plastic-wrapped bouquets scattered around and candles in various stages of burning, it looked a little like a trash dump.

I walked around the circle collecting burned-out candles. When I had an armful I took them to the trash bin. It took me three trips to clear them, then I started on the bouquets. Mick's moving them to the tree was good, because it kept them mostly inside the circle of candles, but they had slumped this way and that and looked untidy. The oldest ones were buried, and I left them be, but any visible flowers that were faded I pulled out, and I did my best to straighten the remaining ones. As I was doing this work, I noticed an SUV pulling up to the curb beyond the picket fence.

Phillips again? No—it wasn't marked, but it was bristling with antennae and looked suspiciously like a cop car. My suspicion was confirmed when Zeke Walters came out of the driver's door and started toward the gate, carrying a manila envelope.

11

EEP BREATH. MISS MANNERS ZEN. I kept working on the flowers, keeping a peripheral eye on Zeke to see if he would go to the door or come to the tree.

Tree. He turned off the path. I ignored him until he reached me, when I looked up with a polite almost-smile.

Tree. He turned off the path. I ignored him until he reached me, when I looked up with a polite almost-smile.

He touched his white Stetson. "Morning."

"Good morning," I replied, and turned to extract a bouquet of faded carnations from the pile.

"I'd like to ask you a couple of questions," Zeke said.

A bundle of tired daisies joined the carnations. "I'm rather busy today. Perhaps you could give me your number and I'll call when I'm free."

Silence as I kept working. Then, "I brought this back."

He opened the envelope and took out Kris's letter opener. I met his gaze.

"Thank you. You should return it to Kris. And it would be nice if you apologized."

His eyes narrowed slightly. The wind played with his mustache, and he reached a hand up to smooth it. "If I do that, will you talk to me?"

I straightened, my arms full of dead flowers. "All right. Come in."

Heading toward the back door, I paused to dump the flowers in the trash bin. Rosa was getting out of her car, and she hesitated as she caught sight of Zeke.

"Good morning, Rosa," I said, smiling to reassure her. She hurried inside, and we followed.

Zeke fell in behind me as I went up the stairs. At the top, I took off my coat and hung it on the coat rack. Zeke continued into Kris's office. Shamelessly eavesdropping, I took my time removing my scarf, then stepped through the doorway and used the small, oval mirror hanging just inside my office to tidy my hair.

"I'm returning this, ma'am," Zeke said.

A muttered "Thanks" from Kris.

"I'm sorry I bothered you about it. We're sure it had nothing to do with the hanging."

"Like I told you to begin with," Kris said.

"Yes, ma'am. I apologize for the inconvenience."

Adequate, if not very heartfelt. Zeke stepped out into the hall and I joined him.

"You can hang your coat there, if you like," I said, indicating the coat rack. "Would you like some tea? It's Irish Breakfast."

He shot me a wary glance as he hung up his coat and hat. "Um, no thanks."

"Very well." I poured myself a cup and led him to the sitting area, where he again took the chair while I sat on the sofa. Zeke got out his phone and set it on the table.

"I gather you've talked with Tony," I said.

"Yes, ma'am. I visited with him last night."

So that was the working late. I was glad Tony had passed along my messages.

"What did you want to ask me?"

He looked appraisingly at me. "Tony said you're a good observer. I wanted to ask if there's anything else you've thought of about the hanging."

Again, a compliment. "Did you look into the cheerleading?" I asked.

"Yeah, that's a dead end, unfortunately. All but one of the other cheerleaders from her senior year have moved out of state, and the one that's here has a solid alibi. Said they haven't talked since high school."

"I can believe that. Margo was not typical cheerleader material."

"No."

"Then it's probably someone in the Goth community, I'm sorry to say. They knew Margo best, as far as I know, and this was a personal crime."

"Yes, ma'am."

I sipped my tea. "It's a large community. I had no idea there were so many Goths in New Mexico. Apparently it's mostly them leaving the flowers and candles." I nodded toward the tree.

Zeke's brows rose. "From all around the state?"

I nodded. "So I heard. If Margo knew even half of them, that would be a huge pool to look at for the killer."

Zeke's jaw worked, then he sighed. "Well, it's most likely someone she knew well, and we've covered that."

I nodded. "Oh, there is one detail you could check, though I don't know if it will help. The jet beads may have come from a shop called Krampus, here in town. They sell a lot of jet jewelry, I'm told."

Zeke picked up his phone and dictated. "Check Krampus shop for jet beads." He put the phone down. "How'd you hear about that?"

"Kris told me. She might have told *you,* if you'd been a little less...assertive." I used a polite euphemism for arrogant.

Zeke's jaw worked again, but he didn't say anything. I took a sip of tea and looked out the window.

"You know, I wonder if it might have been a hate crime?" I mused. "Rather than personal, I mean. Someone who hates Goths?"

"Oh, Lordy. That's a bucket of worms," Zeke said.

"I suppose it is. And there's the kris."

"Yeah." Zeke picked up his phone, stood, and took out his wallet, extracting a business card. "Well, thanks. I'll go check out that shop. If you think of anything else...."

"I'll call."

He left, and I picked up my teacup, pausing to top it up at the samovar before going to my desk. I had just enough time to make a preliminary pass through my messages before the newspaper reporter arrived.

To my surprise, he wanted to interview me out by the tree, and had brought along a photographer, so I put on my coat and we headed downstairs. Good thing I'd tidied up the memorial. We stood talking by the tree in the cold wind for at least half an hour while the photographer took endless shots from various angles, reminding me of my dream the previous night. By the time it was over, my ears were numb from the cold and the tearoom had opened. A steady stream of customers was going in, many coming out shortly thereafter with lavender gift shop bags in hand.

Be grateful, I told myself as I hurried inside and headed upstairs to guzzle tea.

"Tony called," Kris said from her desk as I stood at the samovar.

"Thanks!" I went to my desk and called him back. "Zeke was here," I told him.

"Were you nice to him?"

"I was, but he wouldn't drink any tea."

"Babe, he may never drink tea again."

Allowing that to pass, I gave Tony a brief summary of my

conversation with Zeke. He listened, made no comment, then asked if I was free for dinner.

"Yes," I said. "Shall I meet you somewhere?"

"Yeah, how about at the new place?"

"Oh! All right." Maybe he wanted to get takeout? Or maybe he wanted to make sure I'd come back there after dinner. Sly move.

"I'll be there by…better say seven," I said.

"I'll book us a table someplace nice for seven-thirty."

"Good luck."

I was hungry, I realized after Tony hung up. Still cold. I drank another cup of tea, then went downstairs to check in with Nat and see if Julio had made anything for lunch. He often did so on busy days, or bad-weather days, to make it easy for the staff to stay if they wanted. On *super* busy days, though, he didn't have time. This might be one of those days.

Pausing to look into the dining parlor, I saw three people having cream tea at the table—two women softly chatting and one guy in a really natty suit sitting alone at the far end of the table, absorbed in his phone. The fire had burned down, so I stepped in to pull the coals together and add a log of piñon. The dot Phillips had made on the wall caught my eye.

The women stopped chatting to watch me, making me wonder if they'd seen the TV interview. I gave them a smile as I straightened, then left them in peace.

Nat was at the register in the gift shop, looking cheery in a lemon yellow dress and a multicolored silk scarf. She flashed me a smile as I paused in the doorway. Iz stood beside her, helping bag purchases. Dale was in and out of the alcoves, and I glimpsed Rosa in the main parlor, waiting on the alcoves there.

I noticed the pastry case was getting sparse, so I went to the kitchen for more sweets to replenish it. Julio, Hanh, and Ramon were going full-tilt, and an unfamiliar savory smell filled the air. On a back burner of the stove stood a big stock pot, gently steaming. Soup for lunch! Hurrah!

Extracting a tray from beneath the counter, I filled it with macarons and cookies from the tall, rolling cooling rack. Its shelves were almost completely full of trays of baked goods. My stomach growled.

"That for the gift shop?" Julio called over his shoulder.

"Yes," I said. "They're almost out."

"Don't take any Sachertortes."

"I'm not. Just cookies and macarons."

Carrying the tray to the front, I squeezed past Nat and Iz and replenished the pastry case. A glance at the register screen told me it was nearly noon. I filled two boxes with sweets for customers before escaping to return the tray to the kitchen. Mick took it out of my hands and washed it immediately.

"Um," I said, stepping to where Julio was assembling cucumber sandwiches. "Will lunch be ready soon?"

"It's ready now. Help yourself."

"Thanks!"

"Bread rolls on the cart to go with," Hanh added without looking up from the strawberries she was slicing.

"Yum! Thank you!"

Hanh made phenomenal breads. Julio had once commented that her baguettes were better than his. I found the rolls, which were still warm, and grabbed two: one for me and one for Kris. I put them on a small plate, then picked up the tray Mick had just washed and put the plate on it, setting it on the break table while I added two bowls of soup, a small dish of butter, spoons and knives. The soup was a vegetable stew, with big chunks of potato. I salivated as I carried it upstairs.

"Lunch," I called to Kris as I passed the office entryway. She came out to join me at the sitting area in the hall.

"Thanks," she said as we settled in to eat. "I've been smelling this for an hour. Driving me crazy." She broke her roll in half and slathered one piece with soft butter. "How was the interview?"

"Okay. No surprises. Photographer took pictures from every possible angle. I almost expected him to climb the tree."

Kris laughed, which made me glad. Her mood seemed better today.

"You heard what Walters said to me, right?" she asked.

"I did. I was snooping."

"Good. Thanks for making him return my letter opener."

"I didn't make him do it. I think Tony must have talked him into it."

"Yeah, well, Tony wouldn't have done that on his own."

True.

After lunch Kris insisted on taking the tray downstairs so she could thank Julio and Hanh. I went to my desk and attacked my messages. Gina had sent me a text, pinging me about the wedding venue.

Argh. Couldn't it wait?

I emailed her a copy of my list of the places I'd looked at already, complete with my reasons for rejecting them. Told her I'd get back to it next week.

Louie Cordova had returned my call, so I called him again. Voicemail again. Phone tag. I left another message, giving a few details about the repairs I anticipated needing, and adding that I'd be happy to talk with him about it next week.

Next week for everything not Valentine's-related.

Kris returned with the day's mail in hand, and stopped by my desk to give me a greeting-card-sized envelope that was addressed to me in flowing cursive. The return address was unfamiliar: Houston. I fetched myself a cup of tea and opened it.

The card was a lovely photograph of a garden, with a boardwalk curving through lush wetlands beneath a bright blue sky. On the back, the photo credit said, "Houston Botanic Garden."

Dear Ellen,

I've been thinking about you a lot, so I wanted to write you a note. Jeremy and I are doing well. The funeral was well-attended, and we're mostly through dealing with paperwork and such. Jeremy's handling it all beautifully. He's a lot more relaxed now. It's sad to think about why.

As a tribute, I made a donation in Wesley's name to the botanic garden here. I've been going to meditation classes there and it helps a lot. I also made a donation to an adult literacy program in his name.

I have decided to sell the bars. They were Wesley's thing, not mine, and if Jeremy's going to inherit something I'd rather it not be bars. I'm thinking about maybe opening a tearoom here. What do you think? Would you be willing to advise me? Aunt Rachelle thinks it's a grand idea, even though Houston has a lot of tearooms already. She and I have started going to each one for tea, looking for what we might do that's a little different from them all.

Thank you again for your kindness. We'll be coming to Santa Fe later this year, and I'll finally get to have tea at your place.

Best regards,

Lisette Roan

How nice of her to write. I propped the card on my desk, admiring the photo again while I finished my tea and thought about

Lisette's note. Not many people took the time to write letters by hand these days.

I decided to return the compliment. Getting up, I parked my teacup by the samovar and went into the storeroom to raid the Valentine's cards. We had some with teacups on them, of course, so I chose one with a little spray of violets beside the cup and took it back to my desk, where I added it to the log of my depredations on the tearoom's inventory.

More tea. While I was at the samovar I offered some to Kris, who accepted. The wind was still moaning about the windows, making it drafty, and I was grateful for the warmth coming from the chimney. Settling in at my desk, I took out my fountain pen and opened the Valentine card.

> *Dear Lisette,*
>
> *How lovely to hear from you! Thank you for your note. I love the photo on your card and can picture you in that peaceful garden.*
>
> *Of course I think it would be wonderful if you opened your own tearoom! How could I not? Houston must be big enough to support one more. Good luck with your survey of all the existing ones. Surely you will find a niche that needs filling.*
>
> *Please let me know when you'll be visiting, once your plans are firm.*

I hesitated, wondering if I should mention the date of the wedding. Not that it should matter to her, but I'd hate to miss her if she came while Tony and I were away on honeymoon. I liked Lisette, though she'd been rather reserved at Ghost Ranch (with very good reason). It would be nice to spend some time with her now that her awful husband was gone.

Uncharitable thought, Ellen. Wesley Roan had been a troubled man. At least his troubles were over, now.

Like Margo's. And like Margo—like Gabriel—he'd been hanged. It wasn't a trend, was it? Wesley'd already been dead....

I shook myself out of useless speculations. Wesley Roan had nothing to do with Margo and Gabriel.

> *If you happen to be here in late September, you might be in town for my wedding. I'd be delighted to invite you and Jeremy if that's the case. Please give him a hello from me.*
>
> *All best,*
>
> *Ellen Rosings*

I put the card in its envelope and addressed it at once, before I could chicken out.

Small wedding, Ellen. Remember?

Two more guests wouldn't make that much difference. Adding a "LOVE" stamp from my desk drawer, I got up and dropped the card in the outgoing mail tray on Kris's credenza.

Kris glanced up at me. "Nat just called. They need more Valentines in the shop."

"Thanks. I'll take them."

Grabbing a double handful of cards from the storage room, I went down to put them in the nearly-empty card rack. The shop was crowded with customers, and I spent the next hour restocking displays and occasionally chatting with regulars. On my second trip upstairs (for more loose leaf tea), I collected my coat and scarf, taking them down to hang in the hall in case I didn't get back upstairs before my afternoon interview.

The only empty hook was back by the dining parlor. I looked in; the table was surrounded by cream tea customers. Out in the hall, there were people sitting in the all wing chairs and a couple were loitering by the front door, and I realized they might be waiting for cream tea.

Ay, yi, yi! How many people were in here? Were we over our capacity limit?

Heaters on the *portal*, I decided. By fall, if not sooner.

The gift shop was crammed with customers, and I could see people standing outside through the front windows. I threaded my way through the shoppers and replenished the tea display. The puerh from the Valentine's menu was going like hotcakes—I had one customer take a packet right out of my hand.

As I emerged from the shop, I met Rosa coming out of the main parlor. She cast me a pleading look and I followed her to the butler's pantry. Through the window I saw Mick outside, patrolling the candles and flowers by the tree.

"Ellen, could you help with the cream tea people?" Rosa said as she rinsed a teapot and put on a kettle. "Dee and I have our hands full, and so does Dale. Iz keeps getting caught helping in the gift shop."

"I can help until two, then I have an interview," I said.

"Oh—well—"

"I'll cover the dining parlor until then. Will that do?"

"That'll be great," Rosa said. "Thank you!"

Leaving her making tea, I went to the dining parlor. All ten chairs around the table were full, and three of the customers looked up expectantly as I appeared in the doorway. Smiling, I picked up tickets and processed payments at the register we'd added in the butler's pantry, getting the customers who had finished on their way. Dale popped in and cleared their china, then immediately brought in new customers—people I'd seen waiting in the hall. I fetched the large pot of tea designated for cream tea customers from the butler's pantry. As I filled teacups, I took note from body language of which customers were together.

"Thank you," Dale said softly as we passed in the doorway, I with an empty teapot and he with a tray of fresh cups for the newcomers. "I put the kettle on."

I set up the teapot with fresh leaves, then fetched a tray of scones from the kitchen, plating them while I waited for the tea to brew. When it was done I loaded the teapot onto a tray along with the scones and carried it into the parlor, where I served the new customers from the sideboard. By the time everyone had tea and scones, two more parties were ready to check out. This continued right up until two, and would have continued indefinitely. We needed a server just for the dining parlor on days like this.

Rosa came into the pantry as I was ringing up a payment. "It's two," she said. "Better make your escape. Want me to take that?"

"Thanks," I said, handing her the receipt and the customer's credit card. "It's the two brunettes by the fireplace. Will you be all right for an hour?"

Rosa nodded. "All the alcoves have their food. We should be fine until about three-thirty."

"I'll come back as soon as I'm done with the interview."

On my way upstairs, I met Kris coming down with a couple of boxes of gift shop inventory. "Sorry," I said. "I've been waiting on the dining parlor."

"It's okay," she said. "But we're going to have overtime this week."

"That's fine."

Minuit mewed at me as I reached the upper hall. With a pang of remorse, I ignored her, darting into my suite to tidy my hair and touch up my makeup. I took a couple of deep breaths in the quiet, then gave Minuit a treat before heading downstairs.

The hall was still full of people waiting for cream tea. The gift shop was still full of shoppers. Putting on my coat, I stepped out the front door and saw a news SUV parked across the street. All the spaces in front of the tearoom were taken.

The reporter and cameraperson (male this time) were already by the tree, filming an introduction. I stayed watching by the *portal* until they were ready for me. The wind made the plastic wrappers on the flowers rustle behind the reporter, and the candles flickered like crazy. No wonder he kept his hair cut short.

The interview went well. No surprise questions, all things I'd answered before. Again, I clarified the nature of Gabriel's masquerade, dispelling the suggestion of satanic overtones. The only original question the reporter came up with was whether I thought Captain Dusenberry had anything to do with Margo's death.

I looked at him inquiringly. "You're asking if a ghost might have killed her? I don't know how that could happen," I said.

After that, he wrapped up the interview pretty quickly. I went inside, walked past the customers waiting in the hall, and went upstairs to take off my coat and drink a cup of tea.

The teapot on the samovar was empty. I made a fresh pot. Puerh, because I deserved a treat.

Minuit was sleeping in her playpen. Kris was on the phone. I filled her teacup and drank my own tea sitting on my chaise longue, just enjoying being alone for a moment. My feet were aching, and I realized I'd been on them all afternoon. My appreciation of the servers—and the kitchen staff, too—had been refreshed.

When my cup was empty I sent Gina a text saying "Mission accomplished," then checked my phone for messages. Nothing urgent, and it was almost three-thirty. Customers for the four o'clock seating would be arriving. Time to go back downstairs.

Before diving into the cream tea hamster wheel, I went up to the gift shop to check on Nat. The pastry case was empty, so I grabbed the tray from the shelf beneath it and took it to the kitchen. Julio and Ramon were there making macarons and scones.

"Still here?" I said to Julio as I passed him.

He slammed a tray of unbaked macarons against the counter, which was necessary to eliminate bubbles, but must also have been satisfying. "Gotta keep up or we'll run out in the morning," he said. "I sent Hanh home—she came in at five."

"All right. Shall we order pizza for lunch tomorrow?"

Julio cast me a grateful look. "That would be good."

As I filled my tray with cookies and macarons, Ramon looked up from his work. "Ellen? Got a minute?"

"Sure." I carried the tray over to where he was cutting out scones and set it on the work table.

"I can play until closing on Sunday if you still want me to," Ramon said. "My date got canceled."

"Oh—I'm sorry!"

He shook his head. "We just moved it. She got asked to work, too, so we're going out Tuesday night instead."

"Ah. Well, I would *love* to have you play until closing if you're up to it," I said.

"It's overtime, though. I'm already working extra this week."

"I know, and thank you. Everyone's getting overtime. It's fine."

He smiled, and I took my tray to the gift shop, where I emptied it into the pastry case. Nat nodded at me from the register as I headed for the butler's pantry. Dee was there, setting up pots of tea for the four o'clock seating. I grabbed the big pot and went to the dining parlor.

For the next two hours I served cream tea, with occasional breaks to check on the gift shop. At five-thirty I told Nat and the servers that we would not be seating any more cream tea customers that day.

"Oh, good," Nat told me. "We have a few waiting, though."

"We'll seat them, but any new walk-ins get turned away."

"Right. Thanks, Ellen. You doing all right?"

"Yes, but I'll need a drink after we close."

"You and me both!"

This was like December had been. Possibly crazier than December. I took care of the last few cream tea customers, and escorted the final one out at five after six, when I locked the front door and turned the sign to "Closed."

THERE WERE STILL CUSTOMERS in the parlors and the gift shop, and we were letting them out for another half hour. The door had to stay locked to keep more people from coming in. I glanced out the butler's pantry window at the tree. More or less the same as it had been, although a trifle windblown. Perhaps the tributes were slowing down.

Julio and Ramon had finally gone home, as had Iz and Dale. Mick was washing piles of china, and Rosa and Dee were clearing the parlors. I collected Nat from the gift shop.

"Come upstairs," I said. "Do you have time?"

"No more than half an hour. Manny's making dinner."

"Bless him. This won't take long."

Kris was at her desk, processing a mound of receipts. I collected a bottle of sherry and three aperitif glasses from my suite, and put them on the table by the front window in the hall.

"Would you pour?" I asked Nat.

"With pleasure."

While she made herself comfortable on the sofa, I went to fetch Kris from her office. "Come have a drink with us."

"I'm almost done with this. Be right out."

"Okay."

I stepped into my office for a notepad, and paused to give Minuit a scritch. She purred so loudly I couldn't resist picking her up for a brief cuddle. When I heard Kris stand up, I put the kitten back in her playpen and went out to the sitting area. Nat had poured the sherry, and she handed out the glasses as we sat.

"That was the biggest deposit we've made since New Year's," Kris said.

"Cheers to that," Nat said, lifting her glass.

I sipped, and let out a sigh as the sherry filled my mouth with fragrance and tingling. "Thank you both," I said. "It's been a nutty day. Are we going to make it through the weekend? Is there anything I can do to make things go more smoothly?"

"Yeah, approve as much overtime as the staff will take," Kris said. "Julio already asked for permission to give Hanh and Ramon extra hours."

"Extra hours all around is fine with me. Shall I talk to the servers?"

"Yes," Kris said. "Best if it comes from you."

I made a note on my pad, then bit my lip. "I've got Ramon playing music on Sunday."

"Julio mentioned that. He suggested bringing in his friend Andre that day if he's available. I said I'd check with you."

"Sure." I made another note. "What else?"

Nat cleared her throat. "Would it help if we had two people in the gift shop? So the servers can stick to the alcoves?"

"It would, I'm sure, but who could we get on short notice?"

"I can talk to Claudia if you like."

"Claudia!" Claudia Pearson was a friend, one of the people who had helped me acquire the tearoom. "You think she'd do it? But she works," I said.

"I think she'd find it fun for a weekend. She might be at the

Trust tomorrow, but if she came Saturday that would help, right?"

"Yes! Please do talk to her." I made another note. "Sunday we're not serving cream tea, so it will be a little less crazy, but the gift shop may still be busy."

"I'll call her tonight and let you know what she says," Nat said.

"Thank you." I looked at Kris. "We'll need to do paperwork for her and Andre."

"Minimal. I can have them sign W9s, and we'll treat them as contractors, not employees."

"Brilliant. Anything else?"

"We're almost out of bags in the gift shop," Nat said.

"I'll restock everything—tomorrow morning, if not tonight," I said.

"We're running low on bags, actually," Kris said. "I ordered more yesterday, but they won't be in until next week."

"Yikes. Can we get something in town to substitute?"

Kris nodded. "I'll call around tomorrow. They might not be pretty."

"As long as they'll hold merchandise, it's fine."

I took a sip of sherry. We'd just have to get through the next three days. Just three days.

"Kris, I told Julio we'd order pizza for lunch tomorrow. Can you take care of that?"

"Sure," she said, tapping at her phone. "What about Saturday and Sunday?"

I thought a minute. "Burritos from El Vaquero Saturday?"

"Okay. Sandwiches Sunday?"

"That'll be fine."

"I'll put in the orders."

"Bless you." I looked over my list. "Longer term, we may want to add a second person in the gift shop. Part-time, maybe. Weekends, and special occasions. Or...Nat, would you rather I hired a full-timer, and you could fill in part time?"

"That would be better for me, actually," Nat said. "I'm happy to help, but I don't really want a full-time job."

Hire gift shop manager, I wrote on my notepad. Glancing at Kris, I saw her nod.

"We're there, I think," she said. "We can handle a full-timer. They could take some of the inventory management off my hands. That would be a help."

"What about another server?"

Kris nodded. "I'll run some numbers to make sure, but yes. Our slowest week since New Year's was still busier than November. We can probably support another server. Maybe part-time for now, to keep the busiest times covered."

"Part-time seems to work well for servers anyway," I said, adding to my list. "Kris, remember we talked about outdoor heating, so we can serve outdoors later in the year?"

"Yeah. Want me to get some quotes?"

"Yes, please. I think we should add them by the autumn."

"Okay, but you might want to think about expanding instead. Or in addition."

"Expanding?"

"Adding on to the building. Add a room south of the gift shop, would be my suggestion. No windows in that wall, so adding on would be fairly easy. Either another parlor the size of the main parlor, or a new gift shop and make the current one into alcoves. And if you make it two stories, we could have a storeroom upstairs and maybe a dumb waiter for moving inventory."

Wow. No more carrying boxes up and down.

I took a sip of sherry and stared out the front window, visualizing such an addition to the house. I had roses growing in the area Kris had suggested, but they could be moved.

"Wouldn't it be expensive?"

"If business keeps growing, and I think it will, you can handle the expense. You might have to take out a small loan to cover it. I'll run some numbers for you."

"Okay."

Another sip of sherry emptied my glass. I set it on the table and looked at Nat and Kris. "Thank you. For your help today, and for your advice."

Nat smiled. "Congratulations, honey. You're a hit, and you haven't even been open a year!" She looked at her watch. "And now I have to get going. I'll come in early tomorrow."

"Can you plan to stay late again?" I asked.

"I'll warn Manny."

We all stood, said good night, and went downstairs together, leaving the sherry and glasses for later. Kris headed off to deposit the bank bag. Nat went to check the front door and get her coat and purse from the gift shop. I grabbed my coat and exchanged a wave with Mick who was alone in the kitchen, finishing the dishes. I drove to the townhome, pulling up at the curb at two minutes past seven.

Shutting off the engine, I let out a sigh and sat still. Crazy day.

The porch light sent out a friendly gleam over the dark shapes of sleeping shrubs and flowers in the small front yard. I had mostly been here at night, I realized. I'd have to come in the daytime and check out what was growing in the garden.

As I stood fishing in my purse for my key, Tony opened the door.

"Hi," he said, stepping out and pulling it closed behind him. "Time to go."

"Okay."

Back to the car. "Where are we going?" I asked as we got in.

"Chez Mamou," Tony said. "You know where it is?"

"I do."

I drove there, setting my expectations for a savory French meal. The restaurant was small, and there were people waiting outside, but Tony had snagged a reservation and we were seated right away. We ordered a bottle of red wine, which came promptly. I took a sip, glad that I'd had the sherry and was therefore not tempted to bolt the wine.

"Long day?" Tony said.

I nodded, and told him about it while we waited for our food. "I'm going to be crazy busy through Sunday, and I'm sorry, but I haven't done anything about Valentine's Day. I'm sure it's too late to get a reservation."

"Don't worry about Valentine's. I've got it covered," Tony said.

"Bless you," I said, smiling at him. "I'll probably be working until seven or so."

"No problem. I figured you would." He refilled my wineglass.

A plate of crab cakes hit the table along with a basket of warm bread. We shared them and I began to relax. I'd been hungry, I realized. It had been a long time since lunch.

"Guess that interview you did brought you some business," Tony said.

"I did two more today."

"Like you're not busy enough?"

"Gina thought it would be good to talk to more than just one TV station, so as not to look like I'm favoring the one."

Tony shrugged. "Okay."

Our entrees arrived: steak *frites* for Tony, seafood *vol au vent* for me. A white wine would probably have been better with that, but I didn't care. The red was comforting, like a warm hug.

"How did the bullet hunt go?" Tony asked.

"Oh, I didn't tell you! We found something—well, Phillips did—in the wall next to the fireplace. He thinks it's a ball."

"He didn't get it out?"

"It'll make a hole in the wall. We'll have to do it on a weekend. Not this weekend."

"Right."

I ate a melt-in-your mouth scallop and sighed. "Thank you, Tony. This is wonderful."

"I figured you're not going to have time to make dinner for the next few days, so I made us reservations. Eight o'clock every night."

"Bless you! I'm amazed you found any for Friday and Saturday."

He grinned. "It took some work. It's not big fancy places—those are all booked solid."

"That's fine with me. Food that I don't have to cook is all I want."

"You got it, babe."

"You're so good to me."

He held my gaze, smiling softly, then ate a fry. They looked good, I realized as I watched him chew it.

"Want one?" he offered.

"Yes."

He fed it to me across the table. Salty and crisp. I nipped the tip of his finger and he waggled it at me.

We finished our entrees and shared a chocolate mousse, then went back to the townhome. I had meant to pack an overnight bag, but I'd forgotten. Just as well—I'd have to get up early, so it was best if I slept at the tearoom.

"Hot tub?" Tony said as I parked at the curb.

"God, yes," I said, "But I can't stay. I have to get up early."

"You'll sleep better if you soak first."

He left me undressing in the still-empty master bedroom while he fetched a couple of towels. I put my clothes on a shelf in the walk-in closet and went outside, gasping at the cold night air.

Must bring a robe over here, I thought as I pulled the cover off of the tub. Shivering, I climbed in and turned on the jets.

Bliss. I sank to my chin in the hot water and closed my eyes. The jets roared and the water burbled around my ears. Tony joined me and handed me an Old Fashioned glass.

"What's this?"

"Whiskey."

I took a cautious sip. Whiskey is not my favorite beverage, but this was smooth as silk, and the single ice cube in the glass brought out a touch of sweetness. "Ohhh. That's really good!"

"Owen brought it over when he showed me how to do the tub. Housewarming gift."

"Mmm. Have to write him a thank-you note."

I sipped again, then set the glass down in one of the tub's built-in cup holders. Tony moved next to me and slid an arm around my waist.

"I was kind of surprised to see Zeke," I said. "I expected him to ignore my request."

"He's stalled on the case, and I told him you might be able to help."

"He did ask if I had thought of anything else. I'm afraid I wasn't much help, though."

"Said you gave him a lead on the jewelry place."

"Yes. Did he learn anything interesting there?"

"Haven't heard back from him."

I sighed and took another sip of whiskey. "There are so many possibilities. I do think it was a Goth, but not Kris."

"He's starting to agree with you on that." Tony drank some whiskey and leaned his head back, looking up at the sky. "The M.E.'s report came in. Couple of interesting details."

"Oh?"

"There were rope burns on her wrists."

"So she struggled."

"Yeah, but some of them were older. She'd been tied up before."

I frowned. "Kinky sex?"

"If she was seeing someone, no one's talking about it."

I thought fleetingly of Dale. He might know. Or…could Dale have been dating Margo? But he'd been out of town the night of the hanging.

"And the other thing was the cuts," Tony said. "You know, the kris cut into her chest?"

"Yes," I said, in case he couldn't see me nod.

"There were markings on the edges of the skin. The killer drew the design on her before cutting it."

"With a pen?"

"Highlighter, looks like."

"I guess they wanted to get it right."

"Yeah." Tony sipped his whiskey. "But not exactly a moment of passion. More like cold calculation."

"They wanted to frame Kris."

I could see Tony nod in the darkness. "That's what tipped the scales for Zeke. He thinks you're right that it was a frame job. But he's no closer to finding the killer."

"Well, I hope the jewelry shop yields something. Thanks for telling Zeke to listen to me."

"You look at things differently," Tony said. "That's useful. You notice stuff I don't, and you think of motivations that don't occur to me. You just see people differently."

"True. We have different perspectives."

The whiskey was making its effect known. Might be better if I didn't finish it. I closed my eyes, and Tony pulled me into a hug.

"Um," I said as he rubbed my shoulder blade.

Gently, he turned me to face the side of the tub and started kneading my shoulders. I moaned.

"You need a massage," he said.

"Yeah, but I'm sure 10k Waves is booked solid."

"And all the other spas in town. I tried."

"Aww, thank you! We'll go in a week or two."

The shoulder rub led to—well, more of a full-body-contact massage. I let go of concerns about time and just enjoyed it. Tony moved slowly, sensually, and most effectively, despite the challenge of being in the water. Somewhere along the way the jets timed out and shut off.

We lay still. I became aware of a cool breeze, and Tony's weight on my back. I raised my head and he moved away, releasing me. Turning around, I wrapped my arms around him and kissed him.

"Thank you," I murmured in his ear. "And I'd better go."

He hugged me, kissing me long and slow. "More tomorrow night."

"Ah—uh—yeah."

Tony got out first and fetched the towels, wrapping me in one as I stood up. We set aside the glasses and covered the tub, then hurried inside. The cold air had cleared my head a bit.

"You've got some left," Tony said, offering me my whiskey glass.

I shook my head. "Better not. I need to drive home."

He nodded and downed the whiskey himself. I got dressed, wishing there was a fire in the kiva fireplace in the bedroom. That would be so nice, on chilly evenings. I'd have to bring some firewood over.

"Meet here again for dinner tomorrow?" I asked, rubbing the damp bits of my hair with the towel.

"Uh-huh."

"Okay."

He came with me to the door. A final hug and whiskey-flavored smooch, then I walked down the path though I was sorely tempted to stay.

Two more days. Sunday night I'd stay. I'd pack a bag, and maybe bring some firewood. And the card for Tony.

Since I was tired and had drunk whiskey I drove home slowly, erring on the side of caution. Arriving without incident, I trudged upstairs to be greeted by a plaintive mew.

"Oh, honey, I'm sorry! I forgot to feed you!"

I rescued Minuit from the playpen and cuddled her as I crossed to the suite. She purred like thunder in my ear. After feeding her and cleaning up the litter boxes, I took a quick shower and collapsed into bed.

I dreamed of cream tea hell. An endless stream of customers, teacups in hand, shuffled through the butler's pantry to collect their rations of tea and scones. They then sat anywhere they could to consume them: in the hall, on the stairs, in my office and all over the tearoom, even in the kitchen, where Hanh glowered at me as she worked around customers perched on the counters drinking tea. The Bird Woman kept getting back in line, and when I finally called her on it, she showed me the memorial tree, every branch of which was full of women drinking tea and eating scones that she had given them.

The alarm on my phone rescued me. Clawing my way to consciousness, I became aware that I was hung over. Must have been the whiskey. And the wine. And the sherry.

Okay, I wouldn't do that again.

I dragged myself into the shower, fed the cat, put on the kettle and ate a piece of toast. Drank a glass of water while the tea was brewing, and felt mostly human by the time the aroma of hot chocolate cake drifted up the stairwell.

Sachertortes. Mmmm.

I'd ask Julio to save out two for me for Sunday. That and the card would be my Valentine's gift to Tony. Best I could do.

Friday went a lot like Thursday had, except without interviews. When I needed a break from the cream tea cycle, I swapped with Iz and bagged purchases in the gift shop, with occasional runs upstairs to my office to get more stock and check messages. Kris called around town and dashed out after our pizza lunch break to pick up a couple of cases of merchandise bags she had located: bright purple instead of lavender, but they would do. The phone lines were swamped most of the day with calls that resulted from the two interviews. Half of Santa Fe now wanted to celebrate Valentine's Day at the tearoom, and despite being told we were booked, about a third of them made reservations anyway, for later in the month. Kris handled the chaos like a rock—no moodiness. Zeke must have stopped hassling her.

Mid-afternoon, Gina came by, breezing into the gift shop in a snappy pink and orange tailored dress. "Hi, Ellen," she said as I loaded a pastry box with macarons. "I brought you a copy of the paper."

"Thanks," I said, handing the box to Nat, who gave it to the waiting customer. The gift shop was fairly quiet as we were in the lull between seatings, when most of the customers were busy with their afternoon tea.

"Mind if I disappear for a few minutes?" I asked Nat.

"No," she said. "Now's a good time."

I grabbed two macarons out of the case and took Gina up to my office for a quick cuppa. Kris had made a fresh pot of puerh. We settled in at my desk, and while I dutifully recorded the macarons on my inventory withdrawals list, Gina laid the newspaper in front of me, folded back on page five to display the article. It was fairly short, with just one photo: me by the tree with a black blob over my head (the giant bow).

"Did you see the TV interview?" Gina asked, stirring sugar into her tea.

"No, I was still working at six."

"They ran it at ten," Gina said.

"At ten I was...out with Tony."

"Well, I recorded it if you want to see. It was only a couple minutes—not as good as the one Algodones did."

"Did they include the comment about Gabriel's party not being satanic?"

"They did."

"Good. That's all I wanted. Thanks for setting those up for me."

"You're welcome," Gina said, and bit into her macaron.

To my relief, she didn't suggest doing more interviews. Instead she took a folded piece of paper out of her purse and handed it to me.

"Here are some potential wedding venues. I emailed it, too, so you can just hit the links if you want."

I took the page and glanced over it. "Thanks, Gina. You didn't have to do that."

"Well, you really need to make a decision on this. It's going to affect a lot of the planning."

"I will, when I have a brain again. Next week."

She nodded and sipped her tea. I ate my macaron, grateful for the sugar hit. I'd only had one slice of pizza, wanting to make sure there was enough for all the staff, and I was getting peckish.

I glanced through my messages and found a note from Kris: Andre and Claudia had both graciously agreed to help over the weekend. That was a relief, as was the response of the servers when I'd talked to them earlier—all of them were happy to be offered overtime. We'd get through it, and with Iz freed from helping in the gift shop, I probably wouldn't have to serve cream tea on Saturday.

When I saw Gina downstairs, I found buckets of roses in the hall by the back door: our extra floral order for Valentine's Day. As part of our Valentine's special package, each customer on Saturday and Sunday would receive a fresh rose along with their tea. I had planned to put ribbons on them, but there was no way. There was also no way I would be moving the buckets into the refrigerator before evening, not with the kitchen going full tilt. I stuck them out on the back *portal* and covered them with trash bags, hoping that the cold air would keep them fresh.

That done, I returned to the cream tea/gift shop rotation with Iz. She had come in at nine, so at five I told her she could leave whenever she liked. We were still busy, though, so she stayed another half hour, by which time things were slightly less hectic. Once again, I cut off the cream tea customers early and we managed to clear the tearoom of patrons by six-thirty. With Nat's help, I moved the roses into the walk-in refrigerator for the night. They had survived the afternoon outdoors beautifully.

For dinner Tony had made a reservation at Gabriel's, a New Mexican restaurant north of town, not far from the Santa Fe Opera. I hadn't been there in a few years, and the restaurant's name made me pause for a moment.

Poor Gabriel. Poor Margo. Poor Kris.

Despite being outside of Santa Fe, Gabriel's was packed. I had forgotten how good the guacamole—made fresh table-side—was. I had *one* beer with my enchiladas and *one* small glass of whiskey in the hot tub, and got back to the tearoom without incident.

Minuit, whom I'd remembered to feed, was sleeping in the exact center of my bed. I showered and put on pajamas, then carefully slid into bed so as not to disturb her.

The next thing I knew, it was morning. With eyes still closed, I could tell the light in the room was brighter. Something savory was baking downstairs, and a motorboat was humming somewhere nearby.

Motorboat?

I opened my eyes, to see a furry dome before me. Minuit was curled up on my pillow, purring. I watched the rise and fall of her fluffy fur for a minute, then rolled away, hoping to get up without waking her.

No such luck. She stood, arched her back, yawned, and then mewed.

I got up to feed her, trying to identify what was baking downstairs. Quiche, I decided. I popped a pair of frozen scones in the toaster oven before stepping into the shower.

I really must eat some salad soon. Or fruit. Something besides scones.

With Minuit and myself both fed and ready for the day, I went downstairs earlier than usual to bring roses out of the fridge before the kitchen got too crazy. Everyone was present and busy cooking: Julio, Hanh, Ramon, and Andre, his blond hair covered with a blindingly clean white cap that matched his equally clean chef's jacket. Wondering what the jacket would look like by the end of the day, I paused to thank him for coming in to help us.

"No problem," he said, smiling as he stirred a pot of raspberry curd at the stove. "I'm off weekends at the moment. I got a promotion, and I'm running the kitchen weeknights."

"Andre! That's fantastic! Congratulations!"

"Thanks!"

Note to self: make a reservation at Santacafé soon. On a weeknight.

Julio came over to peer critically into the curd pot. His chef's cap and matching pants today were purple, scattered with pink and white macarons.

"Where did you find those?" I said, admiring them.

He grinned. "Gwyneth found the fabric. She made them."

"Well, they're perfect! Brava for Gwyneth."

Going to the fridge, I brought out two buckets of roses and put them in the butler's pantry, where they were a little in the way but would be handy for the servers setting up the alcoves. Thinking wistfully of the ribbons, I promised myself I'd plan better the next time we did this.

I fired up the hot water urn and went through the parlors, checking on the fireplaces. They were swept clean, with fires laid ready to be lit. Kudos to my staff for setting them up last night.

The gift shop was a little less prepared. I restocked the Valentine's cards and the tea, put out the last of the heart mugs and the little porcelain heart boxes, then went upstairs to see if there were more in the storeroom. While I was there I grabbed a box of the purple bags, since the lavender ones were almost gone.

Dale met me at the bottom of the stairs and immediately took two of the three boxes I was carrying. "Gift shop?" he asked.

"Yes. Thanks."

His vest today was a lavender brocade with touches of pink, and his bow tie was a slightly deeper lavender. As always, he looked dapper and cool. He helped me stock displays and stash the excess in the cupboards.

"Dale," I said as I tucked a stack of purple bags into a shelf beneath the register, "Do you know if Margo was seeing anyone?"

He gave me a long look. "As far as I know, she wasn't. She was still...not over Gabriel."

"I see. Thanks."

"And if you're wondering, I never dated her. We were just friends."

I smiled. "It was good of you to be so kind to her. She must not have been an easy friend."

"Yeah, well. I know what it's like to be an oddball. And it's even harder to be an oddball in a community of oddballs."

"Did she...have enemies in the community?"

"That's too strong a word. She rubbed people the wrong way, though. Kind of a lot."

"But not enough to..."

"No."

I collected an empty kitchen tray from beneath the pastry case.

"And yet, the community is bringing all those flowers and candles."

"I think for some of them it's kind of an apology. They probably regret the way they treated her."

I sighed. "Speaking of flowers and candles, I'd better go tidy them."

"I'll help you. It's kind of my fault—I started it."

It was cold, but there was no wind and the sunlight slanted brightly through the bare tree branches. Dale and I circled the tree, picking up burned-out candles and faded bouquets. A lot more of the candles had gone out, now. As I lifted one, a small piece of paper fell away. I picked it up and unfolded it.

"Rock on, Margo," it said, and an inverted ankh was drawn beneath the words.

That rang a bell. I'd seen the inverted ankh before. I gazed at it, frowning as I tried to remember where.

What should I do with the note? I didn't want to just throw it away. Nor did putting it under someone else's candle feel right.

Well, there was the vase of flowers I had put out—which by the way were faded now and should be removed. I collected that vase and took it inside, then rinsed it and put a half-dozen of the Valentine's roses in it. I had ordered extra flowers, so we shouldn't run out. Returning to the tree, I set the vase back in its spot, then tucked the note beneath it.

Dale approached carrying the vase of lilies I had seen Gwyneth bring. They, too, were faded. "What should I do with this? It's too nice to throw away."

"The vase is Gwyneth's," I told him. "Let's clean it and we can return it to her."

"I'll do that."

I made one more pass around the tree, keeping an eye out for more notes. I spotted several beneath candles that were still lit but burning low. I'd keep an eye on them, and move the notes to the vase when the candles were out. Better mention it to Mick, too, when he came in.

Pausing to look up at the tree branches, I gazed at the big black bow, wondering where Margo was now. Was she looking for Gabriel? Had she found him, and made amends? He'd forgiven her, if one accepted the messages from the séance Kris had arranged as valid. Margo had been alive then, though.

What if Margo had gotten stuck, like Captain Dusenberry had? There had been no manifestations from her at the tearoom, for which I was grateful. I hoped she wasn't stuck, and that she had found peace.

Heading for the trash bin with a couple of faded bouquets, I saw an unfamiliar car coming up the driveway: a silver Mercedes. The driver was Claudia Pearson. I smiled and waved her to a parking place behind the kitchen, as the ones near the back door were already filled.

Chucking the dead flowers in the trash bin, I brushed off my hands and met Claudia on her way to the back door. "Good to see you, Claudia! Thank you so much for coming!"

She smiled. "I've been missing the tearoom anyway," she said. "It's been far too long since I've been here."

"Well, let's find a time to have tea later this month. My treat," I said as we went in.

Claudia removed her coat and hung it on a hook in the hall, revealing an elegant dress of dark rose. Her silver hair was swept up into a French twist, rather like Kris's the other day.

Other day? It felt like a month ago. Ay.

I led Claudia to the gift shop, where she exclaimed over the new arrangement. "This is so much more spacious!"

Nat came in a few minutes later as I was showing Claudia where things were in the shop. I let her take over, and stepped to the register to reserve an afternoon tea spot for me and Claudia. The coming week was pretty solidly booked. I nabbed a slot on Thursday at four in Dahlia (Violet was taken), decided to make it for three people instead of two, and wrote the time down on reservation cards for Claudia and Nat.

"This will be a little thank-you for your help this week," I said as I handed them the cards. "If that isn't a good time, Nat can adjust it."

Next I rang up a gift card for a free afternoon tea for Andre. When I took it to the kitchen, I saw that the raspberry curd was done and Andre was now decorating Sachertortes with exquisite tiny swirls of chocolate and the word "Sacher."

"That's gorgeous, Andre! We hadn't tried to write on them."

"Well, I can't make it as pretty as I'd like. It barely fits," he said, frowning a little at his work.

"It's perfect."

I gave him the gift card, asked Julio to reserve two of the Sachertortes for me for Sunday, changed my mind and requested a third Sachertorte, then went upstairs. Kris hadn't arrived yet, so I filled the samovar and made a pot of Keemun, then took a cup to my desk, trying to remember where I'd seen an inverted ankh.

Gabriel had worn a silver ankh necklace, I recalled, but it wasn't inverted. Where had I seen the inverted one? It had to be connected to one of the Goths. Maybe in a photo?

I brought up Owen's photos of the masquerade and started scrolling through them. There were so very many that I was soon overwhelmed. I had forgotten some of the wonderful costumes. Several of them featured ankhs—including a spectacular Goth Cleopatra costume, all in shades of silver and black—but none of the ankhs were inverted.

Hmm.

Continuing to scroll through, I came across a series of photos of Gabriel, and was struck anew by his gorgeous Sun King costume, and by his presence. Even in still photos, his poise and confidence came through. How tragic that his life had been cut short.

Had Gwyneth made the costume, I wondered? Surely Gabriel had designed it, but it must have taken months to complete, it was so elaborate. Maybe it had been begun when he and Gwyneth were still a couple. That would have been…before June?

Midsummer, I heard Margo's voice echo.

Memory swept back, of Tony asking Margo questions the night of the party, right after Gabriel's death. She was sitting in the downstairs hall of the tearoom, wearing her green costume, a beautiful medieval gown. Why had I not noticed that the hat was missing?

Midsummer was when Gabriel had broken up with Gwyneth, she'd said. And Gabriel had hooked up with Margo after that. They'd been together three months or so, and then Gabriel had dropped her for Kris.

For all his talent and charm, he'd been rather a cad in his romantic relationships.

So he'd broken up with Gwyneth four months before the party. Or—she'd broken it off, I remembered. Mad at him over a photo shoot for a painting, because she'd been sunburned. And yet Gabriel had done the painting anyway—it had been in the show on Canyon Road. Had Gwyneth made the Sun King costume anyway, too? Had their art superseded their personal disconnect?

She might have begun the Sun King costume before the breakup. I could believe that it had taken more than four months to make. It was professional quality—every bit as intricate as the work I'd seen in the Santa Fe Opera's costume shop.

I picked up my teacup, but it was empty. I set it back on the saucer.

Well, that was quite a rabbit hole to wander down, and I still hadn't figured out the ankh. I closed the photo folder and got another cup of tea, sipping it as I went through a batch of messages from the end of the previous day. Nothing remarkable. A couple more interview requests. I set them aside.

Footsteps came up the stairs—sounded like Kris. I got up to greet her.

"Morning," she said, heading for her desk. "Need to get Claudia and Andre to sign forms."

"Tea?" I offered.

"I'll get some in a bit."

I finished my cup while Kris printed out her forms, then accompanied her downstairs. Nat was showing Claudia how to operate the cash register. I fetched a tray of sweets from the kitchen and stocked the pastry case, by which time Rosa and Iz had arrived. They and Dale were setting up the alcoves with china for the first seating.

"We decided to save the roses and put them out just before the seating," Rosa told me in the pantry. "That okay?"

"Yes, that's great," I said. "Do you want help with that?"

She nodded. "Yes, please."

"I'll come back at ten-thirty," I said.

I was tempted to try putting ribbons on the roses, since I had a little time, but I knew that way lay madness. Even if I got it done for the first seating, I probably wouldn't be able to do it for the rest of the day. Instead I retreated to my desk and worked on catching up my messages. Kris had pulled the voicemail, and there was a sizable snowdrift of lavender slips in my in box. When I'd dealt with them, I had fifteen minutes to spare.

Ankh. Ankh. Still niggling at my memory.

Going back to my computer, I surfed on "ankh" and got a bunch of hits describing it as an ancient Egyptian symbol of life. Searching for inverted or upside-down ankhs yielded far fewer hits, and none authoritative. There seemed to be no clear, common meaning for that.

I noticed the folder of photos from the sugar skull party, so I opened it. Again, a lot of photos, but since I had taken them, there were not an overwhelming number. I scrolled through them, appreciating the sugar skulls anew. Gabriel's were gorgeous, of course, but Andre's were almost as good. Most of them were amateurish, but that was okay. They were folk art more than fine art.

Scrolling through, I suddenly stopped on a pair of skulls done all in black. The work was not high-quality, but it was the subject matter that had caught my attention. Lots of symbols, some I recognized, some I didn't. Many were crosses with elongated, pointed bases, and that rang a bell. But the one that had stopped me was a skull with an inverted ankh on the center of the forehead.

Other symbols flanked it. The whole skull was covered with them, rather chaotic in their arrangement. I wasn't sure who had decorated the skull, but the work was similar to the skull with the elongated crosses, and they were on a plate together, implying the same person had done them.

Closing my eyes, I tried to remember where I'd seen those pointed crosses. Two of them, silver, flashing in the light.

Earrings. Earrings that Margo had worn.

Opening my eyes, I looked at the skull photos. If Margo had made those skulls, then she had drawn the inverted ankh. And Gabriel had worn an ankh. By inverting it, had she been wishing him ill?

But his death had been accidental. Margo had regretted causing it, I was certain. Maybe she'd had dark thoughts about him, but she hadn't intentionally killed him.

So who had left the note with the inverted ankh?

Dale might know. If he didn't, I'd point the note out to Zeke and let him try to figure it out. Best I could do, I thought sadly as I saved a copy of the skull photo with the ankh, and closed the folder.

It was time to help put out the roses in the alcoves. I went downstairs and heard a happy chatter of voices from the gift shop, which had now opened. Shaking off the sadness of looking through the photos, I made myself smile as I collected roses for Dahlia and Violet.

From then on, the day was crazy busy. Claudia and Nat waited on an endless stream of shoppers, while I kept the displays and the pastry case stocked. Rosa and Dee handled the alcoves in the main parlor, Dale handled Dahlia and Violet, and I helped Iz with the cream tea customers. The table in the dining parlor was full from the time we opened, and I realized that might create a problem.

As I brought a tray of sweets to the gift shop to replenish the pastry case, I signaled to Nat that I wanted to talk to her. She turned the register over to Claudia and we stepped out into the hall.

"We have a party in the dining parlor at one-thirty, right?" I said.

"Yes," Nat said. "Mrs. Olavssen."

"Then we need to cut off the cream teas at noon."

"A whole hour for cream tea?"

"It takes time to clear and reset," I said. "And some of the customers like to linger. I'd rather have too much time than not enough."

"All right."

"Is Claudia okay on the register alone? Can you two take turns for lunch? We're having burritos delivered."

"She's a pro," Nat said. "We'll be fine."

I gobbled my own burrito at my desk, and hurried back downstairs to check on the dining parlor. Half the seats at the table were still occupied. At twelve-thirty I stood at the doorway and rang the little musical chimes we used to warn the alcoves that their tea time was coming to an end. I rang them again at twelve-forty-five, and smiled sweetly at the two remaining customers.

"Take them their ticket," I said to Iz as I returned the chimes to the pantry. Dee came in and took them out again to ring at the alcoves.

Iz nodded and turned to the register. "Did you get lunch?" I asked her.

"Yes. Thank you."

We left the pantry and went our separate ways. I scouted the front parlors. Our regulars knew the drill, and most of the alcoves were empty. Dale was clearing his two, and Rosa hers. Dee stood talking with the customers in Jonquil. I made a pass in the gift shop (which was *not* empty), restocking displays. Returning to the pantry, I collected roses, carefully drying the stems before taking them to the alcoves where the servers were now setting out fresh china and linens. I placed a rose by each teacup, then went back for more.

The buckets were nearly empty. I fished out the remaining roses, put the two buckets on the back *portal,* and ducked into the kitchen to bring out a full one. It was madness in there, with Mick now washing dishes and four chefs at work. I had to pick my way around them to the fridge.

Stashing the roses in the pantry, I took out enough for Mrs. Olavssen's party: twelve, the maximum the dining parlor could hold. Iz was still setting the table. I helped her, then placed the roses at the settings. There was one extra, and I left it at the head of the table, where the Bird Woman liked to sit. It was twenty-five after by the time the room was ready.

Whew.

I took a deep breath, then went forward to the gift shop. The hall by the front door was crowded with chattering women, and I stopped a short distance away, arrested by the vision of the Bird Woman in a flesh-colored unitard, swathed in white sashes, with a wig of golden curls and a large pair of white wings.

13

SHE'D OUTDONE HERSELF. In addition to the costume, the Bird Woman carried a small short bow painted red, and had a quiver of heart-tipped arrows slung at her back.

Right. Cupid. Okay.

I donned a smile and went forward to greet her. "Good afternoon."

"Hiya, Ellen!" The Bird Woman produced a heart-shaped lollipop from beneath one of the sashes and presented it to me with a flourish. "Happy Valentine's Day, almost!"

"Happy Valentine's," I said, accepting the candy with a slight bow like one of Owen's. "Are all your guests here? Shall I take you to your table?"

"Sure! Come on, everyone. Ellen here's the boss of this place," she added as I started down the hall.

I cringed a little. So many more appropriate words: owner, proprietor, even hostess.

Standing by the dining parlor door, I watched the women file in after the Bird Woman. Some of them cast shy glances at me. Others looked at the table in wonder as they gathered around it. They were from Esperanza, of course: the shelter of which the Bird Woman was a patron.

She had brought women from there to tea at Christmas time, and was doing so again at Valentine's. These women were alone: homeless or refugees from homes that were dangerous to them. She was making sure they knew that they, too, deserved love on this lovers' holiday.

The Bird Woman leaned her bow in a corner and tried to remove her quiver, but the wings were inhibiting her. I edged past the guests to help her. Fortunately, there was a clip on the strap, so I unfastened it and set the quiver in the corner with her bow, then discreetly straightened her cherubic wig.

"Thanks, Ellen!" she said, grinning up at me from beneath the curls. "You're a champ!"

I smiled back. "Isabel will be your server today," I said to the guests, indicating Iz, who stood waiting in the doorway with a large teapot. I was glad it was her, as several of the women in the party were also Puebloans. Esperanza served not only Santa Fe, but the northern Pueblos as well.

"Enjoy your tea, everyone!" I added, and slipped out as they took their seats and Iz began pouring.

A quick stop in the butler's pantry to make sure more tea was brewing, then I got out of the servers' way and went upstairs. Kris was on the phone, and Minuit was attacking the ball in the ring toy, rattling it ceaselessly. I poured myself a cup of tea, added milk and sugar as a reward for surviving the morning, and sat on the chaise longue to drink it.

Two seatings down, one to go. We'd make it, but the cream tea was becoming a problem. It needed rethinking.

With no time constraint, people tended to linger, and that was not cost-effective for an inexpensive cup of tea and a scone. Yet since it was open seating, limiting the time wasn't easy as the customers arrived at different times.

Sipping my tea, I mused about possible solutions. We could set a little hourglass by each place, to remind the customers that they'd have to give up their seats. Impractical, I decided. The servers might forget to start them, and the customers might cheat and invert them to get more time. Or assume they were gifts and take them home.

Would we have to make cream tea by reservation? I liked having an option for walk-in customers, but our seating was so limited. Maybe I'd wait a week and see if it was less crowded after the holiday.

More seating would help. Maybe I really should consider expanding the tearoom. Or, as an intermediate step, we could add a tent in the garden, where we'd had one for Nat's wedding, which was essentially the same area Kris had suggested for the expansion. It was too cold for outdoor seating now, but by April, when we'd be celebrating our first anniversary, the weather should be mild enough.

That raised another question, though. If we added more seating, could the kitchen handle it? We were pretty well maxed out today, with four chefs. Julio had worked every day this week. I didn't want him to burn out. Same for Hanh. If Ramon wasn't interested in a full-time job, we definitely needed another chef, at least a part-timer, and that was with our current capacity, never mind expanding.

These were good problems to have, I admitted, but they still had to be addressed. I was grateful for the tearoom's success, and now I had to manage it.

I drank the last of my tea and put the cup on my credenza before going to my desk. Opening a word processing file, I made a sign, "No Cream Tea Today", and printed it on some paper with a pretty floral border. This I attached to a piece of card stock, then took it downstairs, where I posted it in one of the lights surrounding the front door. There it would stay through tomorrow. Today was crazy enough that we didn't need to be serving any more cream tea. We had already planned on no cream tea on Valentine's Day, since every seat was booked for afternoon tea, but posting the sign would, I hoped, keep us from having to field walk-ins.

Stepping into the gift shop with the intention of notifying Nat of this change, I saw that she wouldn't have time to talk. There was a line of shoppers six deep waiting to check out. Claudia was bagging purchases as Nat rang them up.

The pastry case was empty, so I grabbed the tray and took it to the kitchen. Chaos there as well, with everyone still working and a wild blend of aromas: *bastilla*, scones, chocolate cake, sauteing onions, and asparagus. Yow.

It was actually warm in there, and I saw that the windows were open. Julio was just taking a tray of *bastilla* out of the oven. I waited until he had put it in the rack to cool, then joined him.

"What can I take to the gift shop?"

"No macacons, sorry," he said. "Cookies and scones."

"Okay. Are we on track for tomorrow?"

"Yeah." He shot an appraising look around the kitchen, then nodded toward the back *portal*. I followed him out there, appreciating the cold air.

"I'm going to ask them to stay an extra hour so we can get caught up for tomorrow," Julio said.

"Okay. What can I do to help?"

He sighed. "Nothing, really. There isn't room for another person to work."

"I cut off cream tea for the rest of the day."

"Thanks. That will help. We've gone through all the frozen scones."

"There's no reservation for the dining parlor in the last seating, so you can use it as work space if you need to."

He nodded. "Great. Thanks."

"I want you to be able to take Monday off."

He gazed toward the driveway, thinking. "Maybe a half day. I'll need to make scones for the week. We'll see how tomorrow goes."

"Well, give the others Monday off for sure. I'll help you if you need me."

He gave me a weary smile. "Thanks, Ellen."

"We'll make it."

"Oh, yeah. We will."

We returned to the kitchen and I loaded my tray with cookies and scones. The gift shop was still busy. I put the bakery items in the pastry case, then restocked merchandise. By the time I'd attended to all the displays, the pastry case was empty again.

Back to the kitchen. I heard a roar of laughter from the dining parlor, and glanced in. The Bird Woman was standing at her place, telling a story. Seemed innocuous, and I didn't have time to listen so I fetched more goodies for the gift shop instead.

This continued for the rest of the day. I missed saying goodbye to the Bird Woman, being occupied with extracting a bucket of roses from the fridge for the last seating. I saw the tail end of her party going out the front door as I returned to the gift shop, and paused to look out the lights. Cupid's wings and golden curls were teased by a rising breeze at the head of the small parade. They all climbed into a waiting van and drove away.

The final seating was less chaotic, but the gift shop was still getting walk-ins, and I was busy helping there for the rest of the afternoon. Iz stopped me in the butler's pantry as I was on the way to the kitchen for more cookies and scones.

"Is it okay if I go home?" she said wearily. "I saw the sign you put up."

"Yes. Thank you, Iz. Was Mrs. Olavssen's group well-behaved?"

She smiled. "Yes, and she gave me a huge tip."

"Good. Go home and get some rest."

At six o'clock sharp I put the "Closed" sign in the front window and locked the door to stave off any more shoppers. This necessitated my staying nearby in order to let customers out, and I received many compliments from them on the menu, which I saved up to share with Julio. The line in the gift shop dissipated, and Nat stepped out for a minute to talk to me.

"Thanks for cutting off the cream tea," she said. "That saved us having to show people to the dining parlor."

"Good. Sorry I didn't warn you about it."

"We figured it out." She smiled and went back in to relieve Claudia from the register, while I made a final sweets run to the kitchen. All that was left were rose almond cookies. I put two dozen on the tray and called it good. That should be enough for the departing customers. The day was nearly over.

I locked the door behind the last customer at six-forty-two. Sighing deeply, I closed my eyes for a moment.

We made it.

Tomorrow would be easier, though I was a little concerned about the gift shop. Going in, I saw Claudia and Nat restocking the displays. They both looked a bit tired, but otherwise collected. I marveled at Claudia's appearance, which was as neat and elegant as it had been when she arrived.

"Claudia, thanks so much! We wouldn't have survived without you."

She chuckled as she stuffed valentines into the card rack. "Took me back to my job in a souvenir shop, decades ago."

"Are you wrung out?"

"Nothing a hot shower won't fix."

"All right. See you tomorrow, and thanks again."

Nat paused for a hug. "I think we need to have a management meeting. Yesterday's impromptu one was good, but…."

"Yes, you're right. We'll plan one for later this week."

I checked the pastry case. Three cookies remained. I gave one each to Claudia and Nat, and munched the third as I picked up the tray and made a final round through the parlors. The servers had cleared the tables and were leaving for the day. In the dining parlor, Andre was decorating Sachertortes. Someone had moved the centerpiece to the sideboard and swapped out the tablecloth for the working one for him.

I stepped into the kitchen. "All clear. Last customers are out."

Julio responded by turning on his boom box, sending a blast of salsa music through the kitchen. Everyone started bopping. At the dish-washing station, Mick removed his earbuds and began dancing a samba. I set the tray in the to-be-washed stack and went upstairs.

Kris was working on the deposit. I sat in her guest chair and waited until she was ready to talk.

"Done," she said after a minute. "I think this may be our biggest day ever."

"Wow."

"The cream tea is really profitable."

"Mm. But it's also a problem. We'll talk about it later in the week. I'm going to call a management meeting. Is there a slow time?"

"Not during business hours. We're booked solid all this week and into next. Lot of calls for reservations today."

"Okay. Maybe it can be a dinner meeting. You, me, Julio, and Nat."

"Want me to set it up? I can check with everyone and find the best night."

"Please. Maybe Wednesday or Thursday? See if Santacafé can take us."

"Wow, fancy!"

"I want to thank you all for getting us through this craziness."

She smiled wearily. "It's satisfying."

She left, and I made a quick pass through my messages, then fed the kitten and changed into more comfortable clothes. I was done being Miss Manners for today. One last check on the kitchen, where Julio, Hanh, and Mick were finishing up. The boom box was playing a sultry bolero. I collected the rose bucket from the pantry, with a dozen or so roses left, and put it in the fridge for the night.

"Ramon gone home?" I asked Julio.

"Yeah, and Andre. We're about done for tonight."

"Caught up enough for tomorrow?"

"I think so."

"Okay. Have a good night."

Heading out to my car, I remembered the tree memorial. I had not even looked at it since the morning, and Mick had been too busy, I was sure. I hurried around to the south side of the house.

It was wind-blown, and more candles had gone out, but it didn't look too bad. There weren't a lot of new flowers. I'd deal with it in the morning; no sense having to tidy it twice.

Tony was waiting on the front porch when I pulled up at the townhome. "We're late," he said, getting into the passenger seat.

"Sorry. Crazy day."

"It's okay."

He directed me to drive to the south side of town, to a restaurant I'd never been to: Piccolino. I was dubious of its appearance: the building was a former fast-food chain restaurant, a recognizable design. The drive-up window was still in use, with a line of cars waiting. The parking lot was nearly full, which I took as a good sign.

As we went in, I felt like a time-traveler. The floor was linoleum tile, and the dining room was filled with café tables covered in black and white checkerboard cloths. The place smelled wonderful. It was a good thing Tony had made a reservation, as there was a waiting room full of hopefuls. We were seated after a short wait and presented with menus, a wine list, and fresh baked bread.

The menu was Italian and extensive. Old-fashioned fare, in a good way. I ordered fettuccine Alfredo, and Tony went for spaghetti and meatballs. Looking at the wine list, I saw some nice selections, but decided just a glass of house red was probably wise.

As an attempt at keeping myself from gobbling the bread, I told Tony about my day. He listened sympathetically and without comment.

"How about you?" I asked, taking the smallest piece of bread from the basket.

"Worked on moving. Just some big furniture left—I want to put my chair and the coffee table in the den. And my dresser for the bedroom."

"Okay. Maybe Manny can help."

"I have a buddy who's got a truck. Going to do it tomorrow."

"Ah. Good."

"Then I need to drop off the bed at Angela's. Know anyone who needs a couch? I don't think you'll like mine for the living room."

He was right. His couch had seen better days.

"I can ask my staff."

"As long as they get it before the end of the month."

"Okay. I'll let you know if I get a taker."

Our dinners arrived and we dug in. I was hungrier than I'd realized, and felt a pang of guilt for not ordering a salad, but the carb-fest was wonderful and the portion was huge. I wound up getting a box for my leftovers. The desserts looked tempting, but I had no room.

Back at the townhome, Tony poured whiskey while I stashed my leftovers in the fridge. It was no longer empty; Tony had bought some groceries. A loaf of bread, butter, jam. Small things, but they made the kitchen feel less barren. It was beginning to feel like home.

There were boxes stacked in the master bedroom. We climbed into the hot tub and I sighed with relief.

"One more day," Tony said.

"We're booked all this week, but it won't be quite as crazy. I hope."

He raised his glass. "Here's to success."

I sipped. Despite my full stomach, the whiskey went to my head pretty quickly. I was tired. Tony picked up on it, and after a cuddle and some necking he took away my whiskey glass.

"Time for you to go sleep," he said.

"You sure?"

He nodded. "We'll take our time tomorrow. Go rest up," he added with a grin.

"All right."

I hadn't asked where we were dining for Valentine's. I was willing to be surprised. His dinner choices this week had all been good and interesting. He saw me off with a long kiss at the front door, and watched me walk to my car.

At the tearoom I went through the parlors once more, checking on the fireplaces. They'd been warm when we closed; now they were cool enough that I could sweep out the coals, so I did, then I trudged up the stairs and put myself and Minuit to bed.

For whatever reason—the day, the whiskey—I had trouble getting to sleep despite being exhausted. I didn't want to be groggy in the morning, so I didn't resort to a sleeping pill, but I took a melatonin tablet to help me relax. After going through a long mental list of things I ought to do, I finally drifted to sleep.

I was working on the Margo memorial late at night, carrying buckets of fresh roses out to the tree and collecting dead bouquets to throw away. I had to make a circle of rose buckets all the way around the tree. The Bird Woman, in her Cupid costume, was dancing a samba in the middle of the circle, and Margo in her green dress was waltzing around the outside with Mr. Quentin in his Civil War uniform.

When I had finished the circle of roses, I climbed into the tree to hang giant black bows on every branch. Phillips stood below, handing the bows up to me on the end of his metal detector. As I clambered around in the tree, I kept finding empty whiskey glasses tucked into the crooks of the branches, and I put them on the flat disc of Phillips's metal detector as he held it up. He lowered each glass carefully until Dee could reach it, and gave her a kiss after she collected each one.

When every tree branch had a bow on it, I climbed down. As Margo waltzed past, I realized her partner wasn't Mr. Quentin: it was a man I didn't recognize, with dark hair and a neat mustache, wearing old-style spectacles. As the waltz concluded, he bowed to Margo and led her to the tree, where a door opened in the trunk and she stepped inside.

The strange man in uniform turned to face me, then pointed up at the tree branch above him. Between two black bows a black rope hung down, with three strands of jet beads dangling at the end, glinting a little in the moonlight as they were stirred by a breeze.

The man in uniform looked at me expectantly.

I woke up, then sat up, remembering the stranger's face.

"Captain?"

Shadows moved on my wall: tree branches stirring in the moonlight. I'd forgotten to close the curtains. Wide awake now, I got up and closed them. Minuit, sleeping at the foot of the bed, did not stir.

Had that really been Captain Dusenberry? I had never seen a picture of him, I realized.

Feeling an urge to go downstairs and look at the tree, I pulled on some jeans and a sweater, thinking about the captain. Maybe Sonja at the Archives could find me a photo of him. Or maybe...could Mr. Hidalgo have one? If he had a photo of Maria's music club, perhaps. I'd ask.

Chances of that weren't good. The Hidalgos had disapproved of the captain, and would probably have destroyed any photos that included him, unless Maria managed to hide one. Maybe I should check the other volumes of her journal. It was a long shot: photography back then was expensive and awkward—the subjects had to remain still for a long time during the exposure. Still, it wouldn't hurt to ask.

A better chance would be if there were any military photos that included the captain. I'd get in touch with Sonja...some time.

So much to do. I put on a coat, tiptoed downstairs, and let myself out the front door, pausing on the *portal* to listen to the quiet of the city. Distant machinery hums, an occasional car driving past down on Palace Avenue, the breeze sighing around bare branches. It was very late, or rather very early. A silent cold had fallen, steeping on the dry grass. The light from the crescent moon was feeble, just enough to cast dim shadows.

I rested a hand on the sleeping trunk of a wisteria vine. This house had been my home for over a year. That was changing now; I wouldn't be sleeping here, though I'd be here during the day. I would miss it, I realized. I loved the old house at night, when I was alone, with the occasional visit from Captain Dusenberry.

Remembering the dream, I walked over to the tree and looked up at Margo's branch. Just the one black bow, fluttering a little. What had the captain been trying to tell me?

The jet beads had been suspended by a rope tied to the branch, just as they had when Gina and I had found Margo.

I looked at the tree, reluctantly imagining how I would go about hanging someone in it. It was climbable—there was a lower branch just within my reach if I jumped a few inches—so I could take a rope up there and secure it while my victim lay on the ground beneath, bound and gagged, maybe. She'd have to be gagged to prevent her from screaming and attracting attention. Or maybe drugged.

How would I then get her up in the tree? I'd have to do some kind of pulley thing with the rope. But it would be hard, pulling the weight of another person. And the rope had been tied to the branch as far as I could tell.

Tied to the branch. Not looped over it like a pulley and tied to the tree trunk.

That meant that the killer *had* to climb the tree and get Margo up there as well. Phillips had mentioned that he'd found no evidence of a ladder except the one the police had borrowed from me. It was unlikely that the killer had also borrowed my ladder. For one thing, the police would have had to place it in exactly the same spot or it would have left marks elsewhere on the lawn.

Although—the cops had walked around a bit, and there had been a stretcher. That could have obscured any marks.

Two people *might* have been able to do it without a ladder, if one climbed the tree to tie the rope and the other lifted Margo (not struggling, probably unconscious) up to have the beads looped around her neck. That person would have to be very tall and very strong, though. And the drop from their releasing Margo might not have broken her neck, whereas if she had dropped from up on the branch, the gravitational force would have been stronger. Maybe the tree-climber had pulled her up? But that would have left evidence on her clothes, probably.

Remembering the night we found her, I recalled that her feet had been maybe three or four feet above the ground. Made the two-person scenario unlikely.

I frowned. The simplest answer was usually the solution. I couldn't think of a simple way for the killer or killers to get Margo up onto the tree branch. It would have been troublesome, and taken time that meant risk of discovery.

The simplest answer, then, was that Margo had climbed up herself.

frowned, gazing up at the branch. Margo couldn't have hanged herself. Her hands had been tied behind her back. And there was the kris cut into her chest.

Traced over the highlighter Tony had mentioned. And come to think of it, the kris had been carefully placed above Margo's large raven tattoo, not intruding on it. Who would have cared about that but Margo? God, had she cut it *herself*?

Or had she had an accomplice? Someone to help her kill herself?

I thought of Dale, but felt sure he would not have been willing to help Margo commit suicide. He would have tried everything to persuade her against it.

Gazing at the black bow, I remembered the two Goths putting it there and telling me Margo had been a cheerleader. So unlikely. She'd been accepted because she could do the splits.

Which meant she had flexible joints.

Had she climbed the tree, attached the rope, cut her chest, tied her own hands, and then slid her legs through her arms, up on the tree branch?

And jumped?

A cold rush swept through me. That might just be it.

Tony had mentioned she had rope burns. Older rope burns. She had practiced.

Damn it, Margo! *Why?*

Because she knew she was going to jail. And she'd rather die.

That I could believe, given her emotional state. It was telling that she'd chosen to die here, at the location of Gabriel's All Hallows Eve party. It was here that she had argued with him, and fled from him. He'd followed her to Hidalgo Plaza, where the accident had taken place. But it had all begun here.

And since she'd decided to die, why not frame Kris, who had taken Gabriel away from her? In her wounded brokenness, Margo might even have blamed Kris for Gabriel's death.

It all fit.

I wanted to tell Tony my thoughts, but calling him at this hour would be pretty inexcusable. It wasn't as though time was of the essence. No danger of Margo's killer escaping.

My gaze dropped to the candles and flowers of the memorial. Windblown again. Many candles gone out. Messy. Margo's life had also been messy, at least the last few months of it. I was sorry I'd never known her in her happier days.

My eye caught on the fresh roses I'd put in my vase. Going over to it, I took the little note from beneath it and unfolded it.

Rock on, Margo.

The ankh was a symbol of life. Inverting it implied the opposite: death. Maybe there was no hidden meaning there. Maybe it was just a farewell.

Sighing, I put the note back under the vase. When the sun came up I'd come out and clean up the dead candles and flowers, and if there were any other notes I'd collect them. Right now, though, I was cold. Time to go in. I locked the door behind me, went upstairs, made myself a cup of hot milk, drank it, and went back to bed.

Any subsequent dreams I had did not follow me into the morning. I drifted awake and felt Minuit curled against me, so I tried to slide away without disturbing her, but she instantly woke and bounced away.

The house was silent. No baking smells taunting me yet. I made myself a bowl of oatmeal and a pot of tea. I was tempted to call Tony, but he wasn't a morning person. I decided to let him sleep in on his Sunday.

After dressing and setting Minuit up for the day, I took out the valentine card I'd set aside for Tony. I hadn't written in it yet. I got out my fountain pen and sat at my café table, trying to decide what to say. So much had happened in the months since we'd met. So much more lay before us. We were on the threshold of a new life together. How to condense all my feelings about that into one sentence?

To Tony -

With all my love on our first Valentine's Day together.

Ellen

Not Shakespeare, but it would have to do. I put the card in its envelope, wrote Tony's name on it, and sealed it with a kiss. Leaving it on the table, I packed an overnight bag with my toiletries and a change of clothes, then went downstairs to see if Julio had remembered to save me the Sachertortes.

The kitchen was empty and clean, with the soft light of pre-dawn coming in the east windows. In the fridge I found a small pastry box with my name on it. Peeking inside, I saw three gleaming rounds of chocolate, with Andre's artwork on top.

While I was in the fridge, I moved a bucket of roses to the

butler's pantry, then pulled the prettiest rose out for Tony and took it upstairs. I cut its stem and put it in a bud vase. The pastry box got stashed in my mini fridge.

Ready for tonight. Good.

A rattling sound came from my office as I stepped out into the hall: Minuit attacking her ring toy. I went across to check that she had everything she needed and noticed a giant heap of message slips in my in box. I'd forgotten to check them at the end of the previous day. Before addressing them, though, I went through Kris's office to the storage room and looked through our stock of greeting cards. I was *not* looking for a Valentine this time. I found a predominantly purple, Art Deco card and liberated it, taking it to my desk where I got out my pen.

Happy Birthday, Kris

and many happy birthdays to come.

Love, Ellen

A modern variant of "many happy returns of the day," which no one but me and Miss Manners used any more. Putting the card in the envelope, I wrote her name on the front and laid it on her desk, then fetched one of the Sachertortes from my fridge and put it on a small plate. A quick scrounge through the drawers in my kitchenette produced some birthday candles. I stuck one in the center of the Sachertorte, careful not to destroy Andre's handiwork, and set the plate and a dessert fork on Kris's desk with the card.

Chocolate for breakfast. Not a bad birthday gift.

I went through my messages, pulling out a couple that needed return phone calls. Too early for that still—I'd do it later. By the time

I'd finished, the smell of rose almond cookies was beginning to waft up the stairwell.

Hanh was at work in the kitchen. I exchanged a brief greeting with her, then put on my coat and went outside to deal with the memorial.

Dale had gotten to it before me. He met me with an armful of empty candle glasses, so I opened the trash bin for him.

"Thanks," he said.

"More to do?"

"Just a little."

I walked with him back to the tree. The pile of bouquets was tidy again, and significantly smaller. The candles that were still burning had been gathered around them, and my vase was where I'd left it. Dale picked it up to move it closer to the tree, and the little note fluttered away. I caught it and picked it up.

"There were a bunch of those," Dale said. "I wasn't sure what to do with them." He reached into his coat pocket and produced a handful of scraps of paper.

"They're like prayers," I said, holding out my hands for them. "They should be burned."

"Oh. Okay." He put them in my hands and gestured to the remaining candles. "There are more."

"We'll wait until the candles go out."

He nodded, pausing to look over the memorial. It had been a week now. The community was moving on. He pulled two more tired bouquets out of the pile. I collected a couple more dead candles.

"Dale, did Margo ever mention suicide to you?"

He nodded. "I talked her down a couple of times." Looking up at the tree branch, he sighed. "I wondered...but I don't know how...."

"I have a theory. I'll tell you about it later. Let's go in, it's cold."

We got rid of the trash and walked to the back door. Julio had just arrived and he held it open for us. We traded good mornings, then I stepped into the dining parlor. The lace cloth and flowers were back on the table. Sunrise beamed through the French doors and gleamed on the chandelier.

"Dale, would you lay a fire?"

He did so, and lit it. When the kindling had taken, I began feeding the notes to it one by one.

Farewell, Margo. Rest in peace.

The note with the ankh was last. I watched it curl up in the flames, hoping its message would reach Margo somehow, and give her comfort.

The day was busy, but not as hectic as Saturday had been. A warm, gentle glow filled the parlors as the customers—mostly couples but a few families and groups of friends—celebrated their love. Ramon's guitar music filled the house in the afternoon and made everything more relaxed. I'd have to remember that for the future: live music on days that were super busy.

I circulated from the gift shop to the pantry and kitchen to the offices, keeping tabs on everything and pitching in when my help was needed. As I passed through the hall I was often stopped by customers wanting to chat. Their happy smiles filled my heart with satisfaction.

Toward the end of the day, things wound down. Julio released Andre at four, and as he left I gave him a rose from the buckets in the pantry; we had already set up the final seating and there were plenty of roses left over. All the staff got roses as they departed.

The gift shop was busy up until closing. We still had shoppers seeking last-minute Valentine's Day gifts, and many departing customers bought treats to take home. At five-thirty I handed Claudia a rose, thanked her, and sent her home. I stayed with Nat until six, then locked the door again, though the shoppers had tapered off. Nat went home with two roses in hand (one for Manny) after demanding a hug.

Ramon continued to play until six-fifteen, when I let the last customer out. "Thank you," I said, handing him a rose as he packed up his guitar and sound gear.

"It was fun," he said, smiling. "Better than last time."

The last time he had played here had been at Gabriel's masquerade. I smiled back. "Enjoy your evening."

Mick would be busy for another half-hour or so. Julio had turned the boom box on low, and was shutting down the kitchen.

"Anything I can help with?" I asked him.

"Nah, we're good. I'll be in tomorrow."

"Come in late, if you like. I'm planning on helping you, but I'm going to sleep in. I probably won't be here before nine."

"Okay."

I gave Julio two roses (one for Owen), and gave another to Mick, which he stuck in a glass of water while he worked. Taking a rose upstairs for Kris, I met her on the way down.

"Mind if I take tomorrow off?" she said. "The calls have slowed down. I'll come in early Tuesday to catch up."

"That's fine." I handed her the rose. "Have a nice evening and a restful day off. And happy birthday!"

She held the rose up to her nose, inhaling. "Thanks for the cake and the card."

"You are very welcome. Thank *you*. It's been a tough week."

A fleeting smile, then she caught me in a surprise hug. "Happy Valentine's Day, Ellen."

"Happy Valentine's Day," I said, smiling.

I was touched by her willingness to express the sentiment. Would she spend her evening alone with her memories of Gabriel? Or had she found someone to share it with? Perhaps she'd planned a birthday treat for herself. I hoped so.

I closed my eyes briefly, wishing her healing. Wishing her peace.

She left, and I took Minuit across to my suite for the night. Collecting my gifts for Tony, I thought of one more thing I wanted to do. I put on my coat and carried the card, cakes, and rose downstairs, along with my overnight bag. Leaving them in the pantry, I moved the bucket of leftover roses to the fridge, then extracted one and took it outside.

A breeze had come up, making the candles flicker in the twilight. My vase with its roses stood by the bouquets, but this rose was not destined to join them.

Stepping past the candles, I reached up to the lowest tree branch. My fingers didn't reach it, but I was just able to hook the rose's stem over the branch, and with a little toss it fell against the trunk, catching in the crook of the branch.

Perhaps Margo's story wasn't over, but this part of it was. Wherever she was now, I probably wouldn't hear about her again.

She'd had a rough few months. Messy. She had brought her mess here, which had caused me some grief. I took a deep breath.

And forgave her.

The front window of the townhome gleamed with light as I walked up the path. There were curtains there—Gwyneth had left them when she'd moved out—but they were open and I saw that Tony's modest table—a little fancier than a card table—was set up in the dining room, with two lit candles on it between two place settings.

Oh! We were dining in!

The moon cutout on porch light shone out, making me smile. As I shifted my burdens, reaching for my keys, the door opened.

"Hi," Tony said.

I stepped in and handed him the rose. "Hi. Happy Valentine's Day."

He chuckled. "Finally."

He relieved me of my things, set them unceremoniously on the floor, and enveloped me in a hug and a deep kiss. When he released me, I caught a whiff of something savory.

"Did you order takeout?"

"No," he said. "Come and see."

He led me to the living room, where Santa Fe had begun to glitter through the picture windows. A pair of French doors there gave access to the back yard. At the east end stood a grill that I hadn't noticed on previous visits, and it was giving out amazing mouth-watering smells.

"Wow! I didn't know we had a grill!"

Tony opened it, revealing steaks, jacket potatoes, and garlic bread on an upper rack. He took some asparagus spears out of a bowl and began laying them on the grill.

"This'll be ready in a couple minutes."

"I'll go hang up my coat."

I fetched my things from the entryway and paused to put the Sachertortes in the fridge. The kitchen was clear of boxes and looked inhabited. A bottle of Gruet Blanc de Noirs stood chilling in a wine bucket on the counter. I left the valentine on the dinner table for Tony and carried my overnight bag to the master bedroom.

There were still boxes there, but they were stacked out of the way against the wall. Tony's dresser also stood against the wall by the closets. A fire crackled gently in the kiva fireplace, and near it a makeshift bed lay on the floor, with a deep pile of thick, soft blankets—possibly on top of an air mattress—and a scatter of cushions and pillows.

Oh, my!

I hung up my coat and left my bag by the dresser, then went to help Tony carry in the dinner. He fetched the champagne bucket from the kitchen and poured as I took my seat at the table, then he picked up an envelope from the window sill and handed it to me.

He had made this a homecoming. So many perfect little touches. I opened the card, which had wisterias and butterflies on the front. Nice find!

Ellen-

You are the answer to all of my dreams. I will love you forever, and try my best to deserve you.

Happy Valentine's Day

Love,

Tony

I looked up to find him watching me. He had opened his card and was smiling softly. He picked up his champagne glass.

"Here's to us."

"To us," I replied.

The dinner was fabulous. Tony might not be very interested in cooking, but he was great at grilling. Everything was perfect, and we topped it off with the Sachertortes and the last of the champagne in the bedroom in front of the fire.

Quite a while later, we retired to the hot tub with glasses of whiskey. The night was chilly but calm, and the stars overhead glittered cold and white, competing with the warmer lights of the city.

"Tony, I have a theory about Margo's death," I said.

"Yeah?"

"I think she killed herself. The rope was tied to the tree branch, so I can't see a way for someone else to get her up there. I think she climbed the tree, fastened the rope to the branch, cut the kris into her chest over the highlighter, then tied her hands and slid her legs through them. Maybe as she jumped."

"Pretty difficult."

"She was a cheerleader. She had flexible joints, maybe even gymnastics training. And you said she had rope burns, so she probably practiced."

He was silent for a moment. "You're good," he said. "I hadn't thought of that."

I took a sip of whiskey and rolled it around in my mouth. The champagne buzz was long gone—we had worked it off rather energetically—and I was enjoying the whiskey's mellowing influence.

"You're right about the rope," Tony said. "The tied hands had us stumped for a while, until Zeke remembered your telling him she'd been a cheerleader. Oh, and he checked with that jewelry shop. Only one person bought three strings of jet beads in the past thirty days."

"Margo?"

"Margo. She paid cash, but the owner recognized her photo."

I sighed. "I'm sad for her."

"That's 'cause you're a nice person."

I took a swallow of whiskey.

"Early on we were working on the assumption she was forced to climb the tree," Tony said, "maybe at gun-point."

"If I were going to force someone to hang herself, I'd choose a more remote location. The only person the tearoom mattered to was Margo. It's where her final argument with Gabriel began."

"Could have mattered to Kris for the same reason. And she owns a gun."

"Kris has a *gun*?"

"Yeah. Legally registered. She takes it to a shooting range once a month and practices."

Holy cow. No wonder Zeke had been hounding her.

I took a swallow of whiskey, musing. "That makes sense. She had some rough experiences early on—"

"Oh yeah?"

"—which I'm not at liberty to share with you."

Tony took a pull at his glass. "Well, she pointed out to Zeke that it would be pretty stupid of her to kill Margo on your lawn," he said. "He was annoyed about that."

"Are you going to tell him my theory about the rope burns?"

"Uh-huh," Tony said, and knocked back the last of his whiskey.

He put the glass in a cup holder and reached for me.

"Later."

Rose Almond Cookies

Ingredients:

4 tablespoons butter, softened
½ cup granulated sugar (plus more for decoration)
----
2 tablespoons rose water
1 teaspoon almond extract

¾ cup + 2 tablespoons unbleached all-purpose flour
½ cup almond flour
¼ cup sliced almonds, crumbled (plus more for decoration)
pinch of salt

Preheat oven to 355° F (180° C). Cover a cookie sheet with parchment paper or a silicone baking mat.

Cream butter and sugar together in a medium bowl. Blend in rose water and almond extract.

In a separate bowl, mix flour, almond flour, crumbled almonds, and salt. Add dry ingredients to creamed butter mixture and blend until smooth. Dough may look crumbly but should stick together when handled.

For each cookie, pinch off about a tablespoon of dough and roll it into a ball approximately 1" in diameter. Place on cookie sheet and flatten gently with your palm or the bottom of a glass. Space cookies about 1" apart.

Sprinkle with sugar and crumbled almonds, press them in gently.

Bake 15 to 17 minutes. Remove from oven and transfer cookies onto wire rack to cool.

Makes approximately 15 cookies.

Gabriel's Midnight Toast

Ingredients (for one serving):

   1 shot (1-½ ounce) cinnamon vodka
   1 teaspoon grenadine
   edible glitter (1/4 teaspoon or as desired)

Create a mysterious atmosphere of your choice, using darkness, velvet, candlelight, a red lantern, or whatever appeals.

For a dramatic presentation, place the edible glitter in an empty glass, mix the vodka and grenadine in a separate container (a small pitcher such as a cream pitcher would be ideal), and pour it into the glass to make the glitter swirl up.

Gabriel would want you to shoot the drink, but you might find it appealing to sip it, as the grenadine will then have a moment before the cinnamon kicks in.

Grenadine, being a pomegranate syrup, is highly appropriate for All Hallow's Eve, as the pomegranate fruit was the temptation that led to Persephone's doom. After she was abducted by Hades she resisted all food offered to her, but was finally tempted to eat six seeds of a pomegranate, resulting in her fate of spending six months of the year—one for each seed—in the Underworld. Her mother, Demeter (goddess of the harvest), was heartbroken and caused all plants to die away during those six months (the winter half of the year). When Persephone returned from the Underworld in Spring, Demeter permitted the plants to grow again.

(Note: Gabriel's All Hallow's Eve party is described in *A Masquerade of Muertos*, Wisteria Tearoom Mystery #5).

Wisteria Tearoom

upper floor

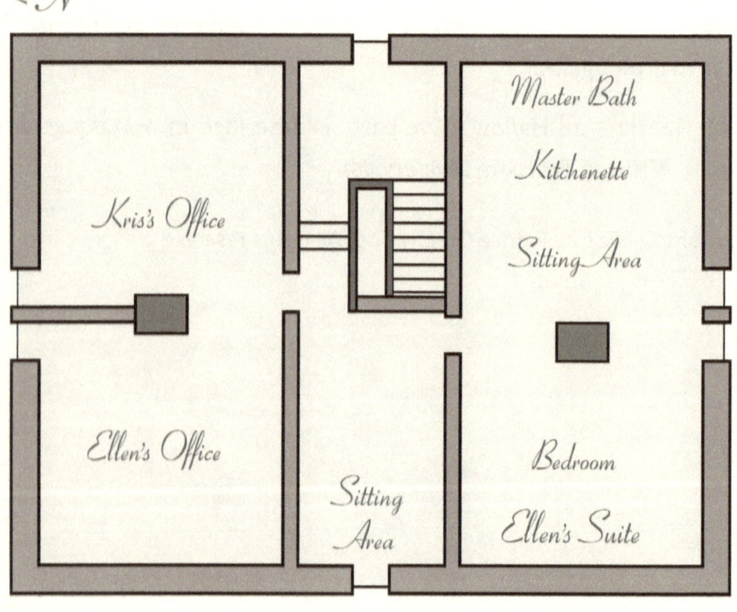

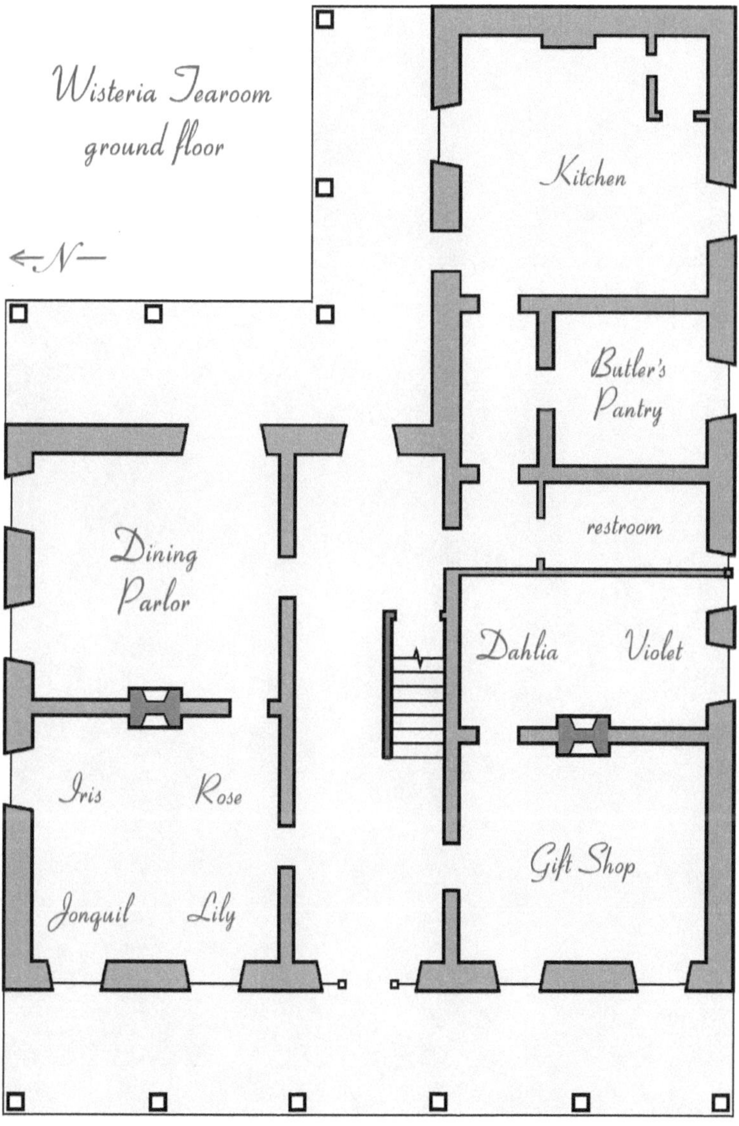

Wisteria Tearoom
ground floor
←N—
Kitchen
Butler's Pantry
restroom
Dining Parlor
Dahlia
Violet
Iris
Rose
Gift Shop
Jonquil
Lily

Wisteria Tearoom Staff

Ellen Rosings	Owner
Kris Overland	Office Manager
Julio Delgado	Chef
Mai Hanh	Assistant Chef
Ramon Garcia	Assistant
Mick Gallagher	Dish Washer
Dee Gallagher	Server
Rosa Garcia	Server
Iz Naranjo	Server
Dale Whittier	Server

Ellen's Family

Joe Rosings	Brother
Nat Salazar	Aunt
Manny Salazar	Uncle

Ellen's Friends & Associates

Gina Fiorello	Bestie
Tony Aragón	Fiancé
Willow Lane	Spirit Tour Guide

Tony's Family

Angela Aragón	Sister
Dolores Aragón	Mother
Abuela Aragón	Grandmother

About the Author

photo by Chris Krohn

Patrice Greenwood was born and raised in New Mexico, and remembers when the Santa Fe Plaza was home to more dusty dogs than trendy art galleries. She has been writing fiction longer than she cares to admit, perpetrating over twenty published novels in various genres. She uses a different name for each genre, thus enabling her to pretend she is a Secret Agent.

She loves afternoon tea, old buildings, gourmet tailgating at the opera, ghost stories, costumes, and solving puzzles. Her popular Wisteria Tearoom Mysteries are colored by many of these interests. She is presently collapsed on her chaise longue, sipping Wisteria White tea and planning the next book in the series.